REVOLUTION

AL ROMERO

With Dave Kelley

PAGE PUBLISHING, INC.
New York, NY

First originally published by Page Publishing, Inc. 2018

ISBN 978-1-64214-552-6 (Paperback)
ISBN 978-1-64214-554-0 (Hardcover)
ISBN 978-1-64214-553-3 (Digital)

Printed in the United States of America

Acknowledgement

THIS BOOK IS dedicated to Joaquin (Pepe) Puebla, Edgar (Jr.) Martin-Rivero and Luis Rueda, the unsung heroes whose courage and sacrifice inspired me to write this story and who were the motivation for this novel, the ones that suffered so much at the hands of that horrible Castro's regime, especially Joaquin who gave his life fighting to get rid of Fidel, his brother Raul and their murdering henchmen like Che Guevara.

To Luis, who to this day suffers the lingering effects of so many years spent in Castro's gulags and to Maria Eugenia, Maria de los Angeles, Maria Elena and Maria Cristina Puebla, (yes they are all named Maria) Joaquin's daughters who made the ultimate sacrifice by losing their father to Fidel's firing squad. And to the thousands of men and women who also gave their lives in front of those firing squads for trying to rid Cuba of the worst dictatorship that it has ever suffered.

I also want to thank my contributing author and long time friend Dave Kelley, who I could not have written this book without his help and who, while doing research for the book, almost got thrown in jail in Cuba for just taking a picture of my childhood home in Havana. To Jim Mendrinos for his input and suggestions that were so instrumental in developing this story, and to everyone who encouraged and supported me to write this novel and tell the real story of how Fidel came to power. To Page Publishing for publishing my book and to Trevor Boyd my publishing coordinator who was so helpful and supportive all along the way.

And to the two beautiful women in my life, my wife Marie and our daughter Alexandra.

Prologue

IT WAS A typical hot and humid September in Miami, and the Magic City was overrun, like so many times in its recent history, by a mass exodus of Cubans desperately seeking to flee the island. The chaotic arrival of so many people from the Port of Mariel had caught the Carter administration totally unprepared and had thrown South Florida into havoc. The tumultuous landing of thousands of Cubans in small boats and rafts was coming to an end, but tensions between Washington and the Cuban government still raged.

Roberto Machado left his home in Havana, Cuba, in 1961 at the age of eleven. He arrived in the United States as a Cuban refugee like hundreds of thousands of others in that first wave of Cubans seeking to escape the Castro regime. Now thirty, Roberto had made his home in Miami, where he grew up watching his father work several jobs to help the family make ends meet.

A naturalized United States citizen since the age of eighteen, Roberto had achieved the American dream, making a life for himself in South Florida's upper middle class. But on this day he paced the living room floor with a heavy heart as he carried on a phone conversation with a funeral director.

The television was on, but no one watched the network report about Cubans fleeing the island. The station showed live footage of the Coast Guard rescuing more refugees from makeshift boats off the coast of Florida.

A copy of the letter he had written to his cousin lay on a desk nearby. The letter read:

September 8, 1980

Dear Elena,

It is with much regret that, after nineteen years, I cannot write you with happier news. Your father is dying in the hospital. He asked to see you one final time. Elena, whatever happened in the past, I beg you to put it aside and come to him so he can die in peace. He has never stopped loving you. Please come.

Your cousin Roberto "Tico" Machado.

"I want the best of everything for him," Roberto said into the phone. He paused. "I know, Mr. Garcia, that yours is the finest funeral home in Miami. I just want to make sure he gets the best. Thank you." Roberto hung up the phone.

There was a knock at the door, but he didn't hear it. At the second knock, he turned and made his way through the living room to the front door, where a young man from Western Union handed him a telegram. After he tipped the delivery man, Roberto opened the telegram and read it.

MR. MACHADO (STOP) REGARDING YOUR LETTER OF 9/8/80 (STOP) I WOULD LIKE TO INFORM YOU THAT I AM NOT INTERESTED IN ANYTHING REGARDING MR DIE-GO QUINTANA (STOP) AS FAR AS I AM CONCERNED MY FATHER DIED IN 1961 (STOP) COLONEL ELENA QUINTANA 2ND UNDER SECRETARY CUBAN COMMUNIST PARTY HALL OF THE REVOLUTION HABANA, CUBA (STOP)

Roberto put down the telegram and picked up a small framed photo. He gazed at the picture of his whole family, each face decorated with a huge smile. It seemed like a lifetime ago when they had all been together and happy in Havana. He studied the photo for a moment and, as tears rolled down his face, hurled it as hard as he could at the wall, shattering the glass.

PART ONE

Chapter **1**

December 2, 1956, Purgatory Point, Cuba

A SMALL YACHT pitched and rolled in the rough waters of the Cuban coast. The gusty winds had turned into a strong, constant gale. On the back of the boat, the name *Granma* was written in black paint, a sharp contrast against the white of the stern. Eighty-two men were crowded on board, all clean shaven and poorly armed, some wearing green army fatigues. As the boat approached the shore, a few of them began to feel seasick. On the horizon, a government patrol boat could be seen. As the patrol vessel got closer, it spotted the *Granma*.

The captain of the ship immediately radioed headquarters and reported sighting the rebels' boat. The colonel in charge of the squadron sounded the alarm and ordered some of his fighter planes to intercept them.

On the *Granma*, quite a few of the men were now violently seasick as the small yacht got close to the shore. Suddenly, the boat ran aground and lurched forward, causing many of the men to be thrown into the shallow water near the beach at Playa Colorada. While they pulled themselves to shore, a military plane seemed to appear from nowhere and began firing at them. In the chaos that followed, some men ran farther up the beach and sought cover, while some hit the sand. Many others were cut down in the hail of bullets.

Their leader, Fidel Castro, was a tall and distinctly charismatic man of about thirty. Some of the surviving men surrounded him, waiting for his order. Camilo Cienfuegos, Joaquin Quintana, and Che Guevara struggled to get to Fidel, who told them to split up, run into the sugarcane fields, and make their way to the Sierra Maestra. The handful of rebels that survived scattered into the cane fields as the plane circled back to strafe the area again.

Camilo and Joaquin separated from the others and were now on their own. They walked, ran, and hid for hours to avoid the strafing and bombing from Batista's pilots. They found their way through the thick of the foothills of the Sierra Maestra to a small shack where a young peasant couple let them in. The dwelling was a one room structure put together with discarded wood, corrugated tin, and palm leaves.

The couple tried to comfort their newborn, who cried as the noise of the bombing came closer. The woman brought cornmeal bread to Joaquin and Camilo, who sat on the dirt floor. She gave them a weak smile, pushed the hair out of her eyes, and walked back to her husband.

Joaquin looked at Camilo. "Do you think they got Fidel?"

"They are still bombing. That means they haven't found him."

Each passing plane brought the bombs nearer until there was an explosion so close to the shack that it lit up the entire inside of the house. The baby let out an ear-piercing scream.

It was December 3, 1956, and Havana was awash in Christmas decorations. Roberto Machado, a nice looking man, walked down a bustling Havana street, carrying Christmas wrapping paper and several toy guns in their boxes. From every store, different Christmas songs filtered through the air. American standards like "Jingle Bells" and "White Christmas" as well as popular Cuban holiday songs added to the festive feeling in the air.

Roberto continued to take in the colorful window displays and exchanged holiday greetings with several people. He stopped to chat with a couple of men, and soon they all burst into laughter, adding to the joyous atmosphere.

December was Roberto's favorite time of the year, when the whole world seemed to be decorated like one huge Christmas tree. He stopped to take in the moment and said to himself, *I can't wait to see my son Tico's face when he opens these presents on Christmas day.*

While Roberto was downtown, his wife, Carmen, and her mother, Rosa, were busy shopping for food and decorations for their annual Christmas Eve celebration at the Machados' home. Although they did this every year, Rosa and Carmen seldom agreed on what to serve for dinner and what decorations to use.

"Ay, *Mami*," said Carmen, "I'm not going to buy those big beans. The smaller black beans are much tastier."

"We go through this every year," said Rosa, looking annoyed. "I have been cooking Christmas Eve dinners since before you were born, and I'm telling you, the bigger beans are better."

Carmen rolled her eyes and walked away, ignoring Rosa, who followed, still arguing her point.

On the other side of the city, a man is thrown half naked out the front door of a modest house. The rest of his clothes followed and landed on top of his head. The man was Cesar, the good looking young uncle of Tico Machado.

He tried to gather the rest of his clothes, which were now strewn all about the sidewalk.

The angry voice of a young woman called out, "Don't ever come back or call me again, you two-timing asshole!" She heaved one of his shoes out the window. Cesar ducked, and it flew past his ear. "You can't keep your dick in your pants for five minutes, and I'm sick of it." She let his other shoe fly, and it bounced off the sidewalk. "And with my best friend, no less, you philandering bastard!" She slammed the door, and Cesar calmly dusted himself off.

"Women. They are so dramatic." He turned and yelled at the closed door, "For God's sake, it was only one time." He paused for a moment. "Okay, maybe two times. What is the big deal?" He waited for the door to open again, but it didn't.

While he straightened his attire, a very pretty girl walked past him. Cesar, like nothing had just happened, caught up to her and said, "Hi there Beautiful! Would you like to get a cup of coffee with me?"

At the prestigious Ursulinas Catholic preparatory school for girls, Elena, Tico's cousin, had just been called to the principal's office. Mother Ophelia, the head of the school, warmly greeted her with a big smile, something quite unusual for the Mother Superior.

"Young lady, I just got a phone call from my friend at the Admissions Office of New York University. It seems that in spite your rebellious nature, you have been accepted to their medical school program. She told me you will receive your acceptance letter sometime this week. Now, Elena, I hope you can put your wild and crazy ideas aside and not only accept this great opportunity but also embrace it and dedicate yourself to becoming the great doctor I know you can be."

Elena, not thrilled with the news, sarcastically told her, "Oh, wonderful, I'm sure my dad will be excited, and I'm sure you are too. After all the trouble you say I have caused around here, I know you cannot wait to see me go as far away as possible."

She stood and walked out of the Mother Superior's office without so much as a glance over her shoulder. Instead of running home to share the news with her dad, she met up with a group of young people.

One of them, Ramon, told her, "I hope you got the stuff we need. We are meeting some very important people tonight."

Inside an office at the Cuban National Phone Company, Tico's other uncle, Diego, was welcoming the newly arrived head of computer operations, Bill Lima, from the United States.

Diego smiled and told Bill, "Boy, am I glad you are here. This computer system they are installing to operate the phone communications was impossible for me to comprehend. I hope you can shed some light for me."

Bill laughed. "Don't worry, Diego. I'll make a computer expert out of you in no time. But before we fill your brain with technical mumbo jumbo, let's get something to eat. I can't wait to try all the great Cuban food I've heard so much about."

The next day, Tico was outside his house, watching as a new family moved in across the street. He noticed a boy his age and waved. The boy waved back and came over to introduce himself.

"Hi! My name is Eusebio, but my parents call me Sebi. What's your name?"

"My name is Roberto, but everyone calls me Tico. You like to play cops and robbers?"

Sebi told him, "Yes!"

"Great!" said Tico. "I'll be the cop, and you'll be the robber."

Sebi, not too happy with that idea, responded, "I want to be the cop. You can be the robber."

Tico thought about it for a minute and told him, "Okay, I'll be the robber first. But later I'll be the cop and then it will be your turn to die."

Sebi agreed, and they shook on it. Tico handed him one of his many toy guns, and they started to play.

But while it seemed life was merrily moving along, not far away, a storm was brewing that would engulf every single Cuban and change their lives forever.

Fidel and the surviving rebels also ran and hid. They had to fend for themselves until they were saved by the peasants in the mountains, like Camilo and Joaquin had been. The Cuban peasants are known as *guajiros* (pronounced *wa-he-rows*) a bastardization of the English term *war hero*.

In the American hemisphere, during the last decade of the nineteenth century, the tension between the aging Spanish empire and the emerging power of the United States had reached its boiling point. The two countries were on a collision course toward war. The American warship, the *Maine*, was blown up in Havana harbor on February 15, 1898. In the United States, many suspected that it was carried out by the Spanish forces occupying Cuba.

William Randolph Hearst, the powerful and highly influential newspaper tycoon, used all his publications to champion the call for war between Spain and the United States. His battle cry, "Remember the *Maine*," repeatedly appeared on the front pages of all his papers. After an official US government investigation, the United States blockaded Cuba on April 21. On the 23rd, Spain declared war, and two days later, the United States invaded the island.

During the Spanish-American War, as the conflict was known, Teddy Roosevelt's Rough Riders came to Cuba to fight against the Spaniards. The Cuban peasants who fought at San Juan Hill alongside the highly trained and war tested soldiers were fearless. What they lacked in military training, they more than made up for in courage and guile.

The Rough Riders, who witnessed the heroism and patriotism on the part of the Cuban peasants, praised them by calling them war heroes. The Cubans used the term among themselves but were unable to pronounce the words correctly. They repeated the nickname the American soldiers bestowed on them as *wa-he-row*, and the name gaujiro was born.

Those guajiros who fought with the Americans against Spain were largely responsible for liberating the island and throwing the Spaniards out of Cuba; however, their descendants were the ones that least benefited from the liberation of their new country. They had little to show for the courage and patriotism of their ancestors.

Joaquin and men like him left the comfort of their lives in cities like Havana to go into the mountains and fight for the benefit of these very guajiros. These poor souls, who barely had enough to feed their families, now aided the rebels with food, water, and shelter. Information about the surviving rebels spread very rapidly around the mountains. The peasants passed the word among themselves that the rebels had landed as an invading force and were the reason for the attacks by Batista's planes. During those days, when the mountains were repeatedly bombed and strafed, the rebels hid among the guajiros.

Fidel told the peasants that he and his men were there to fight for them and the liberation of Cuba from the clutches of dictators like Batista, who had kept them living in such poor conditions for so long. The peasants continued to hide the handful of surviving rebels and feed them until the rebels could regroup and set up their first camp.

After all the surviving rebels were able to reunite with Fidel, the quest for the liberation of Cuba began. They needed more soldiers plus supplies, weapons, and the resources with which to purchase them. It was a monumental task.

Right after their disastrous landing with only a handful of surviving men, the revolution seemed to have no chance in hell of succeeding. Yet Fidel and his group were not dissuaded. They pushed on and endured.

Once they set up their camp, Fidel gathered his handful of rebels and addressed them. "Men, we have encountered the worst that could have possibly happened, and we are still here. Let's take a minute to think of those who were not as fortunate as us, those cut down by the hail of bullets from that despicable dictator Batista. Today we make a pledge that their deaths will not be in vain."

The men in the camp bowed their heads and said a prayer for their fallen friends.

After a few moments of silence, Fidel continued. "Our first order of business is to rally the peasants in these mountains and encourage them to join us in our fight. Once they do, others will follow."

Camilo interrupted, "Fidel, we need resources so we can feed, supply, and equip an army. Don't we require that first before we can recruit more men?"

Fidel looked at his rebels and back at Camilo. "You are right, my friend, we do need money, weapons, and supplies. But what we need more than anything is the youth of this country to rise against the dictator and join us in our fight. Once that happens, the resources will come, and the weapons and supplies will follow."

After the rebels set up camp, many of the younger guajiros in the mountains joined up with Fidel. They, in turn, talked to their friends and relatives, and the word was spread throughout all the villages.

There were many small cities near and around the mountains of the Sierra Maestra. These places became Fidel strongholds, where secret meetings were conducted at night. At these gatherings, young peasants were told about how Batista's regime and others before him had forced them to live under their present conditions. They were reminded how their lives had never improved, generation after generation. Under these dictatorships, their children had been sentenced to a life of illiteracy, poverty, and misery. The peasants were encouraged to rise and fight against these injustices and to join the rebels in their cause to liberate Cuba once and for all.

After those rallies, a truck usually arrived, under the cover of darkness, at a predetermined meeting place. Dozens of young men, and in many cases women, would jump in the truck, now willing to go into the mountains and join the rebels.

Fidel's army grew, and word spread to the bigger cities. Soon, not only peasants but many students also began to join the fight. Their forces were growing every day.

The battle against Batista and his goons had begun.

Chapter 2

Havana, Presidential Palace, February 1957

PRESIDENT FULGENCIO BATISTA, or as he was better known to the Cuban people, the Dictator, a suave and charming man in his fifties, was enjoying a good laugh. It was carnival time, 1957, and Havana, as it always was during that time of the year, was in a festive, party mood.

Batista had been in power for several years during this, his second time around as president. In 1940 he had risen from a mere sergeant in the army to Cuba's highest office. In his first presidency, 1940–44, he was a freely elected democratic president who, during that first term, ushered in the 1940 constitution. At that time, the Cuban constitution was considered to be one of the most fair, balanced, and progressive constitutions anywhere. It was the model by which the country was to be run.

Batista served his term and retired to the United States, where he lived for several years. During that time, he was constantly encouraged by his friends, many in the Cuban army, where he had been chief general of the armed forces, to come back to Cuba and make another run for president.

The lure of power brought him back in 1952. Like an athlete who didn't know he was past his prime, he ran once again, but his time had passed. During the campaign, the would-be voters soundly rejected him. Facing certain defeat, he ignored the wishes of the people, and on March 10, just before elections were to be held, he took over the government in a military coup d'état with the help of his friends in the army. He immediately declared himself president, suspended the constitution, and became a dictator and a despot.

This night he was surrounded by businessmen from the United States. He was entertaining them at a lavish party with a large orchestra and fine food. The tone of the gathering and the displays of wealth made the partygoers feel like they were attending a big Hollywood premiere. Batista was truly in his element. He had worked hard and ruthlessly to consolidate power over the years and had amassed a great personal fortune at the expense of the Cuban people. He had been very friendly to American businesses and always made sure he got a share of the profits for himself. He had also gotten in bed with the mafia and handsomely profited from their illegal activities.

While the party raged at the palace, Batista was inside a large oakwood conference room where he addressed a select group of highly influential American businessmen. A man from IT&T presented Batista with a solid gold telephone, another form of bribery for the corrupt president.

After the enthusiastic applause died down, Frank, an American businessman in his fifties, cut in with his concerns.

"Mr. President, most of United Fruit's holdings are in the interior of your country, and quite honestly, we are worried about the uprising of Castro and his rebels in the Sierra Maestra."

Batista, calm and composed, answered, "I understand your concern, but this is not an uprising. This is a small group of malcontents. Tell all of my friends at the United Fruit Company not to worry. This will be taken care of very soon."

"When, Mr. President?" Frank asked, a trace of alarm in his voice.

"Not today," said Batista as he looked around at his guests. "We have this beautiful party to enjoy."

Those in attendance laughed heartily. But there were some in the room that privately shared Frank's feelings. Batista continued to work the room, shaking hands and trading pleasantries.

Rebels' Camp, Sierra Maestra, October 1957

In the mountains, the number of men in the camp had grown significantly from the handful who had survived the landing of the *Granma* to the hundreds who had joined them. The place was beginning to look and feel like a real military camp. The disorganization and chaos that ensued shortly after their disastrous landing a year ago had been replaced with discipline and a sense of purpose.

Joaquin, now bearded, as were most of the other men in the camp, led a group of soldiers who opened boxes of ammunition and unloaded a new shipment of weapons. Castro was in the radio room, a small hut not much different from the shack where Camilo and Joaquin hid during the bombing almost a year ago. He admired the room full of sophisticated radio equipment they had been able to acquire.

Camilo acted as a tour guide, welcoming about twenty new recruits who looked like college students. Among other things, he showed them the many guns and other weapons that were stacked neatly around every tree in camp as Joaquin and his men continued to unload and stack more weapons and ammunition.

The ammunition, radio equipment, and other essential supplies were furnished to them by none other than the Central Intelligence Agency. Batista's involvement with the US mafia had come to the attention and concern of the Eisenhower administration. Meyer Lansky, the infamous

Jewish gangster, along with Lucky Luciano, ran the most powerful of the five mafia families. Not only were they profiting from their illegal activities in Cuba, but they were also harboring wanted mafia hit men sought by the FBI.

The American ambassador made it clear to Batista that those associations had to come to an end if the dictator wanted to continue to be backed by the United States. Batista ignored those warnings. He had told the Americans repeatedly that Castro was a communist they would not be able to control, a man who would cause a great deal of trouble for them. He believed the United States government would be much more concerned about losing Cuba to someone like Fidel than any mafia hoodlums he might be helping or harboring.

He was wrong. The blatant way in which Batista offered safe haven to those mafiosos was driving J. Edgar Hoover, the legendary and powerful head of the FBI, crazy. Hoover knew that Lansky wanted to establish a mafia headquarters in a friendly country near the United States.

Cuba was becoming Lansky's launching pad, where he could mastermind and oversee all sorts of gangland activities with no repercussions.

Hoover made this clear to the president. He exerted so much pressure on the Eisenhower administration that the old general had no choice but to react. A CIA operative was dispatched into the Sierra Maestra mountains to meet with Fidel and some of the other rebels like Joaquin and Camilo. Fidel assured him that he was not a communist like Batista insisted. Fidel said he believed in democracy and the Cuban Constitution and that he wanted to bring freedom to the Cuban people. He emphasized that he wanted to liberate Cuba and throw the mafia out of his country.

He told the CIA operative, "Tell your superiors that I will be very grateful for any help your government could provide us, especially weapons, ammunition, and communication equipment, and that I will not forget it. With the help of the United States, we will throw Batista out along with his mafia buddies, and we will always be thankful to America for its cooperation."

The CIA man returned to the States and reported what he had heard and seen. The agent's report was considered at the highest levels, and the decision to help the rebels with some of the requested supplies was approved. Fidel now had the means by which to mount a guerrilla war.

Chapter 3

Machados' home, Christmas Eve 1957

BACK IN HAVANA, Joaquin's family had gathered at his sister Carmen's house for Christmas Eve dinner. In the Machado home, there was a fully decorated Christmas tree in the Florida Room with lots of presents underneath. The comfortable, large middle class house was warm and inviting and looked very much like a typical American house of the 1950s. There were family photos, books, and religious figures about.

Elena, a very bright and pretty twenty-year-old, played by the tree with her seven-year-old cousin Tico.

"Bang, bang! I got you, Tico."

"Aaahhh!" wailed Tico.

He grabbed his chest, closed his eyes, and fell to the floor, pretending to die. While Tico's eyes were closed, Elena seized the opportunity to swoop down and tickle him. Tico's eyes opened, and he squealed with laughter. Diego, a good looking forty-two-year-old widower who had his hands full with his rebellious daughter, Elena, was in the kitchen along with his mother, Rosa. Although Rosa was in her late sixties, she still retained much of her youthful beauty. In the kitchen with them was Diego's sister Carmen, a very attractive woman in her midthirties with long chestnut hair. The women talked and laughed while they attended to the preparations for Christmas Eve dinner.

Rosa moved about the kitchen with the grace of a ballroom dancer while she cooked several dishes at the same time. She had actually trained to be a ballerina from a very young age. When she was twenty, old by ballet standards, she broke her ankle, which ended her dancing aspirations. She then embarked in her new career as the wife of the Honorable Judge Jose Maria Quintana. Theirs was an arranged marriage, typical of the times; he was almost twice her age.

Justice Quintana was a relatively wealthy man, and Rosa's family was very happy to see them married. Over the years, she grew to love him. He was a great legal mind and a truly wonderful man who was taken from her much too soon. She became a widow in 1942 when he suddenly died of a massive heart attack. He left her with three sons, a daughter, and a comfortable trust fund. She never remarried, and she devoted her whole life to her home and children, especially Cesar, who was still an adolescent when the judge died, and Carmen, with whom she eventually came to live.

"It makes me feel so good to hear Elena and Tico play like that," said Rosa.

Carmen searched through the cabinets for her good china and added, "She is really good with kids."

Diego played with a spoon on the table. "That's my little girl. She says she wants to be a pediatrician."

"She can be anything she wants to be," said Rosa. "She was always such a bright child. I remember the first time she read the comics in the newspaper to me. I couldn't believe it. How old was she, three or four?"

"Almost four," said Diego. "I always thought she would grow up to be a veterinarian. When she was about five or six, she knew every breed of dog, what they looked like, where they came from, and what they were originally bred to do. She was a sponge."

"Remember Mr. Lopez?" Rosa asked. "He had that candy shop on Tenth Street, and his dog, Gomez, was always there with him.

"Of course," said Diego. "Elena called Lopez's candy store Gomez the dog's store. Any time we were out, we had to stop in and see Gomez the dog. He was the cutest little German shepherd. She would pet him, and he would lick her face. When we left the store, she would be covered in dog hair."

"You have to take some of the credit for her love of learning, Diego. You spent hours reading to her and teaching her all sorts of things," interjected Carmen. "After Mercedes died, you had to be both mother and father to her. Twelve is such a tough age for a girl to lose her mother. And you have always thought of her education, instilling that thirst for knowledge in her."

"Remember her favorite puzzle?" asked Rosa.

"The world map. How could I forget?" answered Diego. "Her friends were doing puzzles of kittens or fairy tales, and she was putting together the whole world." He laughed.

"You've been a very good father, Diego," said Rosa as she came over to him and kissed him on the cheek.

"I remember when she was little, Mercedes would only let her wear dresses," said Carmen.

"Then she would go outside and play with the neighborhood boys," added Diego. "One day I went out in the backyard to tell her to come in for dinner, and she and the boys were all blowing on their forearms, making fart noises. Elena was giggling more than anyone. Her dress would be all soiled, and Mercedes always had a fit about that. Elena was tough, and she still is. She never took any crap from those boys. I remember when she decked that kid Julio because he told her she could not play with them because she was 'just a girl.'"

"Sometimes you would leave her with me when you and Mercedes went to work," said Rosa. "Then when you guys came to pick her up in the early evening, she would run and jump into your arms, and you would grab her and swing her around. I will never forget how Mercedes would carry her over to me, and Elena would tell her all about everything we had done that day. She was a joy."

"Too bad they have to grow up," said Diego.

"Now, stop that," said Carmen. "They can't stay little forever."

"True, but one day she became a teenager, and the arguing began."

"They all do that," said Rosa. "You are going to have to accept the fact that she is an adult."

"I know, I know." Diego lost himself in thought for a moment. It seemed like she had been his little girl one day, and the next she was a grown woman with opinions and ambitions of her own. He thought back to the first time she had walked into her school without looking back to wave goodbye. It gave him a little lump in his throat. "She's very independent. She always has been."

"Maybe she'll meet a nice young man in New York," said Rosa.

"Mom," said Carmen, "she's a very bright girl. She is not going to the United States to socialize. She is going to study."

"I'm just happy I was able to convince her to study medicine in the United States," said Diego, "so she can avoid all the turmoil in Cuba."

Diego and Carmen's baby brother, Cesar, came into the kitchen and took a seat at the table. He was a goodlooking man of twenty-four with a joy for life and not a care in the world.

"Hey, hey, enough of this talking," he said with a big smile. "I'm getting hungry."

"Ay, Cesar," said Carmen, "do you always have to think with your stomach?"

"I think, with Cesar, you have to aim a little lower," said Diego as he playfully smacked his brother below the belt.

Rosa gave Cesar a small piece of chicken and said, "Don't tease my little boy. He needs to gain some weight if he is going to find a wife."

Cesar rolled his eyes, having heard this many times before. Diego, relishing Rosa's comment, sat smiling at Cesar. Carmen's husband, Roberto, a small-framed forty-year-old with the determined look of a driven man, came into the kitchen, found a seat at the table, and began to pick at the food.

"Yes, please find a wife soon so you'll stop mooching food here all the time."

Carmen, running late, feeling crowded, and in desperate need for some space, advised those gathered in her kitchen, "Anybody who is not out of here in one minute has to help me set the table."

Cesar glanced at Roberto and Diego. "I think we should retire to the living room."

They all stood up at the same time, tripping over one another on their way out.

Tico, the cute, smart, and chubby seven-year-old son of Roberto and Carmen, walked into the living room along with Elena, the very bright and idealistic daughter of Diego. They joined Roberto, Cesar, and Diego, who were watching a variety show.

The show's host, dressed in a tuxedo and surrounded by scantily clad showgirls, looked into the camera and said, "Partagas cigars, the best cigars in all the world, presents *El Show de la Alegria*."

"This is such a bad show. What else is on?" asked Diego.

Cesar replied, "No, no, don't change it. I heard Elvis is going to be on tonight."

Tico looked up at the others and announced, "Shh! This is it."

"Ladies and gentlemen," said the host, "today, on our Christmas special, we're proud to introduce a young man who is sweeping the nation. Direct from the San Souci Nightclub, Elvis Perez!"

The studio audience clapped and screamed while Elvis Perez, a very Latin-looking young man trying his very best to resemble Elvis Presley, sang "Hound Dog" in Spanish. *Tu eres un perro callejero. Llorando todas las noches.*

Everyone in the Machado living room burst into laughter.

Cesar started clowning around. "Hey, this guy is good!"

"You can't be serious," said Diego. "He's terrible!"

"You know, you are right. I think I can do better." Cesar stood up in front of the TV. He sang and gyrated his hips in a wonderfully exaggerated Elvis impersonation. "Tu eres un perro callejero."

Elena did a mock swoon. "Oh, Elvis!" She pretended to faint.

Everyone else laughed and threw sofa pillows at Cesar. He grinned and kept singing while he ducked and deflected the soft projectiles. Tico fell on the floor laughing his head off.

Later, everyone moved into the dining room, which was brightly decorated for the holidays and where the China cabinet had been replaced, like it was every Christmas, by a very large and detailed Nativity scene of Lladro figurines. The family sat down for the splendid Christmas Eve dinner.

Elena brought up the subject of Uncle Joaquin. "Don't you think that, before we eat, we should say a prayer for *Tio* Joaquin?"

Rosa replied, "Oh god, I hope he is not going hungry on Christmas."

"I just hope he is safe," said Carmen.

"I can't understand what the hell he is doing there in the first place," countered Diego.

"Dad, he believes in justice of the law, and he wants to bring it back to Cuba. Tio Joaquin wants justice, freedom, and a legal system that is fair to all. He believes like Grandpa believed, in following the constitution. *Abuelo* was very

36

much involved in the drafting of that constitution when he was a justice, and he deeply believed in it. He instilled that in Tio Joaquin, and I believe in it too. I want to be part of a Cuba that's run by a fair government, not live under this oppressive dictatorship."

Cesar, trying to lighten the mood, said, "Can somebody please pass the nonoppressive plantains?"

Roberto continued, "I know what he is doing is noble, but he wasted so many years of education. Who is going to trust a rebel as their legal counsel?"

"They will only call him a rebel if he loses, and they are not going to lose," said Elena.

Diego was not able to hold his tongue any longer. "If they lose, they won't call him a rebel, they will call him dead."

Rosa made the sign of the cross. "God forbid! Don't say that."

Diego looked at Rosa. "I'm sorry, Mom, but this has gone on for generations, and I'm sick and tired of it. We all know when Dad was a superior court judge, he was very much involved, like Elena said, in the drafting of the constitution. That *great* document," he said with mock reverence, "that everyone worships but no one ever follows. And I know he believed very much in getting involved in the politics of this country. He would probably still be heavily involved if he had not died of that heart attack." Diego paused for a second. "I understand why Joaquin wants to follow in those footsteps, believe me. I remember all too well how hard Dad tried to get me involved and tried to instill in me the same ideas he did in Joaquin. But, unlike them, I've always known that getting involved in any kind of politics in this country is a complete waste of time." He shot a look at Elena and said, "And it's a very dangerous game to play. Every time we overthrow a dictator, he is replaced by another one, and only the good people end up dead. I don't want that to happen to Joaquin." Again he looked at his daughter. "Or anyone else in this family."

Elena ignored his scare tactics and countered, "It's different this time. This revolution comes from the common people."

Diego looked at her with exasperation. "What common people? Joaquin is a lawyer. Fidel is a lawyer. Jesus, he and his brother come from money. That doesn't sound like the starving masses to me."

Cesar, again the jokester, tried to change the mood of the conversation. "I don't know about the masses, but I'm starving."

He reached across the table and grabbed a piece of chicken. Cesar truly did not care anything about politics. He was the baby of the family or, as they jokingly referred to him, the judge's last sentence. He had heard his family argue about politics at the dinner table all his life. But he had been too young to fall under the spell of the old man's political universe, and unlike Diego, he didn't care so much about not caring. He truly had never had any desire to get involved or even talk, let alone argue, about anything political. He figured he had just one life to live and was determined to enjoy it. Because he was Cesar the bon vivant, he always got away with it.

Elena said, "There are people starving in Cuba."

"Enough!" shouted Carmen.

She smacked her palm down on the table, spilling her glass of water. She too grew up listening to the same political arguments and hours of political discourse by her father, and she did not want this evening to turn into one of those nights, not because she hated politics, but because she was terrified for Joaquin and what he might be going through and did not want to bring up the subject, especially in front of Rosa.

"I did not invite all of you here to have a political argument," she said while trying to clean up the mess. "God bless Joaquin. Now let's eat."

Cesar kept looking at Diego with a smile on his face. He always got a kick out of seeing his brother get so mad about politics, something Diego swore he cared so little about. Diego ignored him.

After dinner, Elena put Tico to bed and came downstairs, where all the men were seated and talking. She joined them just in time to hear her father kid Uncle Roberto.

"Roberto, I am surprised you're not working today. How many jobs do you have now, four?" Everyone had a good laugh.

"Laugh all you want, but I'm saving my money. Not all of us are fortunate enough to work for a big American company running, what do you call them, computers?"

The doorbell sounded, and Elena went to answer it.

"Computers? Don't you work for the telephone company? I thought you were a repairman," said Cesar, not wasting an opportunity to rib his brother.

Diego countered, "Hey, I want you to know I'm one of the few people in this country who knows how to use a computer. Maybe if you stopped wasting so much time chasing women, you wouldn't have to deliver mail and wear that silly uniform."

Before Cesar had time to respond to Diego's dig, Elena walked into the living room with Bill Lima.

"Merry Christmas, everyone!" said Bill.

He was a big, portly, joyful American man in his midthirties with blond hair and freckles. Diego stood up, walked over to Bill, and shook his hand.

"Merry Christmas, Bill. I'm so glad you were able to make it. Let me introduce you to everybody. You've met my daughter, Elena. This is my brother-in-law Roberto, and that one over there is my brother Cesar. Carmen, Mom, there is someone here I want you to meet."

Carmen and Rosa came in from the kitchen, wiping their hands on their aprons.

"This is my sister Carmen and my mother, Rosa. And this is Bill Lima. IT&T sent him here to train and supervise me on the new computers."

"Thank you for having me over. I hope I didn't come too late. I brought you this." Bill handed Rosa a bottle of Dom Perignon champagne.

"You didn't have to do that," she said, admiring the very expensive gift. "Please, sit down. Are you hungry?"

"Ma'am, I'm always hungry."

"I like this guy." Cesar smiled. "I'm always happy to meet a fellow glutton."

Bill let out a big jovial laugh and said, "That's me. I see it, I eat it. Oh, Diego, I just came from the office, and I brought you these papers so you wouldn't have to wait until Wednesday for them."

He handed Diego a folder.

Carmen motioned to Bill. "Come sit at the table, Bill, and have something to eat."

They walked into the dining room. Bill took a seat at the table as Cesar walked in from the kitchen with a plate of food for himself. Diego came over, sat down with them, and stared at Cesar and his full plate.

"What?" said Cesar when he saw the look on Diego's face, "I can't let him eat alone. That's bad manners. Bill, try the plantains. They're great and totally nonoppressive."

Again, the doorbell rang, and this time Rosa went to answer it.

"Roberto!" she called from the foyer, "There are some people here to see you."

Roberto got up and went to the door, where a small group of students stood outside on the front steps of the house. They were obviously poor; anyone could tell by the way they were dressed. Most of them black and mulattos. The students began to sing "For He's a Jolly Good Fellow."

When they finished singing, one of the students, Ignacio, a tall, skinny young black man with an intense yet noble look, handed Roberto a package and said, "Professor Machado, we took up a collection and got you this."

"Thank you, Ignacio."

"We figured it would be nice to come over and give you something for a change," said one of the girls in the group, a perky, pretty brunette.

"Thank you, Delia. This is so nice of all of you. You didn't have to do this."

Ignacio interrupted Roberto, "And you don't have to tutor us for free, but you do. If it weren't for you, most of us wouldn't graduate this semester."

"What can I say? And as much I cherish this gift, it's even more gratifying to see all of you graduate. Thank you. Thank you all very much. Please come in."

Ignacio jumped in before anyone could accept the invitation. "Oh no, not today. Today, you and your family should all be together without us around."

He wished Roberto Merry Christmas and led away the group of proud students. Roberto waved goodbye to them and tried to choke back a tear. Then he returned to the dining room, where the others were still talking.

As he entered the room, Roberto said, "So, Mr. Lima, how long have you been in Cuba?"

"A little over a year now, and I really love it. It's a beautiful island, and I have to tell you, I love the weather. I'm from Detroit. Right now it's about ten degrees at home."

Rosa asked, "Are you married?"

"Oh, no," mocked Cesar, "she's trying to marry off somebody else."

"Right now I'm married to my job," answered Bill.

"Good answer," said Cesar. "Why didn't I think of that?"

"Bill met Batista," said Diego.

"What do you think of our president?" asked Roberto.

Bill laughed. "You're the first person I've heard call him president. All I've heard since I've been here is the Dictator this, the Dictator that. As a matter of fact, I was invited to a party at the presidential palace, and when I met Batista, I almost said, 'It's a pleasure to meet you, Mr. Dictator.'"

Everyone laughed.

"I heard a great joke today," said Cesar. "Batista is talking to Pepito and says, 'Pepito, I heard that when I die, you are going to spit on my grave. Is that true?' Then Pepito says, 'Mr. President, that's a lie. Do you think I want to stand in such a long line?'"

Again, everyone laughed loudly.

When the laughter died down, Bill said, "Let me tell you a joke I heard at the presidential dinner, of all places. Batista is flying in his plane, and he says to his pilot, 'Maybe I'll throw a hundred-dollar bill out the window and make some Cuban happy. Or maybe I'll throw out five twenty-dollar bills and make five Cubans happy. Or maybe I'll throw out a hundred one-dollar bills and make a hundred Cubans happy.' Then the pilot says, 'Mr. President, why don't you throw yourself out the window and make every Cuban happy?'"

This brought huge laughter from the group.

Between laughs, Roberto said, "Let's keep it down. Batista's minister of labor lives right across the street."

Elena got serious and changed the mood of the group. "That's how bad things are in this country. We are afraid to even tell a joke. That's why our men and women have to go and fight in the mountains."

"Bill," said Diego, cutting Elena off, "you'll have to excuse my daughter. She's young and excitable. Soon, thank God, she'll be going to New York to study." He turned to his daughter and told her, "Elena, Bill went to NYU."

"Congratulations on getting accepted to medical school, Elena. You'll love it there," said Bill. "NYU is not only a great school, but it's in a great city. I think you'll really like New York."

"That's what I keep telling her," said Diego.

"Trust me, Elena, you won't regret living in New York." Bill looked at his watch and stood up. "Well, I have to run," he said to everyone as he looked at Diego. "I had a great time, but I have to pick up Beth. Happy holidays."

They all wished him Merry Christmas and said their goodbyes. After Bill left, Roberto took the wrapping paper off the present his students had given him. He opened the box, and inside was a plaque. It was engraved, and the inscription read:

> By the powers granted to us by no one, we
> the students of the University of Havana,
> on this day December 25, 1957, bestow
> the doctorate degree of import/export law
> to Professor Roberto Machado."

Cesar, always the wise ass, grinned and said, "Can students really do that? Maybe they can get one of those for me."

Roberto was still looking at the plaque and smiling when he answered, "I don't have a PhD, and there have been a lot of complaints from some students about the university appointing instructors without doctorate degrees. This is my students' way of showing their support."

Elena noticed there was something attached to Roberto's present. "What's that stuck to the back of the plaque?" she asked.

Roberto turned the plaque around and saw an envelope taped to the other side. He opened it and read the note to himself.

"I don't believe this. It's a letter from Joaquin!"

"What is it doing there?" asked Carmen.

"Read it! Read it!" said Rosa.

Roberto began to read out loud.

My loving family,

I wish you all a very merry Christmas. You don't know how much I love and miss all of you. If only I could be there to enjoy Carmen's delicious chicken and rice.

Here in the mountains, we feel we are making great strides toward the liberation of Cuba. I know that my decision to join the revolution is very difficult for all of you to accept, but please realize it was not a decision I made lightly. However, it is one I am very proud of.

My friend Camilo has turned into our greatest military leader. The men in the mountains have learned to respect him as much as they respect Fidel. He is always saying that the world will not turn its back on us just because we are a small island in the Caribbean.

What mother in the world would not cry when she hears of a government that condones thirteen-year-old girls working as prostitutes? Who would not be angry knowing the police see this every night yet do nothing? Who would not be a brother of Cuba when they hear of our young men being murdered in the streets near the mafia-owned casinos?

In some parts of the country, people are starving, while the Dictator dines with gangsters at fancy state dinners. We will let the world know of the peasants' hunger so that the world will hunger for the peasants to be fed. I long for the day when I can hold each and every one of you in my arms in a free and fair Cuba. *Viva Cuba libre.*

Love,
Joaquin

Diego wanted to look at the letter, so Roberto handed it to him.

Elena's emotions were roused by her uncle's words. "That's what I've been trying to say. That's what it's all about. I should not be going to the United States to study. I should stay in Cuba and fight."

Diego jumped out of his chair and told her, "Well, I have news for you, young lady. You're going to the United States. One idealist in this family is enough."

Elena glared at her father. "Just because you don't give a damn about Cuba doesn't mean I don't."

She knew her father wanted nothing to do with changing the situation in their country. He was aware that things were not fair and Batista was corrupt, yet he was willing to just go along. She was angry with him but also disappointed that he could feel that way.

Diego gave her a dirty look and told her. "Well, you can give a damn all you want from the university in the United States."

"Elena, don't you do anything foolish," said Carmen. "I don't need two people to worry about."

Roberto turned to Diego and asked him for the letter back. "We better get rid of this. If anybody sees it, we could get into a lot of trouble."

Cesar was running late and had grown tired of listening to all the political debate. He smiled at Rosa. "Well, I better get going. It's time for me to get myself into trouble." Rosa gave him one of her looks. "Hey, if I don't socialize, how will I find a wife?"

Rosa, knowing where he liked to hang out, asked him, "What kind of wife will you find in the types of places where you go?"

Cesar knew what was to follow. He replied, "Oh, no, not again. I'm getting out of here before you people drive *me* into the mountains. Goodnight, everyone."

He motioned to Elena as he sprinted for the front door. Cesar was Elena's uncle, but because of how close they were in age, they had grown up more like brother and sister. He walked out to the driveway, lit a cigarette, and waited by his car. Shortly, Elena came out to say goodbye to him.

"I may not see you before you leave for the United States," said Cesar, "so I want to give you this." He handed her an old expensive looking box. "Your grandfather gave this to me, but I want you to have it."

Elena opened the box to see a rosary inside. "It's beautiful. Are you sure you want me to have this?"

"I hope it brings you lots of luck in the United States. Besides, what am I gonna do with it? Wait until I get married and give it to my kid? I don't think the beads will last that long."

They both laughed and hugged each other.

"I will cherish it and keep it with me forever," said Elena as she tearfully said goodbye to Cesar.

He was about to get in his car when he turned, looked back at her, and said, "Please don't go and do anything crazy. Your father might be a pain in the ass…" he paused for a moment and smiled. "Actually, he *is* a pain in the ass." They both laughed. He looked at her and told her, "But he is right. You need to go to the United States and finish your studies. Don't stay here and waste your time with all the bullshit that is going on. They have given up on me, but there is still hope for you."

He flashed her one of his winning smiles, got into his convertible, and sped off, honking the horn all the way until he turned the corner. Elena shook her head, laughed, and wiped her eyes.

Chapter **4**

The Tropical Brewery Dance

CESAR PULLED UP to the Tropical Brewery and could hear that the festivities were in full swing. He parked his car and hurried to meet with his friends as he danced to the beat of the music that could be heard all the way to the parking lot. It was truly a beautiful scene. Lush, colorful gardens surrounded the brewery, and there was an outdoor stage with a full Latin band playing music loud and fast.

Those who attended the dance were a mixture of the middle and lower classes. Everyone was neatly dressed, and there was electricity in the air. Two of Cesar's friends, Alberto, a good looking mulatto, and Armando, a blond and blue-eyed fellow, saw him and waved. Cesar walked up to them, and they greeted one another with handshakes and hugs.

"Cesar, you're late again," said Armando. Cesar was constantly late, and Armando always kidded him about it. "How the hell do you ever manage to deliver the mail on time? You're lucky you still have a job."

"The family dinner ran longer than I thought it would. What can I say?" Cesar continued, tongue in cheek. "I'm a very busy man."

"Yeah, very busy delivering the mail late and banging every chick on your route," said Alberto. "Armando is right. There's no way you will last much longer."

"First of all, I have not banged every chick on my route," said Cesar, "just the pretty ones." They all laughed, and Cesar continued, "All I need to do is hang on for a couple of more years delivering, let's say, *most* of the mail, and I will have enough money saved up for art school."

"You are really going to be a painter?" asked Armando.

Before Cesar could say anything, Alberto jumped in. "The only things Cesar is going to paint are houses."

"I'm not going to be a painter. I want to be a commercial artist, you morons." Cesar shot them the bird, and they all laughed. As their laughter died down, Cesar asked, "Where is Jose? Did he get lucky already?"

"Are you serious?" said Armando. "He is the only guy I know who can come to a place like this and not get laid."

Just as Jose, a homely looking young man, returned to the group, a huge commotion broke out. A beautiful and very sexy young woman was screaming and fighting with a much larger man. Because of them, the festivities came to a standstill as people looked to see what the noise was all about. They were so loud even the band stopped playing. The big man had her by the wrists. He was shaking her and cursing while she flailed and kicked at him. That was when several policemen charged over to the disturbance, hit the big man a couple of times with their nightsticks, and tried to drag both of them away.

"Wow," said Armando. "I wonder if she has that much fire between the sheets." He was impressed as he watched her do a pretty good job of defending herself against the much larger man.

"Well, let's find out," answered Cesar, and he started to walk toward them.

The woman would not stop struggling. "Let me go, Maricon! I'll scratch your eyes out if you don't get your filthy hands off me!"

"I've heard just about enough out of you," said the policeman. He raised his nightstick up over his head, ready to strike a blow.

Cesar stepped between them and showed the cop a twenty-dollar bill. He stuffed it in the policeman's pocket and said, "Excuse me, Officer, the lady is with me."

The officer took the bill out of his pocket, examined it, and a big smile lit up his face. "No trouble at all, sir."

The officer let go of the woman and went to help the others drag her attacker away. He was such a big man it took all the policemen to control him. They were finally able to hustle the huge man out while she watched. The young woman stepped back a little, and her eyes slowly looked Cesar up and down. What she saw in front of her was a good looking man dressed like someone with money and status.

"Thank you. My name is Juana, and you?"

"Cesar. Are you okay?"

"Yeah, fine," she said as she straightened her dress and tried to fix her tousled hair.

"Is that guy your boyfriend?"

"Pablo? Not anymore."

The band started to play again, and she slowly walked close to Cesar, grabbed both of his hands, and said, "Let's dance."

When they danced past Cesar's friends, they all hooted, cheered, and shouted encouragement. The band played a very hot, very fast Latin number, and Juana reveled in all the attention. The longer they danced, the sexier and more provocative she became. After the fast song ended, the band eased into a ballad, and Cesar and Juana embraced, dancing to the slow music. Soon, they were groping each other more than they were actually dancing. Cesar held her tighter against him and told her how much he liked the way she danced and moved.

In a very sexy voice, Juana whispered in his ear, "Why don't we get out of here, and I'll show you what other moves I've got?"

At first Cesar was taken aback by her boldness. But when he looked at her face, he smiled, picked her up, and carried her off the dance floor. As they passed his friends, he winked at them and continued to carry Juana all the way to his car, leaving them stunned and speechless.

Jose, amazed at what he had just seen, asked the others, "Where are they going?"

Alberto looked at his incredulous friend and answered, "Where do you think, dummy?" Then he smacked Jose on the back of the head.

The next morning, Cesar awoke in Juana's bed. Her small apartment was located in one of the poor sections of the city. He looked at his watch and saw that it was already 11:00 a.m. He realized he was all the way across town and would barely have enough time to make it to the stadium.

There was no way he was going to miss the biggest baseball game of the year. It was the Havana Lions, which Diego rooted for, against the Almendares Scorpions, which was Cesar, Tico, and Roberto's favorite team. He was supposed to meet them at the ballpark no later than eleven thirty for the game that started at noon. He had no chance of getting there on time, but he figured he was always being told he was late anyway, so why should he start disappointing people now?

He quietly got up from the bed, trying not to wake Juana. But it seemed women had a sixth sense about these kinds of things, and of course, she immediately woke up.

As he quietly dressed, she said, "Good morning."

He looked back at her and, with one of those bright smiles of his, told her, "It's the best morning." He continued to dress.

"Where are you going in such a rush? Don't you want me to make you some breakfast?" asked Juana.

She was still lying in bed, looking very inviting, giving him one of those "I don't want you to leave" looks. Part of Cesar wanted to jump right back in the sack with her, but he really had to get to the game.

He finished putting his clothes on, came over to the bed, gave her a passionate kiss, and told her, "I would love to stay and have breakfast, lunch, and dinner with you, but I have to meet my asshole brother, my nephew, and my brother-in-law. We're going to the game."

She shrugged her shoulders and looked at him blankly.

"The game?" he said, "The Lions against the Scorpions? The biggest game of the year?" He looked around in search of his car keys. "My Scorpions have been trailing the Lions all season long, but they have been able to climb from ten games back in last place, all the way into a tie for first."

She could tell how excited he was as he continued, "If we beat Havana today, we take sole position of first place. And there is no way," he laughed while he laced his shoes,

"I am going to miss the look on my brother's face when we beat his beloved Lions."

Juana laughed and told him how silly men were with their little boy games. "Go ahead and have a good time," she said. "When will I hear from you again?"

Cesar reached over and planted another big kiss on her beautiful, full lips.

"After the game. If we win, I'll come back and take you out to celebrate. If we lose, I will be in jail for killing my brother."

He smiled, gave her one more kiss, and walked out. Cesar got in his car and drove like a mad man to the baseball stadium, not because he was concerned about being late, but because he could not wait to watch the game. Like all Cuban males and many females too, baseball, or as it was called locally, *beisbol*, was in their blood. Cubans did not watch baseball, they *lived* it. And a game like this brought out all of Havana, especially today, Christmas Day, when everyone was off.

Baseball was played in Cuba during the winter and was properly called winter ball. Many American Major League players would come to Cuba and play in the Cuban winter league. To the Cubans, it wasn't winter ball; it was *El Campeonato de Beisbol,* and today it seemed like almost everyone in the capital was at the game. Those who could not get tickets hung around outside the park and cheered or groaned, listening to the stadium announcer from the parking lot.

At the Machado's, Diego, Tico, and Roberto were getting into Diego's car to go to the game, and the ribbing between Roberto the Scorpion fan and Diego the Lion fan had already begun. On their street, they could see the other fathers and sons in the neighborhood sporting the hats and shirts of their own respective teams, getting in their vehicles to go to the big game. People from all races and social classes melded together at these events, and they cheered as one for their beloved teams.

Diego, Tico, and Roberto drove to the stadium, pulled into the parking lot, walked to the gate, handed over their tickets, and went to their seats.

Diego told Tico and Roberto, "You guys better hope and pray the Lions win, or I'm going to make you walk home."

Tico turned to him with a mock "I don't care attitude" and told him, "That's okay. Uncle Cesar will take us home in his car. His is nicer. It's a convertible."

Roberto piped up, "Yes, who wants to ride in the same car with a guy that rooted for the losing team? How depressing would that be?"

Diego looked at them and chuckled. "Well, we all know Cesar. Who knows when, or if, Cesar will show up? So you might be stuck with me and have to walk home after all. Besides, trust me, the Lions are not going to lose."

Roberto fired back, "We'll see about that. And believe me, there is no way Cesar is going to miss this game."

Just as Roberto said that, Cesar arrived and sat next to Tico.

"Well, well, look who is here. It's Mister I-Can't-Be-on-Time-for-Anything," said Diego.

Cesar looked past his brother and asked Roberto, "So what did I miss? How many runs are we ahead already?"

Roberto laughed and Tico told him, "It's just about to start right now!"

The Cuban national anthem was played, and as soon as the umpire at home plate yelled "Play ball!" the place erupted in cheers.

The game was a nail biter. It was one of those pitchers' duels that kept the crowd on its feet because every at bat could mean the game. The Machados and Quintanas drank beer and ate medianoche sandwiches, and of course, Cesar had to have two of everything. Tico had Coca-Colas and feasted on hot dogs that were sold at the Cuban stadium, very much the same way it was done at the American ballparks.

In the bottom of the ninth, the score was 2-1 in favor of the Lions, and Diego wore a smile of confidence. But the Scorpions were the home team for this game. Because all the clubs played at the same stadium, the famous but old El Parque del Cerro, the teams switched back and forth for home field advantage. Today it was the Scorpions' turn. All the Havana club had to do was hang on for three more outs, and the game belonged to them.

On the mound was their young fireballer, an American kid that had been called up to the majors by the Yankees at the end of the season. The guy was a can't miss phenom who threw close to a hundred miles an hour. The Yankees, who played a lot of exhibition games in Cuba during spring training, usually sent their young prospects to Cuba to get more seasoning in winter ball. He was now on the mound, ready to mow down the Scorpion hitters.

The first two batters for the Almendares team made easy groundouts. But the next batter was a seasoned veteran of both the major leagues and Cuban winter ball, a guy who was able to work the count against young pitchers. He sliced several foul balls until he managed to wrestle a walk out of the frustrated young hurler.

The crowd cheered as the Scorpions' potential winning run stepped up to the plate. He was Conrado Rivera, the aging slugger for the Scorpions that had always been Roberto's idol. He was the reason Tico's first middle name was Conrado. Tico came close to being named Cesario because he was born by a very difficult cesarean section. Roberto, for whatever crazy reason that must have made sense to him at the time, promised God he would name his son Cesario if he was born alive and healthy. Carmen said there was no way she would ever saddle a child of hers with that name, so they settled on Cesario as his second middle name. Cubans traditionally gave many middle names to their children. The Machados gave Tico his first as Conrado in honor of Roberto's idol, the great Scorpion slugger.

Rivera walked to the plate amid the roar of the Almendares fans. He approached the plate, took a couple of practice swings at the air, and prepared to take his at bat. The young pitcher was throwing smoke, and the aging slugger missed the first two pitches badly. The Scorpions fans groaned, and the Lions fans cheered. Conrado stepped away from the plate and looked at the crowd for a few seconds. It seemed as if he wanted to muster all the accolades and cheers he had received throughout his great career into his next swing. He listened to the roar of the fans for a few more seconds and stepped back into the batter's box.

"Here it comes," said Diego. "Strike three, and you're all out!" He laughed.

The pitcher waved the catcher off a couple of times, insisting on throwing the fastball that he was sure the aging slugger could not catch up to. The young player wound up and delivered the heat. When the ball reached home plate, Conrado made perfect contact and launched it out of El Cerro's park. The Scorpion's fans were delirious. Their team had just won the crucial game, 3-2, on one swing of Rivera's bat.

Diego was about to lose his mind. Not only had his Lions lost, but he knew the three of them would ride him like a pony all the way home, and that was exactly what they did. Cesar, Tico, and Roberto were merciless. They taunted Diego and teased him all the way out of the stadium and to his car in the parking lot. Outside the ballpark, the Almendares fans celebrated, cheering and screaming, ribbing the Lions fans as they marched quietly out of the stadium all the way to the streets.

As if that wasn't enough, Diego's misery was compounded by one of the comparsas, the Cangrejeros. They were practicing for carnival, which was quickly approaching, and had come to cheer for their favorite club. The comparsas were groups of dancers, singers, and musicians who would dance, strut, and shuffle their way along the carnival parade route much like the groups that performed "When the Saints Go Marching In" during Mardi Gras in New Orleans.

For close to fifty years, the tradition had been passed from generation to generation. The oldest and most famous of all the comparsas were the Cangrejeros. Their symbol and their name was the crab, and they would go from one end of the carnival parade route to the other, marching, dancing, strutting, and shuffling to the beat of their own signature song.

It just so happened that most, if not all, of their members were Scorpions fans. And today, just as they did for other important games, different Comparsas that were preparing for their carnival performance would show up at the stadium. They came dressed in their fancy comparsas' attire to root for the team of their choice while they performed and partied outside before and after the games.

Today the Cangrejeros were celebrating their team victory, and as they did during carnival, they made their way around the outside of the stadium, playing their drums, timbales, and other musical instruments, marching and dancing to the beat of their famous song.

"Mirala que linda viene, mirala que linda va, la comparsa cangrejera, mira la que linda va."

Diego, being a Lions fan, hated that damn song with a passion. He could not wait to leave the stadium and all the Scorpion celebration. Tico and Roberto got in the car and continued their teasing of Diego on the ride back. Since Diego did not follow through with his threat of making them walk home, Tico sat in the back seat, making meow noises to mock a lion's roar, while Roberto kept asking Diego, "So what was the final score again?"

Tico had a wonderful time and loved all the fun he had with his father and uncles.

Cesar rushed to pick up Juana and made good on his promise to take her out and celebrate. He was surprised at how much he wanted to see her again. It wasn't only because she was a knockout and great in bed, *boy, was she good in bed!* It was something about the way he felt so soon after meeting her that he could not figure out. Unlike all his other romantic conquests, Cesar did not mention her to his brother or Roberto. He just said he had to go, and off he went.

Chapter 5

University of Havana

THERE WAS A meeting being held in a basement room at the University of Havana. It was a small group made up of both men and women. Ignacio, the student who had given Roberto the plaque, sat near the back. Elena was in the front right next to Ramon, a passionate young man who spoke to the group.

"Remember," he said, "we must keep moving supplies to the Sierra Maestra. The success of the revolution depends on it." He glanced down at Elena. "As some of you may know, Elena is going to the United States. While there, she will be in contact with our people to get medicine and supplies. It is very important that each of you provide mailing addresses

:ver been used before." He paused. "I know all
ngerous, but it is nowhere near as dangerous for
r the rebels in the mountains. At any time, they
could be hit by a surprise attack, even shot in their sleep.
The better equipped they are, the better they will be able
to tend to their wounded, and the less often they will have
to bury their dead."

He thanked them all for their courage and patriotism
then dismissed them with a warning to always be alert.

Meanwhile, in the mountains, the battle against
Batista's forces continued. A surprise attack by the army was
intense, though short, because the rebels were able to push
back the assault. They had become a force to be reckoned
with, a formidable foe. The battle for the liberation of Cuba
slowly began to take a turn in their favor.

The rebels had not only made strides on the battlefield
but in the public relations arena as well. More and more
men and women were joining them in the mountains. It
wasn't only peasants who, in many cases, had to be educated
as to how horrible their plight was. (Sometimes ignorance
really is bliss.) The rebels were also joined by young men
and women from middle and upper middle class families
that were angry about the injustices in their country. They
were sick of the dictatorships that had ruled and plagued
Cuba almost from the very beginning of its independence.

In the United States, Fidel and the rebels' fight in the
mountains had begun to get some attention, and many

newspapers had to decide whether to send their reporters to cover the story. The *New York Times* was the first one to dispatch a correspondent to the Sierra Maestra to meet with Fidel and his rebels. The *Times* reporter came to Cuba, made contact with the underground in Havana, and was secretly escorted to the Sierra Maestra mountains to have his interview with Fidel. Fidel was very eager to meet with the American reporter and have a chance to explain his motives and ideals to the American public.

The reporter from the *Times* was very impressed and captivated by Fidel's charisma and believed that Fidel was sincere when he told him he was not a communist or a terrorist like Batista had painted him and his men to be. He assured the *Times* reporter that he was for democracy, following the Cuban Constitution, and open and fair elections. He emphasized that he and his men were fighting for the liberation of Cuba, to rid her of its history of dictatorships and abuse. He told the reporter they wanted to create a more fair and equal system for all people, especially the guajiros, who had always been ignored and taken advantage of. The article was not only printed in the pages of the *New York Times*. It was picked up by the wire services and appeared all across the United States.

The favorable article with its glowing characterization of Fidel by the most influential newspaper in the country created a small groundswell of support for Fidel and his men. That translated into donations that were desperately needed by the rebels.

The initial help from the CIA was starting to dry up due to the US government's dissatisfaction with the rebel attacks on several sugar refineries that were owned by United States industries, like Hershey and the United Fruit Company. Those giant influential companies were not happy with the disruption and loss of income to their businesses due to the recurrent attacks by the rebels. Fidel reasoned that they had to attack the production of enterprises that were vital to Batista's ability to generate income and run the country. Those attacks also hurt the dictator personally because the disruptions cut into Batista's kickbacks.

The CIA began a retreat from their involvement with Fidel and his rebels and took a more cautious approach. They had some agents in Cuba already but now decided to send others to spy and keep tabs not only on the rebels but the situation with Batista and his ability to stay in power.

Thanks to the *Times* and other glowing newspaper and magazine articles, Fidel had become a cause célèbre not only in the United States but in many other parts of the world.

Havana, February 1958

It was carnival time once again, and like every year, Havana was full of tourists and locals ready to party and enjoy the amazing parade. The uprising in the mountains was proceeding at full strength, but the people of Havana continued to enjoy life as if nothing had changed.

Although the carnival in Cuba could not compare in size with the one in Rio De Janeiro, it made up for that in style and exuberance. The floats were magnificent. They were sponsored by private businesses that tried to outdo one another with one float being more extravagant than the next and all of them costing a great deal of money.

One could find the king and queen of the carnival and many beautiful ladies waving to the crowd from those floats, just like in New Orleans or Rio. On board other floats, there were all kinds of celebrities. Famous Cuban singers belted out popular songs to their adoring fans over loud speakers mounted on the floats as they traveled the parade route. Cuban actors and actresses as well as some dignitaries also rode on the floats and waved to the excited crowd.

The parade route went all through the city before it turned onto the boulevard along the Malecon, the famous seawall that surrounded Havana Bay. It continued all the way to the bridge that crossed the Almendares River, which connected Havana with Miramar, the affluent suburb on the other side of the Almendares. In addition to the floats, the parade consisted of the many comparsas that strutted along the parade route, playing their instruments and singing their songs. There was also an opportunity for private citizens to join in. Some people who owned convertibles were selected and invited to participate on the carnival route and fill their cars with friends and relatives to become part of the festivities, waving to everyone along the parade route.

This year Cesar was one of the lucky ones chosen to bring along his convertible full of friends to join the parade and act like they were important people waving to the eager crowd. Cesar, Armando, Alberto, and Jose, along with some of Jose's cousins, were going to pile into Cesar's car and join the carnival. But an hour before they were to line up with the rest of the floats and comparsas, Jose and his cousins had to bow out. Jose got word that his father was ill and heading to the hospital. Jose and his cousins broke the bad news to Cesar and went to meet up with the rest of their family.

Cesar and his buddies felt bad for Jose, but they were now screwed. They did not have enough people to fill their car and would no longer be able to be part of the parade. Cesar and his two pals ran to the nearby payphones and tried to contact some other friends. But everyone they knew was already at the parade. They had come to watch and wave at them. Cesar thought about calling Juana but decided that would not be such a good idea. He knew he would never hear the end of it from his buddies. Cesar didn't know what to do. He had applied to be in the carnival parade ever since he had gotten his convertible three years ago. This year he had finally been accepted and was not about to let the opportunity slip by.

Then he remembered his family was not coming to the parade this year. Instead they had decided to gather at Carmen's house and watch it on TV. Rosa was getting too old to fight the crowds, and Carmen did not want to leave her alone. Besides, Carmen had a cold and wasn't feeling too well. They knew Cesar was going to be part of the carnival, and they wanted to get a good look at him on television. Cesar and Armando decided to take a chance, and they headed for Cesar's sister's house.

They left Alberto with the convertible to make sure the parade officials would not disqualify them. Armando sped toward Carmen's house in his jalopy, and he and Cesar both prayed they would be able to talk the group into joining them. When Cesar got to his sister's house, he rushed in and found all of them sitting by the TV, waiting for the parade to start.

Out of breath, Cesar panted, "Thank God you are all here!"

The family was stunned to see him.

Carmen saw both he and Armando gasping for air, and she asked Cesar, "What's wrong? Are you two okay? What are you doing here? Aren't you supposed to be getting ready to be in the parade?"

The others wondered the same thing.

Cesar tried to catch his breath and told them, "Jose's father got sick and had to go to the hospital. We are at least three people short of what we need to qualify to be in the parade. We want all of you to come and join us."

Rosa asked, "What happened to Jose's father?"

"I'm sorry, Mom, I don't really know," answered Cesar. "But please come with us, or we will be thrown out of the carnival. If I don't show up with at least three more people in the next thirty minutes, we are out. I have been waiting three years for this, so please come with me now."

Tico immediately jumped up and said, "I want to go! I want to go!"

The kid could not believe his good luck. He was so excited. He couldn't wait to be part of that parade and have a chance to be on TV. Roberto also said he would go. Diego was the first to say he wouldn't. He was not in a celebratory mood. His beloved Lions had just lost the championship to the Scorpions by just one game, and Diego was in no mood to be in a parade.

"Count me out. I'm not going to be part of any silly parade. I just want to stay here and watch it on TV."

Rosa did not want to go either, and Carmen's cold was worse than before, so she was not up to it.

Cesar was upset. "Oh, come on, I'm going to be one person short. I can't believe you are going to let me be thrown out of the carnival because I'm missing one body. He turned to his brother. "Come on, Diego, don't be such a sourpuss. Just because my Scorpions beat your Lions, you are going to let me lose out on this?"

Cesar knew his brother was annoyed with him. He had been driving Diego crazy, celebrating the Almendares victory. His Scorpions had come out of nowhere to not only catch but pass Diego's Lions and wrestle the trophy right out of their hands. Cesar was constantly making fun of his brother's Havana team, which had lost the championship.

Diego defensively told him, "It has nothing to do with that. I just don't feel like waving at a bunch of strangers from a car."

Tico turned to Diego and pleaded with him, "Please, Uncle Diego, come with us. We need you to come, please."

Tico was overcome with excitement and would not stop asking Diego to come with them.

Roberto also said to Diego, "Come on, come with us. You will have a great time, and you'll get to be on TV. If you don't want to wave at the crowd, just sit there and look at the pretty girls. It will take your mind off your loser team."

Cesar and Armando heard this and smiled at each other. Now Rosa and Carmen started to put pressure on Diego so Cesar wouldn't lose out on this fun opportunity. Diego kept trying to get out of going, but after all the pleading by everyone, he finally and reluctantly said yes.

They all piled into Armando's wreck of a car and rushed like a bunch of lunatics to Cesar's convertible. When they got there, Alberto was involved in a heated discussion with one of the parade officials that kept asking him to produce the rest of his people. He insisted that Alberto at least give him the names of everyone that was going to be in the car.

"If your people are not here in five minutes, I'm disqualifying this vehicle."

Alberto saw them coming, turned to the official, and pointed to Cesar and the rest of them. "There they are.

You see? I was not lying. They all just wanted to go to the bathroom first."

The official turned to them, asked their names, wrote them down on the official form, and left.

"Thank God you got here when you did. That prick was threatening to throw us out if you guys didn't show up soon," said Alberto.

"Well, we are here now, so let's get in the car and go," said a very happy Cesar.

"Yeah, let's go!" echoed Tico.

They all got in. Tico wanted to ride shotgun, so he and Roberto sat in the front with Cesar, who drove. Armando, Alberto, and Diego all got in the back, and they eased their way toward the parade route. Diego, still not too happy about being there, tried to make the best out of the whole situation. The car inched up, and Cesar was given the spot right behind the float with the queen of the carnival. Besides the queen herself, the float was full of pretty girls making up the queen's court.

Roberto turned back to look at Diego and told him, "See? What did I tell you? You have the best spot in the whole parade. You get to look at all those beautiful women for the entire afternoon."

Cesar also turned back and said, "That's not all. There is a big surprise that you are going to love."

"What is that?" asked Diego.

"It's a surprise. If I tell you, it will ruin it."

Cesar positioned his car right behind the king and queen's float as they moved up to where the parade was to start. The first few blocks of the route were great. They all waved, and Tico blew kisses at the crowd. He had just turned eight-years-old and was having the time of his life. Diego started to relax a little and decided it was not so bad after all. He even kind of enjoyed waving at all the people who lined the street.

This went on for a few blocks until they turned onto a wide avenue. That was when the comparsas joined in and blended into the parade along with the floats. Diego had just begun to feel comfortable and enjoy himself when, to his horror, he heard the sound of the Cangrejeros. The comparsas marched and strutted their stuff then broke into their famous song that Diego abhorred. He turned around, saw the Cangrejeros, and could not believe that stupid comparsas had joined in right behind them, blasting that damn, rotten song. Diego was mortified. He would have to be in front of the Cangrejeros the entire parade route, listening to that god-awful sound.

As soon as the comparsas broke into their song, Cesar turned to Diego and, with a devilish smile on his face, said, "*Surprise!* So how are you enjoying yourself? Having a good time?"

Diego looked at his brother, wanting to kill him. The bastard had known all along that the Cangrejeros were going to be right behind them, and he swore Cesar had planned the whole thing just to make him miserable.

"You asshole!" was all Diego could get out.

Immediately, all of them, together and unrehearsed but right on cue, turned to Diego and sang at the top of their lungs: *"Mirala que linda viene, mirala que linda va, la Comparsa Cangrejera, mirala que linda va."*

Tico was laughing his head off along with the rest of the guys in the car. Diego just sank into his seat, fuming. The others swore they saw smoke coming out of his ears.

After they all got their kicks singing to Diego, he addressed everyone in the car, "You fucking bastards, you will all pay for this."

Of course, that made them all laugh harder and sing louder. Diego almost jumped out of the car; he was so annoyed. But he thought the better of it and just sat there and brooded while the Cangrejeros continued to sing, block after block after block. As if that was not enough, Cesar took out a bunch of Almendares hats and banners he had in his glove compartment and passed them to Armando, Alberto, Roberto, and Tico. They put them on and waved their pennants to the crowd that cheered as they drove by. Diego sank deeper into his seat.

If you had asked Diego for how long this went on, he would have answered, *"Forever."* But after a while, even he had to chuckle at the situation and kept repeating, "You are all going to pay for this, I swear."

But he said it with a smile on his face as he settled in and tried to make the best of it. He still could not believe that he was stuck in a car with a bunch of Scorpions fans with their hats and championship banners and that stupid song in his ears. He knew the time would come when things would be reversed and he would be the one gloating.

The parade ended at the bridge in front of, of all places, the Almendares River, from which the team took its name. Armando and Alberto said their goodbyes and left in Armando's car.

Diego got back in Cesar's car and told them, "I swear if any of you start to sing that song again, I'm going to kill you all, and that goes for you too, you little runt." He said it while looking right at Tico.

So, of course, they sang the song over and over all the way home. Diego sat shaking his head and mumbling under his breath, "God I hate you, Scorpions fans. Just wait till next year, you bastards."

Chapter 6

New York City, March 1958

ENRIQUE WAS NERVOUS. He was nineteen years old and had worked as a janitor at the hospital for several months. As he took a large bag of trash outside to the dumpster, he looked both ways down the hall and went out the back door. After taking a few steps into the alley, he saw Elena waiting for him.

He walked up to her and whispered, "Elena, I can't keep doing this. Some people at the hospital are starting to notice things that are missing." He took a large plastic bag out of the trash he carried and handed it to her.

Elena ignored what he said. "Were you able to get all the medicine I asked for? It's very important, Enrique. We both have family in the mountains. They might be the ones who need this the most."

"But what if I lose my job?" he told her, nervously looking around.

"The hell with the job. Don't you want to go back to a free Cuba? Do you want to be a janitor in the United States for the rest of your life?" She moved closer and pleaded with him, "They need medicine, Enrique, and they need it now. Get as much as you can for as long as you can. We need to save as many lives as possible. That's what we're doing, Enrique. We're saving lives."

Enrique ran his fingers through his thick hair and paused for a moment. "Okay, okay." He searched through his pockets and handed her a piece of paper. "Here is my friend Rolando's telephone number. He works at Mount Sinai. He says he is willing to help. Come back tomorrow. I'll get what I can."

Back in Havana

Now that Elena was at school in New York, Diego was spending more time hanging around his sister Carmen's house, especially on the weekends. He was a lonely widower and empty nester who found staying at home by himself too depressing. He missed Elena terribly. They had been very close ever since her mother died, and Diego was having trouble coping with Elena's absence. A love life was something he had not even thought about.

He was a good looking man with a great job and a very bright future. There were plenty of women, beautiful women, that had made it clear they wanted him, but he felt nothing. Diego had not once tried to meet or date a woman since his wife, Mercedes, had passed away. He had resigned himself to the fact that there was only one woman for him in this lifetime and Mercedes was the one. He had said it to Elena over and over whenever they reminisced about her mother, and she had grown to expect that from her father. After all these years, it was unthinkable to Elena that her father would be with any other woman.

One Saturday when Diego was visiting his mother and sister, Tico was scheduled to have his first of four sittings for a portrait. It was to be painted by a young artist a friend of Roberto had recommended. Roberto had planned to take Tico to the studio, but he had to go to the port instead because one of the shipments he was brokering for a client was held up by a hard nosed customs agent. Diego had no plans for the day, so he volunteered to take Tico.

Carmen thanked him over and over again. She could not take Tico herself, and they did not want to cancel the first sitting, especially at the last minute. The young up-and-coming artist was named Alejandra Visquel. Doing the painting of Tico was a favor for the Machados, as she had stopped doing portraits and was involved in developing her own style. But Roberto had known her uncle Marcelo ever since they met at the university. The two men had remained friends after graduation, given that both of them opened their own import-export businesses and continued to stay in touch. Due to Roberto's friendship with her uncle, Alejandra agreed to do the project.

Diego drove Tico to the studio and told him they would have ice cream afterward if Tico promised to sit still so they could finish quicker. "The quieter you are and the less you move around, the bigger the ice cream you will get," Diego told the boy.

Tico gladly agreed, and they shook on it. Diego parked the car right in front. He and Tico walked up to the studio, where they were met by the artist, Alejandra, a beautiful woman in her early thirties.

From the moment their eyes met, there was a noticeable electricity between them. Diego could not believe what was happening to him. He had known this woman for mere minutes, yet he was experiencing the same reaction toward Alejandra as when he had first met Mercedes. Long ago he had forgotten what that was like. He felt lost. He was stunned and full of a feeling that could only be described as giddiness. And by the look on Alejandra's face, it was evident she felt the same way.

She was a beautiful woman, and there had been many suitors, especially in Paris, where the men were so good looking and sexy. But there was never any real love. As an artist, she longed for a spark, something to bring out passion and emotion. Yet after all this time, she had never met *the one*. But there was something about this man she could not explain. She had just met him and instantly knew she wanted to see him again.

She went about setting up for the portrait and Tico was a champ. He sat for the entire two hours and hardly moved. All he could think about was the giant ice cream he was going to get out of this deal. Alejandra painted, and Diego acted like a schoolboy, trying to be funny and charming. He could not believe he was acting that way, but he had no intention of stopping. For the first time in a long time, he felt something inside him that he thought had died with Mercedes. He was not about to let it go.

From that day on, Diego became Tico's official portrait chaperone. By the third sitting, he got up the nerve to ask Alejandra to dinner, and she gladly accepted. Within a couple of months, the two were inseparable. Diego felt alive again.

Diego had recently made his relationship with Alejandra known to most of the family. They were all very happy for him, especially Rosa, who knew how lonely he had been since Mercedes died. For a long time, she had hoped he would find someone new in his life. Cesar did not know about Alejandra since he was not around much anymore, spending most of his time with Juana. Elena was not aware of Alejandra either. Diego had failed to mention it to her in his letters or in their phone conversations.

He did not want to break the news to her while she was away at school by mail or over the phone. He decided to wait and tell her in person when she came home during her upcoming spring break. He had told Elena so many times that Mercedes was the only woman for him that he felt almost ashamed to admit to her that he had fallen in love again. But he was happier than he had been in years. He was truly in love with Alejandra. He was going out, having fun, and living life again.

One night Bill Lima invited Diego and Alejandra to join him and his girlfriend, Beth, at the famous Tropicana nightclub. Bill had mentioned to Diego that Beth was a secretary at the US embassy. They met while he was there taking care of some immigration issues, and they hit it off.

Havana, at that time, was considered the Paris of the Caribbean with one of the best night lives anywhere. There were many great nightclubs and casinos throughout the city, but the Tropicana was the cream of the crop. The nightclub was a world-famous tourist attraction. People from all over the world came to Cuba, and they had to visit this amazing showroom for its grand performances and unique atmosphere. It was all done up in good taste but very much over the top. The décor was all glitz and mirrors, more extravagant than many showrooms in Vegas, and had some of the most amazing and beautiful sets, along with the latest in electronic stage equipment. Showgirls emerged from the ceiling and from under the stage, with waterfalls and fire appearing and disappearing. It was truly spectacular.

The Tropicana also boasted some of the most magnificent and striking women in very flamboyant and revealing costumes. The skimpy outfits were as famous as the showgirls due to how provocative they were, especially for the mid-1950s. The ladies performed amazingly choreographed dance numbers with moves that seemed to defy gravity because of their elaborate attire. The costumes were wildly extravagant with plumage and enormous headdresses that cost a fortune. The showgirls were mostly from Cuba, where they were called vedettes, but some were recruited from all over the world, a few coming from as far as the famous Lido in Paris and other equally renowned showrooms. All the women were beautiful and stunning.

The club also brought in entertainers from the United States. Sometimes there were famous singers and other types of performers that catered to the large American crowds that attended the Tropicana. This particular week, they had a comic by the name of Johnny Ray performing in between the big productions.

When the showgirls took their first break, Johnny Ray was introduced, assumed the stage, and proceeded with his show. His act consisted of a set of prepared jokes and comedy bits, but Johnny was the type of comedian that also liked to play with the audience. This night he went around to the poor souls who had seats in the first row at the front of the stage, trying to find something to make fun of and play around with them. Bill and Diego's table was ringside but way off to the side in a corner. Johnny moved from table to table, making jokes and comments, but he hit gold when he saw the amount of food in front of Bill. He immediately noticed the many main course dishes Bill had ordered. As Bill devoured his cuisine and listened to the show, Johnny Ray took one look at Bill with his enormous amount of food and tore into him.

"Ladies and gentlemen, I read in the paper today of the many children that go hungry each night throughout the world. Well, folks, now I know why." He pointed at Bill. "This guy right here is the reason. Look at all the food this man is consuming. No wonder there is nothing left for the rest of the world."

Everyone laughed and look toward their table.

Johnny leaned over to Bill and said, "Sir, don't you think five steaks, three salads, four rolls, and six deserts are enough? Maybe we should call your waiter and order some more. Oh, wait, now I get it. You're trying to break the world record!"

The audience was howling. Some people even stood from their chairs, trying to get a better look at the pile of food and the person Johnny was referring to. Bill, with his fair skin and freckles, turned beet red. Beth, Diego, and Alejandra wanted to hide under the table as the audience would not stop laughing and looking at them. Johnny Ray went on for a few more seconds about Bill's food intake before he moved on to his next victim.

The show went on, but Bill had lost his appetite and slowly pushed the plates away.

When he did that, Diego, Alejandra, and Beth all looked at one another and then back at Bill and started to laugh. At first Bill was not too happy with them, but even he had to chuckle. The comedian was right. He had ordered enough food to feed an army.

Beth leaned over and planted a big kiss on his cheek and said to Bill, "Don't pay any attention to that bad man, honey. You need to eat. You are getting too skinny."

They all laughed again, with Bill joining them this time. The rest of the show went on, and it was spectacular, every bit as amazing and entertaining as advertised. When the show ended, Bill insisted in picking up the tab, and they all went out to get their cars. Bill was not ready to go home yet, and while they waited for the valet to bring their vehicles, he suggested they all go someplace else for a nightcap.

"Hey, guys, I know of this nice little bar that has great daiquiris, and nobody will make fun of me there."

They all laughed at Bill's comment, but the girls were tired, and instead they all went home. Diego drove to his house, and Alejandra stayed with him. She was practically living with Diego. It was a bit bold for the times, especially in Cuba, but the love birds did not care. They were no longer children. They were totally in love and were planning on getting married sometime in the future anyway. Diego was very happy but could not stop thinking of how the hell he was going to break the news to Elena. He felt like a little kid with his hand caught in the cookie jar, and he could not figure out a way to break the news to his daughter.

The same night that Diego went to the Tropicana nightclub, Cesar had finally been talked or, more accurately, shamed into going out on the town with his buddies. Cesar was spending all his time with Juana, and his friends were constantly giving him hell and calling him pussy whipped. Cesar kept deflecting their ribbing, but deep inside, he knew he was really getting hung up on Juana He did not know how to react or what to do. He had been with many women and had had a few girlfriends. But he had never been really hooked on any one person.

He was always in control and spent as much time with his friends as with his girlfriends, whether the girls liked it or not. But this was different. It wasn't that Juana objected to him going out. He could still go and hang around with his friends, but to his surprise, he didn't really want to. He not only enjoyed Juana in bed, but he really liked hanging around with her. She was fun, kind of crazy, and totally into him. He wanted to spend all his free time with her. But after being ribbed so much by his buddies, he decided to go out with them and put an end to their jokes.

In Havana during the late nineteen fifties, the night life not only consisted of the great nightclubs like the Tropicana and the San Succi and other famous night spots that catered to the predominantly American audiences.

There was also an underbelly side to the tourist experience that Havana was famous for. That was the wild, live sex shows and houses of prostitution that also catered to the tourists as well as the locals.

The most famous entertainer in all those shows was Superman. He was a fellow endowed with an enormous penis that was almost impossible to believe. American tourists flocked to this show to see the perverted and physically impossible acts that Superman put on. The place had started as a bordello. The owner, lucky for him, stumbled onto this young man with his incredible penis, and soon people were coming to the bordello more to gawk at the young man's member than to actually go to the whorehouse. Soon women began coming with their husbands or boyfriends to marvel at Superman's unbelievable proportions.

The exhibition of Superman eventually morphed into a show where he would perform sex acts on women that were mind boggling to watch. It was impossible to comprehend how the hell the women could accommodate this young man's penis in the various places he inserted it into them. It was the show everyone told their friends could not be missed. The owner of the whorehouse had to build a special showroom for all the people who wanted to attend because they could no longer be accommodated in the bordello.

After the show, the many unaccompanied young men like Cesar and his friends would move on next door and end up at the whorehouse, where they would partake in the company of the girls that worked there. The whorehouse was doing a brisk business thanks to the many people who showed up to watch Superman and his amazing antics.

Cuba was a conservative Catholic country at that time, and young men were not able, in many cases, to have sex with their girlfriends because most of the ladies tried to save themselves for marriage. Most of the young couples had to go out accompanied by chaperones. These were the elderly aunts or grandmothers who volunteered to go along with the couples on their dates to make sure the chastity of their young female relatives was guarded. Bordellos did a big business to accommodate the many horny young men who were not able to fulfill their desires with their respective girlfriends.

Cesar, Armando, Alberto, and Jose decided to attend this unbelievable show because they had heard so much about Superman for so long. Alberto knew a bouncer/doorman who worked at the showroom where Superman performed, and he was able to get them all in for free.

They went in and sat down, mesmerized like all the other patrons. From time to time, women could be heard gasping and shrieking. Some ladies actually fainted watching Superman do his unbelievable routine.

Jose was not poor, but he was rather cheap. He always sneaked in a bottle of rum with him so he would not have to pay the exorbitant prices that were charged for drinks at all the tourist attractions. He generously passed it around to his friends so they could get a buzz while watching the performance. The show went on for a while, and when it was over, Cesar and his buddies all gathered outside, smoking, laughing, and carrying on about Superman and the ladies Superman had serviced.

Cesar lit a cigarette took a puff, laughed, and told his buddies, "Those poor women are ruined for life. How the hell will they ever be satisfied by any man after that animal?" He looked at Jose. "Especially you, Jose, with your three inch dick."

They all laughed, and Jose gave them the finger.

Then Jose suggested, "Why don't we stop the bullshit and go inside the whorehouse and enjoy some of the girls that have not been ruined by that guy yet?"

Armando and Alberto were all for it. But Cesar was hesitant. He really did not want to go. He kept thinking about Juana and wanted to run back to see her.

He told them, "You guys go ahead. I'm going to call it a night."

Armando looked at Cesar and told him, "You pussy-whipped asshole. You are going to run back to her, aren't you? What did she give you, a curfew?"

They all laughed, and Cesar just put his hands in his pants pockets and looked at the floor. Jose told him, "I have another bottle of rum that we can finish inside. Come on, don't be such a party pooper. Come in with us."

Cesar mulled it over and shuffled his feet, but he really had no desire to go and bang some whore. He looked up and told them, "You guys go ahead and enjoy your night.

I'm going home. I don't care how much money you guys will spend in there. No one woman inside that place can compare to what I have waiting for me."

Alberto looked at Cesar and said to him, "Hey, asshole, don't you go and get married on me. This guy," he pointed to Armando, "is betting you will be married soon. I have my money on you staying single, so don't go surrender and marry her."

Jose spoke up and told Cesar, "I have my money on you staying single also, so don't be stupid and make me lose."

Armando smiled and rubbed his thumb and index finger together and told Cesar, "Go ahead. Get married. I need to make some money."

Cesar smiled and told them, "I can guarantee all of you that I will never get married in a million years, and you can bet all your money on that. Now go pay for your lousy lay, while I enjoy the best piece of ass in the city."

They reluctantly hugged Cesar, shook his hand, and said goodbye. When his friends went in, Cesar ran to his car. He could not wait to see Juana.

Chapter 7

IT WAS APRIL, and Elena was home for Easter break and her twenty-first birthday. The Machado family prepared to celebrate the happy occasion. The house was decorated, and festive music played on the hi-fi. Most of the family was in the living room, chatting and having a good time while Carmen and Rosa were in the kitchen.

Diego had invited Bill Lima and Beth Donahue, Bill's girlfriend, a pleasant, jovial big woman in her thirties, to join them for the party. While his friends and the rest of the family sat chatting in the living room, a very nervous Diego walked in the kitchen, looked through the cabinets for a bottle of liquor, found some whiskey, and poured himself a drink.

"Diego, you're drinking?" asked Carmen.

"I need something to calm me down."

"Don't worry," said Rosa. "Alejandra will be here soon. I'm sure Elena is very happy for you."

"I haven't told her anything," said Diego as he took a sip of his whiskey. "I've wanted to, but every time I try, we get into another argument. It seems like we've been doing nothing but fight since she got home."

"Well, don't argue with her anymore," said Rosa. "Today is her birthday." She walked over to Diego and kissed him in the forehead. "I'm sure she will love Alejandra."

Carmen tried to reassure Diego. "Today is going to be a great day. Even Cesar is bringing a date."

"He is?" said Diego, finishing his drink. He was stunned to hear that his brother would bring a woman to meet the family. During all these years and the many girls Cesar had dated, he had never bothered to bring any of them to the house. "Who is she? Have you met her?"

"No, but she must be special. He's never brought anyone home before."

Rosa stopped stirring for a second. "I'm so happy. All of my boys are finally settling down."

The doorbell rang, and Rosa went to answer. She opened the door to find Cesar standing there with Juana.

"Mom, I want you to meet Juana. If you can teach her to cook, I'll marry her in a minute."

Rosa was startled by Juana's appearance. With her bright red lips, very high heels, and an overly tight dress that accentuated her cleavage, Juana looked like a slut.

"Uh, uh, come in," Rosa stammered.

Juana replied, "Nice meeting you." She slowly looked around and remarked, jabbing Cesar with her elbow. "Boy, this is a nice house. Your brother-in-law must be rich."

The three of them walked into the foyer, where they were met by Diego and Carmen. Cesar introduced them.

Juana said hello and continued to check out the surroundings. "Boy, this is some house."

In a courteous yet terse tone of voice, Carmen said, "Nice to meet you too. Come in and let me introduce you to everyone."

She let Juana go ahead of her, turned back, and gave Cesar a dirty look.

Cesar looked at Diego. "What was that look about?"

"What about? It's about your girl! Where the hell did you find her?"

"Well, you have all been bugging me to bring a woman home. She's been bugging me to meet my family. So I killed two birds with one stone." He spread his arms out and went, "Ta-da. I think my future wife should meet my family, don't you?" He grinned.

Diego gave Cesar a tap on the head. "We were hoping you would choose a woman with *this* head."

A little while later, Elena sat alone in the kitchen, and Diego walked in.

"Oh, there you are," he said.

"Listen, Dad, I know we have argued a lot since I got back home. We have our differences, but that doesn't mean I don't love you."

They heard the doorbell ring again.

"I know. I just get very upset when you talk about the revolution. Every time you mention it, it terrifies me." He paused for a second and looked into his daughter's eyes. "The thought of losing you kills me. You remind me so much of your mother." He took her hand. "We lost her, and I don't want to lose you."

"You'll never lose me, Dad. I'll always be your little girl."

She stood up, and they gave each other a big hug. Diego wiped a tear from his eye, and just as he was ready to tell her about Alejandra, Cesar walked into the kitchen.

"There is a woman here who says she is your date, but she has to be lying because I know you are a monk."

In the living room, everyone was talking to the beautiful thirty-two-year-old Alejandra Visquel. She was a tall, raven-haired woman with deep, piercing eyes. Diego was very nervous as he entered the room, followed by Elena. Elena was shocked as her dad introduced her to his date.

"I'm so glad to finally meet you," Alejandra said. "You look so much like your father."

"Most people say I look like my mother," replied Elena, giving Alejandra a hateful stare. She crossed her arms in front of her and shot her father a dirty look.

Carmen, sensing the tension in the room, smiled a big smile and said, "Elena, let me show you the portrait Alejandra painted of Tico. It's really beautiful."

Tico jumped up. "It's in my room. I'll get it."

Cesar, who felt the tension in the room was making the others uncomfortable, tried to lighten things up. "Bill, don't you think it's time to get something to eat?"

"Oh, yeah. It's always time to eat as far as I'm concerned."

"Don't get him started," said Beth. "Last month, we went with Diego and Alejandra to the Tropicana nightclub, where Johnny Ray was performing. Bill ordered so much food Johnny Ray did a whole comedy routine about it."

That got laughs from everyone except Diego and Elena.

Juana said to Alejandra, "Cesar is a painter too."

Cesar jumped in, "No, no, I'm not a painter."

"He draws beautifully," interjected Juana.

"I want to be a commercial artist."

"My first job out of art school was as a commercial artist," said Alejandra.

Tico returned with the painting. "Look, Elena, it's me!"

Elena looked but said nothing.

"Alejandra is a serious painter," said Diego. "She lived and studied in Paris for many years."

Elena looked at Alejandra. "Really? What brought you back to Cuba?"

"I came back when my father was dying. We never got along very well, but I wanted to be there for him. Then I fell in love with Havana all over again." She paused a moment. "Elena, I would love for you to come over to my studio so I can do a portrait of you for your father."

"Oh, great." Elena stared at Diego. "You can hang it right next to the one of my dead mother."

During the awkward silence that followed, Cesar left the room.

"Everybody must be starving," said Rosa. "Elena, come help me in the kitchen."

"I'll join you two in a minute," said Carmen. "Let me just put the portrait back. It's really beautiful, Alejandra."

Elena and Rosa left the room, and Juana followed Cesar.

Looking at Alejandra with apologetic eyes, Diego said, "I'm sorry, Alejandra. This is my fault. I never prepared her for this. She has not seen me with a woman since Mercedes died. I never told her about you."

Roberto softly patted Diego on the back. "Diego, don't worry. She'll get over it. I'll bet Elena and Alejandra are going to become great friends."

"I'm sure we will," Alejandra said, taking Diego's arm. "There is nothing I would like better. But you should have told her."

"I know, I know. I'm sorry. I tried, but I didn't know how."

Alejandra leaned over and gave him a soft kiss on the cheek.

Upstairs in the bathroom doorway, Cesar and Juana were talking. "I get the feeling your family doesn't think I'm good enough for you," she said.

Cesar grabbed her around the waist. "Oh, baby, you're more than good enough for me." They embraced and passionately kissed each other. Then Cesar playfully slapped her on the ass and told her, "I'll see you downstairs."

He went into the bathroom, and Juana mischievously followed him and closed the door behind them. As Carmen walked down the hall with the portrait, she passed the bathroom and could hear them both.

"No," said Cesar, "this is not the place."

"I bet I can make you change your mind," Juana purred.

"No," he said firmly, "I mean it. Not here, not in my sister's house."

Carmen got upset hearing this and stormed into Tico's bedroom with the painting. Tico followed a few steps behind her, and as he passed the bathroom, Juana opened the door. When she came out, Tico saw that Cesar was still inside.

Tico continued to his room, where Carmen was hanging the portrait. "Mommy, why were Tio Cesar and Juana in the bathroom together?"

Carmen was fuming but tried not to let Tico know how angry she was. "They were washing their hands before dinner, sweetheart. You better wash your hands too. Dinner is almost ready. Hurry up. Everybody must be starving by now."

Downstairs, Rosa and Elena were setting the table. Alejandra brought dishes and trays from the kitchen to the dining room, and Carmen once again checked on the food. Juana was trying to help, but Carmen ignored her.

Juana, sensing the cold shoulder from Carmen, asked, "Is there something wrong?"

Carmen put down the spoon she was using to stir the rice, took a deep breath, and told Juana, "I don't know how to say this, and please don't take offense, but I have a young child, and he saw you and Cesar in the bathroom together."

"We didn't do anything," said Juana defensively.

"That's not the point," said Carmen, trying not to appear angry. "Tico is at the age where he notices everything. You're welcome in my house, but you have to watch your behavior."

Angry and embarrassed, Juana pursed her lips and put her hands on her hips. "That's not what's bothering you. I could tell from the moment I walked in this house your whole family thinks I'm not good enough for Cesar. Fine! You won't have to worry about my behavior anymore. I'm leaving!"

She stomped out of the dining room and into the living room with Carmen close behind.

"That's not what I meant, Juana."

Juana walked right up to Cesar. "I'm not wanted in this house. I'm leaving." She picked up her purse and hurried out the door.

"What? Juana, stop!" yelled Cesar as he chased after her.

Roberto asked, "Carmen, what the hell was that all about?"

"Roberto, I . . . I . . . I said something to her, and I think I offended her. I didn't mean to, I swear."

To no one in particular, Rosa said, "Cesar needs to find himself a nice girl and stop running around with women like her."

Diego looked at Rosa. "I'm sorry to say it, Mom, but my brother has always been attracted to low-class women."

Elena got very upset by what her father had just said and raised her voice. "That's exactly what's wrong with you, all of you! You divide people into classes. Look around at this house and all that we have. Just because Juana is less fortunate than us, you look down on her."

"You don't know what you're talking about," fumed Roberto. He had come from nothing and was tired of hearing the same old excuse for people's bad behavior. "It's about how she carries herself, the way she comes across. Don't talk to me about being poor. My family never had any money, and I lost my mother at fifteen. I tutor students that really have nothing, and they still manage to look respectable, wearing clothes that are practically rags. There may be something wrong with this country, but it has nothing to do with the type of person she is. Your mother and grandparents were poor too, but that did not keep them from being respectable people."

Diego yelled, "We haven't seen you in months, and this is the way you talk to us?"

"Don't yell at her, Diego! It's her birthday," said Alejandra, trying to calm him down.

"Butt out! You are not my mother!" shouted Elena. "This is between me and my family."

"I've had enough of you and your behavior," roared Diego, angrily pointing a finger at her.

"Well, I've had enough of all of you too!" Elena grabbed her jacket and rushed out the door.

Later that evening, Elena met up with Ramon at his small one-room apartment near the university. Ramon wanted to talk some sense into her.

He sat down next to her and put his arm around her shoulders. "Elena, it's too dangerous for you in the mountains. You're a very smart woman. Open your eyes. This is not the way for you to help our cause. You are much more valuable to the revolution by helping to keep up the supply line from the United States. Not everyone has to go into combat to help defeat Batista."

Elena would have none of it. "There are plenty of other people who can do that job. It's time for me to fight."

Ramon sighed. Elena had told him about the argument she just had with her family. He didn't want her to leave and join the rebels for the wrong reasons. He leaned over, took her by the arms, looked directly into her eyes, and said, "Elena, I help people go to the mountains to fight for our liberation, not to run away from home."

Elena jerked away from him. She was mad at Ramon and insulted by his comment. "I have proven my dedication to this cause, and I will get to the Sierra Maestra whether you help me or not. If I wanted to run away from home, I wouldn't need any assistance from you."

She quickly got up, stormed out of his apartment, and slammed the door. Ramon tried to go after her, but it was too late. She was already gone.

Elena walked the empty streets, not knowing what to do, but she knew she would not go crawling back to her father and his new girlfriend. Instead, she hailed a cab.

"Take me to the Central Bus Station," she told the cab driver.

He looked at her funny and advised her, "Miss, there are no more buses leaving at this time of the night."

She told him to take her there anyway.

Elena spent the night on a bench at the bus station, and when morning came, she bought a one-way ticket to Holguin, said goodbye to Havana, and headed for the mountains.

Chapter 8

IT WAS A very long ride from Havana to the mountains on the eastern end of the island, giving Elena the opportunity to spend a lot of time alone with her thoughts. Out the window, she watched sugarcane fields and tall palm trees rush by. She thought about the beauty of Cuba, how much she loved her country, and how much bounty there was.

Why can't everyone share in the riches of this land? There should be plenty for everyone. Why must there be a peasant class? Why should anyone here not be able to read or write? How can people in power, like Batista, sleep at night when they enjoy such privileges but cause so much pain and suffering and so many go hungry?

There were so many things that were unfair and didn't make sense to her, and she wanted to be part of the revolution that would change all that.

Several times she started to write a letter to her father and tried to explain all her feelings. But each time she began, she couldn't move past her anger. It wasn't only about her father's new love, which was hard enough for her to accept. She was not able to process the thought, let alone the reality, of seeing him with any other woman besides her mother. But what bothered her even more was his indifference to what was going on in Cuba. Her uncle was risking his life for the liberation of their country while her father did nothing. She would get about half a page written before she would have to wad up the paper and start over. After four or five attempts, she gave up.

A woman about the same age as Elena was in the seat across the aisle. She couldn't help but notice Elena's futile attempts at correspondence.

"Are you writing to your boyfriend?" she asked.

Elena looked up to see the girl's big eyes and warm smile. "No, my father."

"Ah, yes. I always have trouble talking to mine."

"He's a good man," said Elena. "He's just so stubborn and set in his ways. I feel like he doesn't understand me, and I certainly don't understand him. I don't think we will ever understand each other."

"Is that why you're going east?"

"Partly, yes."

"And what's the other part?"

"Well," Elena hesitated. She wasn't sure how much she should tell this stranger. "I'm going to see my uncle. I'm studying to be a doctor, and he thinks I can help the peasants in the mountains."

"Well, whaddaya know? I'm studying to be a nurse. I'm Miriam." She extended her hand.

She shook Miriam's hand. "My name is Elena."

Miriam crossed the aisle and sat in the empty seat next to Elena. "I'm going to the mountains too." She looked around the bus to see if anyone was listening and continued in a whisper, "I want to help the soldiers, the rebel soldiers. I've heard they need nurses and anyone with medical experience."

Elena, still not sure if she could trust Miriam, asked her, "Why do you want to help the rebels?"

"Because I think this country could be so much more than it is. I have a little brother, and I want him to grow up in a better Cuba, a free and fair Cuba."

Over the course of the bus ride, they got to know each other and discovered how much they had in common. After hours of talking with Miriam, Elena eventually confessed to her that she also was headed to join the rebels.

The Machado Home

It was Sunday morning. Almost a week had passed since Elena had run out, and nobody in the family had heard from her. They were all very worried about her safety and whereabouts. Diego and Alejandra were at the Machados, talking to Roberto and Carmen. While Rosa and Tico were at church, the rest of the family took the opportunity to discuss what to do about Elena.

"It's been days since we heard from her, Diego," said Carmen. "You have to call the police."

Diego was visibly exhausted and depressed. He sat with Alejandra, who was equally exhausted and feeling some guilt about Elena's reaction to her.

Diego held her hand as he spoke. "I can't do that, Carmen. We don't know whom she's been hanging around with, but I'm sure it has something to do with the anti-Batista underground, that student movement."

"*The Student Revolutionary Directory,* they call themselves the SRD," said Roberto. "They are all over the university."

"This is the very reason I sent her to New York," said Diego. "If the police find her amongst the SRD or some other revolutionary group, God only knows what Batista's animals would do to her. And I'm not just worried about Elena. If they go digging and make the connection to Joaquin, the whole family could get in a lot of trouble. We don't need that."

Alejandra interjected, "The best thing we can do right now is wait and hope she calls."

"It's not enough," said Roberto. "What if she doesn't get in touch with us? Somebody should be out looking for her.

If you don't want to call the police, hire a private detective. To hell with the cost. I have money saved." Carmen agreed.

"I really appreciate it, Roberto," answered Diego. "That is very generous of you and Carmen. But you don't have to do that. Bill has offered me the use of the company's detectives. Also his girlfriend, Beth, has friends at the US embassy, checking to see if Elena has gone back to New York."

Cesar walked in, but he wasn't acting like his usual joyful, playful self. "Any news of Elena?"

"Not a word," said Diego.

"I'm so sorry this happened," said Cesar. "I feel like it's all…"

Diego interrupted. "Don't blame yourself. It's not your fault. This was bound to happen sooner or later."

"But if I hadn't brought Juana here, there would not have been an argument, and none of this would have happened."

"Look, Cesar," Diego said, "Elena and I had been fighting from the moment she got off the plane. What happened with Juana was just a convenient excuse. Had that not happened, she would have found another reason to leave."

Alejandra jumped in. "If she was upset about anything, it would be me."

"I'm the one who had the argument with Juana," said Carmen. "But who cares why Elena left? That's not important. The important thing is that we find her." They all agreed but shared the helpless feeling of not knowing what to do.

Several days later, Elena and Miriam found themselves in a dark basement in Holguin, Oriente, with a few other would-be revolutionaries who were also making their way to the mountains. They were listening to the field radio, waiting for the orders to rendezvous with their escort. Elena was excited and ready to go. She saw no reason to wait any longer. She knew one of her comrades, Francisco, the man who was coordinating their way to the Sierra Maestra, knew the way to the camp.

"Why can't we just go ahead?" she asked.

"We don't operate that way," said Francisco. "The organization in the mountains runs like clockwork. It's because of our very careful planning that we have the edge. We leave nothing to chance. Nothing. We will meet at a predetermined time and place. Some of the rebels will draw Batista's patrols away from us while another group comes to pick us up."

The radio came on again, and the rebels transmitted their position. Shortly thereafter, Francisco led the new volunteers to meet up with them.

Chapter 9

FRANCISCO WAS RIGHT. The group that came to get them waited until they were sure Batista's men would be away from the area. When they joined them, Elena, Miriam, and the others were told to stay close together and to be as quiet as possible. There was no moon, and the woods were very dark, even after their eyes adjusted.

Francisco told them, "Watch yourselves. If you see something dangerous, try to get our attention and quietly back away. But don't get loud or make sudden movements. Any animal will fight if it feels threatened or cornered."

Miriam stayed close to Elena and tried not to show her fear. "I've never been through a jungle at night," she said.

"Me neither," said Elena. "Just follow the group. I'm sure everything will be fine."

They walked for miles. Even though it was night, the air was warm and humid. Perspiration dripped down the side of Elena's face as they trekked up a small hill.

"How much farther?" asked Miriam. Never before had she walked so far. The sounds of the woods at night made her nervous. The thick underbrush was difficult to get through. She was getting tired.

"We'll be there soon," answered Francisco. He could sense the new arrivals' apprehension and knew they were near exhaustion.

The group was making their way up another hill when someone stepped on a dry, brittle twig, and it snapped loudly. That was when they heard the grunting of the wild boar. Locals called them jabalinas because of their unusually long tusks that looked like two long spears or javelins.

"Stop, everyone," Francisco whispered. "We must go off to the left. The wild boar is probably eating something it has just killed. If we leave slowly and quietly, it won't bother us."

Francisco went over to make sure it was just a wild pig.

Everything happened so fast. He parted some of the branches and leaves, and then, in a flash, the jabalina charged. Francisco tried to move out of the way, but the wild boar was able to slash his leg. Francisco screamed from the pain. He tried to fend off the jabalina, to keep the animal's tusk away from his femoral artery. The wild boar got a hold of his ankle and tried to slash Francisco's leg.

Before anyone reacted, Elena grabbed a soldier's machete. She swiftly came up from behind and swung the machete at the pig but missed, just nicking the boar's tail. The pig let out a small squeal, let go of Francisco's leg, and made a move toward Elena. She stepped back, the pig barely missing her, and she slashed again at the jabalina with the long, sharp blade. This time, she connected. The animal let out a loud squeal and fell to the ground. Some of the soldiers grabbed Francisco and pulled him away. Another soldier shot the animal and killed it.

Francisco hopped over to Elena. He could not believe what she had just done. "Look, that was very brave of you, but you shouldn't have done that. You could have gotten yourself killed. If that pig cuts one of your arteries, you, of all people, should know that you will bleed to death out here." He pointed to the soldiers. "You should have let them handle it. One of my men would have killed the pig."

"I know." Elena was gasping for breath. "I'm sorry, I just reacted."

Francisco fixed his eyes on Elena, shook his head, laughed, and thanked her while she began treating his wounds.

He looked around and told his men, "Guys, you just got outdone by a nurse recruit."

The soldiers chuckled a little, trying to hide their embarrassment. None of them could believe that this little girl had the balls to do what they had just witnessed.

Elena examined Francisco's ankle. Luckily, it had been partially protected by his boot and no arteries were severed, but it was still cut and bleeding. Elena and Miriam both worked on the ankle and were able to stop the blood flow. Elena bandaged the wound, and they all continued to move toward the camp in the mountains. Now, more than ever, they had to move fast and quiet. If any of Batista's patrols were around, the rebels had just given away their position when they discharged the gun. They moved out as fast as possible, Francisco hopping along as best he could, leaning against one of his men.

Miriam moved over and said to Elena, "Girl, you are crazy."

The next morning, Elena and Miriam were in a compound in the Sierra Maestra. Miriam seemed nervous and apprehensive as they dressed in their newly issued fatigues. Outside the tent, there was a lot of activity. Soldiers were exercising, cleaning weapons, and talking about what to expect. Miriam rolled up her sleeping bag and stowed it in the corner on the dirt floor of the small bare tent.

She ran her fingers through her thick dark hair, looked at Elena, and said, "I wish we had a mirror in this room."

Elena smiled. "I'd settle for a nice, long bath."

Vilma Espin, a tough looking, no-nonsense twenty-five-year-old woman, entered their tent. Strong and proud, she was one of the soldiers in charge of the female rebels. She was also the girlfriend of Fidel's brother Raul.

"Correct me if I'm wrong. Elena Quintana? Miriam Torres?"

Both girls nodded. She took a second look at Elena. "Are you related to Joaquin Quintana?"

"He's my uncle," replied Elena. "Is he here?"

"He'll be returning later today."

Vilma took the two women to the makeshift hospital; it was a shack but a much better constructed one than what the rebels had built in the earlier days. There were several beds inside the shack. Vilma walked up to a doctor who was attending to three wounded soldiers.

"This is Dr. Andujar." She pointed at the girls. "Miriam Torres, Elena Quintana."

He was much older than most of the other rebels yet no less dedicated to the fight. Dr. Andujar talked while he bandaged a soldier's arm.

"Do either of you have any nursing experience?" he asked without looking up.

Both women said yes.

"Good, we are going to need you to help train the soldiers in first aid. Also, when we begin our next offensive move, we are going to need some of the nursing personnel to go into combat areas with the troops." He secured the soldier's bandage and moved to the next patient. "If either one of you feels up to it, we could use some volunteers. As far as your duties here, I'll leave that up to Vilma. Any questions?"

Elena raised her hand. "I'll volunteer to go with the troops. I was studying to be a doctor. I think I could be of some help."

"And I'll be glad to show the soldiers how to administer first aid," said Miriam, relieved that Elena had volunteered to be the one to go into combat.

They walked out of the makeshift hospital, and Vilma took them to a nearby shack that was full of peasants. There were men and women, both young and old, learning to read and write. Vilma led the two women to the back of the classroom to observe.

"The teacher is Celia Sanchez," Vilma told them. Celia was Fidel's girlfriend, a woman about the same age as Vilma. "She is in charge of all the women here, and today she is teaching this class. As part of our responsibilities, we teach the peasants how to read and write." Vilma looked at Elena. "Whenever possible, as we travel with the columns, we continue to teach the illiterate soldiers."

The class ended, and the peasants began to file out, some stopping to ask the teacher questions. Soon after, Celia joined the three women.

"I take it these are the new soldiers?" said Celia. She shook the girls' hands.

"Yes," said Vilma. "This is Elena Quintana and Miriam Torres. They both have nursing experience."

"Good," answered Celia. "I have a full workload mapped out for you two. As you can see, we don't have much free time around here."

"Elena has volunteered to go into combat with the column," said Vilma. "She is going to need extra weapon and surgical training."

As a new group of students came into the shack, Celia looked at Elena and said, "That is very brave of you. All right then, Vilma is going to take you to get some weapons training. Miriam, I want you to stay with me, and I will show you how to teach the next class."

Later that afternoon, Elena was in a field with targets scattered about, learning how to use a rifle with a scope. Her instructor was Sergeant Gustavo Vela. Gustavo was a young, very handsome, and overly eager soldier.

He handed her the rifle and said, "The most important thing for you to remember is that by using the scope, we have an advantage. We can hide in the thick of the mountains and pick off Batista's soldiers before they even get a chance to see us. Now, remember, every bullet counts. We cannot waste what little ammunition we have. So look through the crosshairs, pick your target, and shoot."

Elena raised the rifle and took careful aim. "The Coca-Cola bottle on the left." She squeezed the trigger and felt the gun's kick as the blast rang out, hitting the target.

"Good shot," said Gustavo. "You've done this before."

"The SRD taught us how to shoot a rifle, but I've never used one with a scope before. It's easier."

"Not when you're shooting at a live person," he replied. "Remember, they will also be armed. They will be moving.

You'll be naturally nervous, and you won't have much time to aim." His eyes narrowed as he continued, "And when you shoot them, they die." He paused and smiled. "But you'll get used to that."

Just then, a voice came directly from behind them.

"Don't ever get used to that." It was Camilo Cienfuegos who had just entered the range.

Gustavo was surprised and immediately saluted. "Comandante Cienfuegos!"

"Relax," he said, giving Gustavo a look of contempt. Camilo looked at Elena and tipped back his big cowboy hat. "You must be Elena Quintana."

Elena snapped to attention. "Yes, sir."

Camilo kept talking to Elena, but his gaze was firmly set on Gustavo. "I've been in these mountains for almost two years, and I haven't gotten used to killing anyone. But learn how to use that weapon because your life may depend on it. That's the saddest part of this revolution, Cubans killing Cubans." He looked back at Elena. "By the way, Miss Quintana, did you bring us any of that chicken and rice?"

"Huh?" Elena didn't understand his question.

Camilo gave a hearty laugh. "Every time we sit down to eat with Joaquin, he brags about his sister Carmen's cooking, especially her chicken and rice. Most of us want to taste that chicken and rice more than we want to see our own families. If you didn't bring any with you, we're going to have some pretty disappointed soldiers around here," he said with a smile. "All right, I'll let you get back to your training. By the way, Joaquin should be in camp tonight. Carry on."

Camilo walked out, giving Gustavo a dirty look.

That evening, Elena sat near the campfire, eating dinner amongst the other soldiers, Fidel, and most of the platoon leaders, Raul Castro, Che Guevara, Camilo, Huber Matos, Ramiro Valdez, and Juan Almeida, the only black comandante. Needless to say, she was a bit awed to be in their presence.

"Camilo," Fidel said, "when we make the final push into Havana, I'm putting you in charge of the lead column."

"Wait a minute," interrupted Che, trying to kid his friend, "I don't think he can lead anything."

Everyone around the campfire enjoyed a good, loud laugh.

Camilo countered, "Well, Che, after we win this revolution, we're sending you back to Argentina. I'm sure their government misses you."

Raul, who did not get along with Camilo and resented his charisma and popularity, jumped in. "As far as I'm concerned," he sneered, "Che is Cuban."

Camilo, who had grown tired of Raul's subtle digs but was trying to keep things lighthearted, asked, "Fidel, do you have to bring your little brother everywhere?"

Fidel smiled and took another bite as Joaquin and his men arrived.

Elena saw her uncle and called out to him. "Uncle Joaquin! Uncle Joaquin! Over here!"

Joaquin was stunned as Elena ran up to him. She put her arms around his neck, and they hugged.

"What are you doing here?" asked Joaquin. "Are you okay? Is everybody back home okay?"

"Get your butt over here, Captain Quintana, and eat your dinner," said Camilo. Joaquin and Elena walked over and sat next to him.

"I see you have all met my niece, Elena. Now I wish she would tell me what the hell she is doing here."

"She seems to be a fiery one, just like you," said Che.

"She even volunteered to join the columns," added Celia.

"What?" Joaquin was a bit riled. "I can't let you do that! It's too dangerous!"

"No more dangerous for me than for anybody else."

Joaquin was very upset by this and glared at Elena while the food was passed around.

Camilo took a big bite and said, "Fidel, I would like Elena to join my column."

Fidel thought for a moment then said, "No, I think Joaquin and Elena will be distracted worrying too much about each other. I think she will be safer in Che's column."

"Well," replied Camilo, "I don't know how safe she'll be with the way Che shoots."

The other soldiers laughed. After the laughter died down, Camilo, taking the opportunity to get under Raul's skin, suggested, "Hey, let's put her in Raul's column. He never sees any fighting. That way, we'll know for sure she'll be safe."

Everyone laughed except for Raul and Ramiro. They both stared angrily at Camilo, who just winked and smiled at them.

Che picked up a piece of meat and asked Elena, "So how does the food here in the mountains compare to your aunt's?"

The others chuckled a little.

"Not bad," she said. "What is it?"

"What does it taste like?" asked Camilo.

"Chicken?" she asked, not sure what kind of meat she was eating.

Camilo looked around at everyone as they started snickering. "Well, it's kind of like chicken, isn't it?"

"It's Camilo's favorite," offered Fidel. "It's a four-legged chicken."

"What is it?" Elena asked Joaquin.

"Cat."

"What?"

"It's a cat, just like Midnight," Joaquin answered. "Remember Midnight?" He hoped this would impress upon her the reality of life in the mountains.

"Really? Well, I never thought Midnight would taste so good." She looked at Joaquin, smiled, and took another big bite.

Everyone laughed, and Camilo gave Joaquin a good, solid pat on the back. "Joaquin, this is one tough little woman you've got for a niece, my friend."

Later, as Joaquin and Elena were walking toward her quarters, Elena looked up at her uncle and said, "I thought you would be proud of me for coming here."

"I am proud of you. But I'm concerned for your safety. This is not the world you are used to."

"I can handle it," said Elena, trying to show her uncle that she was not a little girl anymore.

"I have to admit," said Joaquin, "it makes me happy to see you. Does your father know you're here?"

"No."

Chapter **10**

The University of Havana, Roberto's Classroom

THE BELL RANG, signifying not only the end of class for the students but the end of their university years. Roberto raised his hands and asked them to stay a few moments. He paced the floor for a second or two to collect his thoughts and cleared his throat.

He began by telling them what a privilege it had been to be their instructor and how proud he was that they were the first class in over ten years to graduate every single student. He reminded them of how much they had accomplished, challenged them to always strive to do their best, and assured them that he would always be there if they needed him. He thanked them and wished them well.

The classroom exploded into cheers and applause. Some chanted "Professor, Professor!" alluding to the title they had bestowed on him. When it finally died down, the students began to slowly file out. Some stayed and went over to Roberto to shake his hand and say a final goodbye.

In the midst of this, Ignacio was able, without being noticed, to drop an envelope on his teacher's desk. He hung back and was one of the last ones to approach Roberto. When he did, he shook the professor's hand, hugged him, and thanked him for all his help and generosity. Roberto told Ignacio that he reminded him so much of himself, that he expected great things from him, and they said their last farewell. Ignacio and the remaining students walked out to the hallway, where the others students cheered and howled.

Roberto, now alone in the classroom, could hear the students celebrating. He smiled to himself and started to gather his papers when he noticed the envelope. He opened it and realized it was a letter from Joaquin.

Later that night, the family gathered at the Machados' home. Alejandra stood next to Diego as he read the letter.

> Dear Diego,
>
> I know you must be sick with worry about Elena, not knowing where she might be. Stop worrying. She has reached me in the mountains, safe and feisty as ever. I have tried to talk some sense into her, but like you, she is both proud and stubborn.

I realize this letter won't give you much comfort because of her whereabouts, but as long as I breathe, I will keep her safe and in good health so I can bring her home to you.

I know you must be angry with her, but if you could see her, you would be more than proud. You may not understand why she came here. But I have spoken to her, and she came for the same reasons I and so many others have come. We all want to give Cuba the bright and just future it deserves so the next generation can grow up free of oppression in a Cuba where the people have the right to choose their own course, free at last from dictatorship.

I love you, my brother, and I hope the whole family can be reunited soon. Until then please give everyone our love and let them know we are safe.

Viva Cuba libre!

Your loving brother,
Joaquin

Diego finished reading the letter, and tears rolled down his cheeks.

"Thank God she is safe. God has answered my prayers," said Rosa.

"But for how long can she be safe there?" lamented Diego, trying to hold back his tears.

Alejandra reached over and gently squeezed his hand. Roberto took the letter, to the kitchen and burned it.

Che Guevara's column of soldiers was slowly moving through the thick brush near the south side of Cuba's central highway. Elena was at the front of the column, walking with him. Che was addressing her but also directed his comments to a small group of young soldiers who closely followed them.

"A new order is coming into the world, Elena. Your uncle Joaquin still clings to outdated concepts. Don't get me wrong. He means well, but this revolution should be fighting for, as Lenin said, 'the salvation of the working class.' To achieve this, we have to do everything that is necessary to stop the further development of capitalism. Even at its best, capitalism helps only the privileged few at the expense of the masses."

"We studied a little about socialism in school," said Elena, "but I really don't know much about it. It sounds like a more fair system." The young soldiers nearby murmured in agreement.

"If Cuba were to follow the ideals of Marxism, Cuba would finally realize its full potential. Under capitalism, dictatorships have flourished. Unless we break completely from those outmoded economic ideas, Cuba will never be more than a playground for the bourgeois of the United

States." His voice got lower, and he took a more serious tone. "Not many among us share my ideals, but it's only because they, like you and them," he pointed to the soldiers behind them, "are not familiar with socialism. Once we are victorious, even the skeptics like your uncle will embrace it."

Elena, impressed and inspired by Che's ideals and his interest in her thoughts, told him, "I would like to learn more about it."

"We're not going to have much free time, but whenever you have a chance, you should take a good look at this." Che pulled a notebook from his backpack and gave it to her. "It's a collection of quotes by Marx, Mao, and Lenin." Some in the group of young soldiers asked Che if they too could get a copy.

A sudden flurry of gunfire broke out, and one of the soldiers near Elena was hit in the shoulder. Elena, Che, and the rest of the soldiers hit the ground and crawled through the brush, seeking cover.

To the north, the soldiers in Camilo's column could hear gunfire in the distance. Joaquin, Camilo, and Omar, a skinny twenty-two-year-old with thick glasses in charge of the radio, got into a tight circle.

Omar adjusted his glasses, looked at the other two men, and told them, "Che's column is under fire. They're pinned down."

"How bad is it?" asked Camilo. "Find out if they can handle it."

"Dammit! I lost them."

"Get them back!" Camilo turned to Joaquin. "Get some men up in the trees and see if they can find out what's going on."

Joaquin motioned to a couple of soldiers to follow him, and they all took off.

"It's no use, Comandante. They're not responding."

"Try all the channels. See if you can pick up Batista's soldiers communications."

While Omar tinkered with the radio, Joaquin returned. One of his men had climbed to the top of a tree and informed him that they could not be very far away. The soldier could see the gun battle right on the other side of the highway.

Omar interrupted them. "Comandante, I just heard Batista's men calling for reinforcements. I think I can get their coordinates."

"Good. Let's round up the men and gear up."

The soldier who climbed the tree had just returned, and Camilo asked him to point on the map to the exact spot where the fighting was taking place. The young soldier pointed and told him what he saw.

Camilo thanked him and addressed his men while still looking at the map. "This is what we are going to do. We'll split up. I'll take half the men and cross the highway from this direction. Joaquin, you approach them from the east with the rest of the column. With Che still engaging them from the south, we'll be able to surround Batista's soldiers before their reinforcements arrive. We have no time to waste. Let's go!"

Che's column was under heavy fire from the army. Their radio had been hit, and Orlando, a big and burly forty-year-old, was trying to repair it.

"Isn't that damn radio fixed yet?" yelled Che.

"It's dead, Comandante. It's no use."

Che turned to Elena. "How many wounded?"

"Four wounded, two dead."

"As soon as you take care of the ones who got shot, get your rifle. We're going to need everyone." He stopped and looked at her. "Are you ready for this?"

Elena nodded yes. He gave her a quick salute and left to lead his men. The sound of the guns was deafening as the rebels and Batista's soldiers furiously fired back and forth. Suddenly, bullets from a machine gun whizzed past Che and some of his men. They were now trapped by the barrage of bullets. Che's troops got as low as possible and tried to hide in the thick vegetation, fighting back as best they could.

Elena had just finished dressing the wounds of the soldiers who had been hit. She got her rifle and quickly crawled through the brush up a small hill away from where Che and his men were pinned down by the machine gun fire. When she got to the top of the hill, she slowly crawled to a big pile of leaves and hid behind it. She waited and listened for a few seconds.

She rolled to her right and parted some of the leaves. She now could clearly see the fire from the barrel of the machine gun. Slowly, steadily, she fixed the gunman into the crosshairs of her scope. She took a deep breath and held it. With a gentle squeeze of the trigger, a sharp clap rang out, and the gunman fell backward to the ground.

"I got him! I got him!" she cried.

Thanks to Elena's sharp shooting, Che's men were no longer held up and were now free to move and fight back.

Tomas, one of Che's lieutenants, looked through his binoculars, trying to appraise the enemy's strength and location. In the distance, he recognized Camilo by his distinctive cowboy hat. Camilo had led his men around Batista's soldiers and came up from behind.

"Comandante, we have help! It's Camilo's column. He is attacking their rear flank."

Shortly after Camilo's surprise assault, Joaquin and his men came up from the east and immediately engaged the army soldiers. Che's column once again started to fight back from the south, and soon they had surrounded Batista's soldiers just as Camilo had planned. The tide of the battle turned and Batista's men began surrendering. The battle came to an end, and Camilo approached Che.

"Do I always have to save your ass?" joked Camilo as he embraced Che.

Che grinned and told him, "I just wanted to make you look good." He turned to Orlando and ordered him, "Round up all the prisoners and take them, along with our injured men, over to Huber's column. Pick up all the captured weapons and radio equipment and leave it with us. We need it. Now, let's get the hell out of here before the reinforcements for these sons of bitches show up."

Joaquin saw Elena and ran up to her, threw his arms around her, and hugged her tightly. "Are you okay? I was so worried about you."

"You were worried about her?" said Che as he approached them. "Batista's soldiers should worry about her. Not only did she take care of the wounded, she took out a machine gun all by herself and saved half my column. I only wish we had more like her." He turned and saluted Elena. "I think you've earned your stripes, Sergeant Quintana."

Elena was exhilarated and stunned at the same time, trying to digest all that had just happened when she felt Joaquin staring at her.

When she turned to look at him, he stood with a proud smile, nodded, and said, "Sergeant Quintana. It has a nice ring to it."

Elena burst into a bright smile, snapped to attention, and saluted him.

Chapter 11

Violence in Havana

THERE WERE OTHER groups aside from Fidel's forces that had been fighting to oust Batista from power. One of them, the Student Revolutionary Directorate (SRD), had been fighting against Batista's regime in the streets of the larger cities for several years, and they were beginning to make a dent on Batista's hold on power.

Also in the Escambray Mountains, a group of rebels not associated with Castro was led by Eloy Gutierrez-Menoyo. He had started a second front of attack against Batista's forces, and his rebels were causing big headaches for Batista's army. Because of Menoyo and his men, the army was forced to take attention and manpower away from fighting Fidel in the Sierra Maestra mountains.

Also, Menoyo's rebels in the Escambray Mountains were much closer to Havana, creating a geographical problem for the army, which had to fight in two completely different locations, one of them much closer to the capital. Batista found himself fighting two guerrilla wars, one in the Sierra Maestra and another in Escambray. Add those to the urban war that the daring, if not reckless, SRD was mounting in the cities, and it was all beginning to strain Batista's forces to their limit.

The SRD, headed by student leader Jose Antonio Echeverria, was made up mainly of students along with some professionals and union workers. They were determined to push Batista out by mounting an urban guerilla war against him.

The SRD pulled off a daring assault and killed Colonel Antonio Blanco Rico, the head of Batista's secret service. After hearing about this successful attack on such a close member of Batista's inner circle and because of the attention it brought to Echevarria and the SRD, Fidel was furious. Some believed he was jealous and afraid that Echevarria might beat him to the punch and remove Batista from power before Fidel and his men could be the liberators.

He dispatched Faustino Perez to deliver a letter to Echeverria. Perez was a close confidant of Fidel and one of the original surviving members of the *Granma* landing. He was familiar with Echevarria, having been the liaison between the rebels and urban guerilla groups all over the island. He had met with Echevarria many times before. In that letter, Castro condemned the killing of Blanco Rico, accused the SRD of being assassins, charged them with treason, and called them all cowards, especially Echeverria.

Echevarria was livid. He approached Faustino, screaming at him, "Who the hell does he think he is, calling me a coward!" he raged. "He who is too much of a coward to deliver this note to me in person!"

Echeverria lunged for Faustino, but others kept them apart. After he had calmed down, Echeverria wrote a letter back to Fidel, rejecting all the charges. In the letter, he made a series of accusations against Fidel, accusing him of hiding in the mountains and playing Boy Scout while the real rebels fought Batista's goons in the cities every day.

Echeverria was still furious and yelled at Perez, "Get the hell out of my sight and give this letter to that two-faced coward Fidel. You tell him that no member of the SRD will ever help or join his guerillas again!" He lowered his voice and looked Faustino in the eye. "Make sure you tell Fidel not to show his face around Havana after I throw Batista out and liberate this country."

Echevarria, having pulled off the assassination of the head of Batista's secret service, one of the most well guarded men in Havana, was feeling very confident. Determined to end Batista's dictatorship before Castro's forces could reach the capitol, he set out to mastermind another even more daring plan.

Around three o'clock on a March afternoon, two automobiles and a red delivery truck arrived at the presidential palace. Several men jumped from the vehicles, firing point-blank at the soldiers guarding the entrance, and raced up to Batista's office, only to find it empty. The attackers never found the president. He was checking on his son, who was sick that day.

After the unsuccessful attempt on the president's life, Batista's security forces regrouped, and the members of the SRD found themselves trapped in the palace, surrounded by Batista's guards. The rebels fought for their lives, but after an intense firefight, most of the would-be assassins were killed inside the palace. In the streets, the shooting continued for hours.

At the same time his men attacked the presidential palace, a group led by Echeverria himself, captured the studios and control rooms of Havana's most influential radio station. When Echevarria took control of the mike, he was overcome with excitement as he was sure his men had killed Batista and could not wait to announce it to everyone. With Batista dead, his plan was to arouse the Cuban people and send a mass of human bodies into the streets of the capital and overwhelm the authorities. Echeverria shouted into the microphone, informing the Cuban people that rebel forces had occupied the palace and that Batista had been killed. But he was talking into a dead mike.

He was so carried away with emotion that his shouting triggered the automatic devices that cut off the microphone whenever anyone spoke too loudly. When Echeverria, still unaware that his radio address was never heard, left the radio station, Batista's forces were waiting for him.

He and some of his men jumped into an awaiting car and tried to get away, but by that time, the military had arrived and opened fire. In the fierce gun battle that followed, Echeverria was killed when his driver was shot, lost control of the car, and collided with a patrolling police vehicle. After Echevarria's death, the SRD was left without a leader and in disarray. Faustino made contact with the remaining guerilla leaders, and the SRD went back to cooperating with Fidel.

In the summer and fall, there was still much discontent. Homemade bombs exploded in theaters. City buses were burned. Rebel bands blew up businesses and homes of people associated with Batista. Students demonstrated, and Batista's police led brutal assaults on them to squelch dissent and to make examples of people in hope of stopping the protests.

The minister of education, Jorge Montes, wanted to close the University of Havana. He said the students were not there to learn and accused them of being there only to protest illegally and disrupt all university classes and proceedings. He had had enough and demanded all student protests cease immediately. If the protests didn't stop, he threatened not only to close the university but to nullify the degrees of all the students ready to graduate.

When he came to see the president of the university, students came out in large numbers to protest. Among them, leading two different groups of students, were Ignacio, from Roberto's class, and Ramon, Elena's friend. They were furious about his threats and wanted Montes to meet with them, but he refused, dismissing the students' requests as irrelevant.

When he wouldn't talk with them, the student demonstrations outside the university buildings quickly turned ugly. The group led by Ignacio smashed some windows, while the group led by Ramon was more violent. They rolled over cars and set some on fire. When the police started shooting, people ran through the streets, and some were trampled by the large crowds while trying to get to safety. Ramon was shot in the leg running away from the police. He barely escaped being apprehended thanks to one of his friends, who shoved him into the back of a car and sped away. Ignacio fared better although he did get hit with a healthy dose of tear gas.

From that day forward, all the houses of the ministers in Batista's cabinet were guarded by the army around the clock. Havana became a different city. Tourists were still coming, and the casinos were open, but there was an ominous feel all around. The level of fear among the citizens of the capital could be felt in the air.

Chapter 12

IT WAS CHRISTMASTIME 1958. Across the street from the Machados' home, many armed soldiers were guarding the house of Eusebio Mujal, Batista's minister of labor. The presence of the armed men, along with a machine gun nest perched atop the Mujals' roof, gave a dark, somber air to the neighborhood. In the Machados' front yard, Tico was playing with his friend Sebi, the Mujals' spoiled nine-year-old son. While they played, two soldiers armed with machine guns stood close by. The boys used the men like shields as if they were trees or parked cars.

"Bang! Bang! I got you," yelled Sebi.

"You missed. You'll never take me alive," countered Tico.

"This is your last chance to surrender."

"Never."

Tico moved away from his safe spot behind one of the soldiers and ran across the lawn, firing his toy gun. Sebi chased after him. Tico turned around to take a shot, but before he could take aim, Sebi clicked his trigger, and the blast from the toy revolver went off. Tico pretended to be hit. He let out an agonizing screech and dropped his gun. Tico dramatically grabbed his chest, turned around a couple of times, and fell to the ground.

Just then, Carmen came out the front door and spoke to the boys. "Sebi, your mother just called. She is coming over to pick you up."

Sebi, disappointed, replied, "Okay."

Tico jumped up. "Aw, you got to go now? It's your turn to die."

Sebi's mother, Alicia, was a professional woman and a successful doctor before she married Eusebio. But over the past couple of years, due to her husband's politics and the danger of exposure to all the violence in Havana, she had become a bored and reclusive woman. With an air of despondency, she walked over to the Machados' house to pick up Sebi, two soldiers in tow behind her.

"Sebi, it's time to come home now," she said.

"Do I have to? Tico doesn't have to go yet."

"I'm afraid so. Come on, get your stuff together. It's getting dark."

AL ROMERO

While Tico and Sebi went to gather their toys, Alicia approached Carmen.

"Merry Christmas, Alicia," said Carmen as Alicia hugged her and kissed her on both cheeks.

"Thank you, Carmen. Merry Christmas to you too." She paused for a moment, trying to find the right words. "Carmen," she said, "I really want to thank you for letting Tico play with Sebi. Most of the parents in the neighborhood aren't letting their kids play with him anymore."

"Oh, that's silly. Sebi can play with Tico anytime," said Carmen. Still, the thought had crossed her mind because of how bad things had gotten in Havana and the fact that Sebi was the son of such a high profile member of Batista's cabinet. But she reasoned that the kids had soldiers guarding them all the time while they played, and she felt bad for Alicia because she always looked so unhappy.

"Well, I just want you to know that I appreciate it. If it wasn't for Tico, Sebi wouldn't have any friends at all."

"Sebi has nothing to do with politics. He is only a child."

Alicia sensed an opportunity and told Carmen, "By the way, Eusebio and I want to invite you and Roberto to the president's New Year's Eve party."

Carmen was taken aback and visibly surprised by the invitation. Alicia had never invited them to parties at the palace or anything official before.

"I . . . I . . . I don't think we can make it," stammered Carmen. "I'm sure Roberto has already made other plans."

"Carmen." Alicia's voice quivered a little. "Sebi is not the only one without friends. I would really appreciate you coming. I've never liked any of the other cabinet member's wives. You'll be the only one there I'll feel comfortable with. I know we have never been able to get close due to all this crazy political turmoil, but I always have felt a kinship toward you. Please come. Talk to Roberto."

Carmen had no idea what to say. She felt horrible for Alicia, but she knew Roberto would not want any part of it. She wrestled with her choices and finally answered, "Okay, I will talk to Roberto."

Carmen and Alicia continued to chat while the boys were inside, putting away the toys. Tico had dozens of toy guns that looked extremely realistic. The way they were all laid out made Tico's playroom look like an arsenal. The pistols and revolvers were on one side of the room, and the rifles were on the other, where they were stacked army style, forming what looked like a teepee. The grenades were neatly gathered in a small barrel, and the machine guns on tripods were center stage. The boys finished picking up and returned to where their mothers were talking.

"Great," said a very happy Alicia. "I will tell Eusebio you'll come. Thank you, Carmen. Thank you."

The boys waved goodbye, and Alicia, Sebi, and the soldiers walked back across the street.

Near Santa Clara

The comandantes were gathered together in a small hut in the Escambray Mountains, finalizing their battle plans. Camilo and Che met with Eloy Gutierrez-Menoyo, a handsome, passionate man in his late twenties and the head of the Second National Front of Escambray rebels. Menoyo was a Spaniard by birth but a true Cuban at heart; he was also determined to liberate Cuba from its history of dictatorships. His and Fidel's forces had finally come together and agreed on a mutual plan of attack. Menoyo's group was still independent of Castro's forces, but the two groups were now working in tandem. All three men were confident and happy. Their meeting felt like a celebration.

Che said, "I hope Santa Clara is easier to capture than Camaguey."

"We should be grateful things have gone as well as they have," said Camilo.

Eloy stroked his chin. "I'm afraid the most difficult one will be Havana. But once Santa Clara falls, half of the island will be free."

"Once Santa Clara falls, Batista is done," said Che. "Havana will be easier to take over than you think." He stood up and announced, "I'm going to the radio room to let Fidel know and bring him up to date on what is happening."

After Che left the hut, Camilo looked at Menoyo and, with his bright smile, said, "We have come a long way, my friend."

He and Eloy firmly shook hands. Menoyo was aware of the many disagreements and bad blood that had existed between Fidel and Echevarria. He was still leery of what was to happen once Batista was eliminated from the picture.

"After Batista is defeated," said Eloy, "I hope we don't begin fighting amongst ourselves. There are many different opinions as to what Cuba should become."

Camilo tipped back his cowboy hat. He understood Eloys's concern and wanted to reassure him. "I don't think you have to worry about that. We are going to follow the constitution, and the people will let us know what they want with their free vote. That is why we are fighting, for what the people want."

"What about the communists like your friend Che? You think they will follow the constitution?" asked Eloy.

"Not many among us are communists, including Fidel. We are not fighting for any single ideology. Nobody is going to impose anything on the Cuban people anymore. Those days will be over."

Eloy sighed. "I hope you are right. It's about time we stopped replacing one dictator with another."

Camilo looked right into Eloy's eyes and told him, "I give you my word, my friend, that no dictator will come out of this revolution. I guarantee it with my life." Camilo burst into a big smile and put his arms around Eloy. "Now come on, it's Christmas Eve. Let's get something to eat."

Christmas Eve 1958 at the Machados' home was a much more subdued family gathering than Christmas Eve the year before. Roberto, Carmen, Rosa, Tico, Diego, and Alejandra were all sitting at the table when Roberto spoke.

"Carmen, how could you agree to go to Batista's party with everything that is happening in this country? And without even asking me?"

Carmen felt defensive. "How could I say no, Roberto? You should have seen her. She seemed so sad and lonely. It broke my heart."

Roberto raised his voice. "Her husband is in Batista's cabinet, for God's sake! I don't want to be around those people. It's an insult to Joaquin and Elena."

"I don't want to be there either, Roberto, but I'm not going to hurt Alicia's feelings because Batista is a bastard. The fact that her husband is a Batistiano didn't matter to any of us when Tico fell from that wall, got a concussion, and we couldn't get an ambulance. Remember that? If it wasn't for Alicia being a doctor, getting us a police escort, and attending to Tico all the way to the hospital, heaven knows what would have happened. Roberto, it's only for one night. Please?"

Roberto kept shaking his head, trying to grapple with the situation. He took a deep breath and finally said, "Fine." He looked up at the ceiling. "I just hope to God the revolution takes over before we have to go to this damn party."

Carmen came over, sat on his lap, put her arms around him, and gave him a big kiss. She looked at him and smiled. "Come on, I'm sure we'll have a good time.

Chapter 13

A FEW DAYS before the big New Year's celebration, Batista was in the presidential palace, stuffing gold bars and bundles of US dollars into trunks and traveling cases. He dreaded the day his presidency and power would come to an end, but he was ready for it.

Meanwhile, in the interior of the island, Batista's forces were demoralized and had lost their stomach for fighting. They were surrendering to the rebels in droves without even firing their weapons.

Early on the evening of the 31st, Batista was in his gaudy bedroom, talking to two of his generals. Besides the tawdry displays of wealth that seemed to be everywhere, the walls were covered with photos and portraits of Batista in full military uniform, adorned with medals that he had never earned. The generals were about to give him bad news and they were obviously scared. Like all failing dictatorships, Batista's had degenerated into finger-pointing and retaliation, and the generals did not want to be the next ones to feel his wrath.

One of the generals nervously cleared his throat and said, "Mr. President, sir, Santa Clara has fallen into the hands of the rebels. They'll be in Havana in a matter of days."

"Days? Days?" repeated Batista sarcastically. "They'll be here tomorrow, you idiots!" Batista rubbed his forehead, paced the floor, and thought about every possible outcome to the horrendous situation he found himself in and came to the conclusion that he had no choice but to flee. "Get out!" he screamed at the generals. Batista reached for the phone. The generals saluted him and quickly left.

"Get me Carlos." A moment later, he said, "Carlos, get the plane ready. We are leaving for Santo Domingo tonight." He listened for a moment. "Yes, tonight! Have it ready in a couple of hours." He hung up, picked up the receiver, and dialed another number. "Get the armored truck and come pick up the boxes," he said into the mouthpiece. "I'll meet you at the plane later tonight."

Just as he hung up, Mrs. Batista came in. She was a tall, attractive brunette, about fifteen years his junior.

Batista hugged her and told her, "Marta, we are leaving tonight."

She knew this day had been coming and was nowhere near ready to accept it, but she was a strong woman, capable of handling the dangerous and sad situation her family found themselves in.

"Make sure the children stay close to us," said Batista.

She steadied herself and held his hand. He looked at her, smiled a somewhat weak smile, and told her, "Go get ready, and let's enjoy our last official party."

Roberto and Carmen were finishing getting ready, as they waited for the Mujals to pick them up. Roberto was angry and nervous, trying to fix his tie while he talked.

"It's bad enough you agreed to go to this party, but now we have to go in the same car with them!" Roberto put his hand to his forehead and said to himself, "My god, the whole world will know we are going to this party."

"Roberto, they don't let taxis into the presidential palace. Even if we owned a car, they would not let us in by ourselves. The only way to get in is in their car."

He was fumbling with his tie, getting nowhere. Carmen came over to fix it for him. He was still mad at her, but while she adjusted the necktie, he thought to himself how beautiful she still was. He had fallen in love with her when she was fifteen. The first time he saw her was when his father delivered coal to the judge's house. He caught up with her years later at the university. He was older than her, and he had gotten a late start with his studies, having to help his father run the coal route. When the old man died, he had to sell the business for mere pennies because coal stoves were quickly becoming a thing of the past. He took what little money he made from the sale of the business and dedicated himself to studying at the university. Roberto could not believe she actually had fallen in love with him, and although she drove him crazy, he counted his blessings that he had her in his life. She had encouraged and helped him achieve so much.

Carmen saw him looking at her with a funny smile on his face and asked him, "What is that look about?"

He just kept smiling. When she finished with his tie, he held her tightly and gave her a deep, passionate kiss.

She straightened herself up. "Wow! I should fix your tie more often." And she told him she loved him. He laughed, and she went to the mirror to touch up her makeup.

"Honey," said Carmen, trying to soothe his nerves, "the party will be over before you know it. It won't be that bad."

A car horn beeped, and Roberto went to the window. He pulled the curtains aside and looked out. What he saw was an official government limousine with two motorcycle escorts in front, two in the back, and a jeep full of soldiers behind it. Roberto kept looking at this scene, not believing his eyes.

After what seemed like forever, he snapped out of his trance, turned to his wife, and told her, "Carmen, I'm going to kill you."

The party was a lavish, black-tie affair. The guest list included a mix of Batista's high-ranking politicians, military men, American businessmen, and their respective wives or dates. Most of them were happily enjoying the party and all its splendor. They were drinking, dancing, and seemed oblivious to all the unrest in the island nation.

While the party was in full swing, a military officer came over to the table where Carmen and Roberto sat with Eusebio and Alicia. He leaned in close to Eusebio and whispered something in his ear. Eusebio excused himself, followed the officer, and joined a group of cabinet members who were engaged in intense conversation with Batista. Batista was not his usual suave and calm self. He was very agitated and wildly waved his hands in front of him as he talked. He addressed his men one last time and abruptly left the room.

Eusebio, as well as the other important men in Batista's inner circle, were left dumbfounded. The color drained from Eusebio's face as the realization of what he was just told sunk in. Carmen and Roberto were on the dance floor when Eusebio and Alicia, along with other cabinet members, were led out of the ballroom by a group of heavily armed soldiers. Suddenly, gunshots were heard outside the palace.

Roberto instinctively pulled his wife close to him and cried out, "What's happening?"

Carmen looked around the room, trying to find the Mujals, when she saw them being escorted out.

"Roberto," she pointed to the back entrance of the ballroom, "those soldiers are rushing the Mujals out of the palace. They are leaving us here by ourselves. What are we going to do?"

"Don't panic. It's going to be all right," said Roberto, trying to reassure her. "Let's just go."

Outside, there were hordes of people leaving the premises. Some had panicked and were running aimlessly through the lawn and gardens of the beautiful palace. In the distance, a huge mob could be seen approaching. By now the gunfire had become constant. Roberto and Carmen walked out of the palace grounds and kept walking away as fast as they could. There was pandemonium in the streets. The parking meters, which had become a symbol of corruption, were being decapitated by gangs of bat-wielding young men.

Before the Machados had time to get very far, they were stopped by one of the gangs. It was led by Pablo, the big man who had been fighting with Juana at the Tropical Dance.

"So the end is finally here for you, filthy Batistianos!" he yelled at Roberto and Carmen. "Did you have fun at Batista's party? Well, we are going to have a little party for you too. Right now!"

Roberto got between Carmen and the group of men in an effort to protect her. Pablo walked over to Roberto, towering over him. Pablo grabbed him, shoved him to the ground, and raised his bat. Carmen screamed. But before he could strike Roberto, a car screeched to a halt right beside them. Juana ran out of the car, followed by Cesar.

"Pablo, stop!" cried Juana. "I know these people!"

Cesar grabbed Carmen and helped Roberto get up. "Are you okay? Get in the car. Hurry!"

Juana talked to Pablo and the men for a few moments. Then she returned to the car, and they drove off.

"Thank you, Cesar," said Roberto. "My god, this is a nightmare. What is going on?"

"We heard on the radio that Batista had just resigned and was fleeing the country and all hell was breaking loose. They announced that a mob of people was heading for the palace. Mom told me you had gone to Batista's New Year's Eve party, so we decided to take a chance and see if we could find you. They are broadcasting that Fidel's forces will be here in Havana tomorrow."

Carmen took Juana's hand. "Thank God you found us. Thank you so much."

"It's a good thing that brute still has the hots for me," said Juana.

"You know that man?

"Pablo? He's the guy Cesar stole me away from."

On the drive back to their home, something caught Roberto's eye, and he yelled, "Cesar, stop the car! That's Ignacio, one of my students, over there."

Cesar slammed on the brakes. A group of Batista's soldiers were searching and harassing Ignacio.

Roberto got out of the car and approached them. "Good evening, officers. This young man is my assistant. We just came from the president's party at the palace. He was supposed to meet us there. I'm sure he got lost and was trying to find his way."

The captain looked at the way Ignacio was dressed and knew that was a lie, but Roberto quickly pulled out a hundred-dollar bill and put it in the captain's hand. "By the way, Captain, you guys better get to the palace. They're rioting over there. I'm sure they could use your help."

The captain inspected the bill and slipped it into his pocket. "You better get your assistant out of here before he gets himself into trouble." He turned to his soldiers. "Let's go, men." The soldiers got back into the jeep and drove away in the opposite direction of the palace.

Ignacio turned to Roberto. "Thank you, Professor Machado. I think you just saved my life."

"Ignacio, what was that all about?"

Ignacio was silent for a moment and finally said, "I guess there is no more need for secrets at this point, Professor. I am in the underground. We got the word Batista might be leaving the country tonight, so the SRD is creating some diversionary incidents around the city to help the rebels get into Havana. I was on my way from one of those incidents to a safe house when the soldiers stopped me."

A look of realization flashed across Roberto's face. "So you are the secret letter carrier that delivered all the mail from Joaquin. I always wondered who that person was, but

I have to admit, Ignacio, I never would have pegged you as a revolutionary."

When they turned onto the Machados' block, it looked like a riot. The soldiers who had been guarding the Mujal house were gone. There was a sea of people, and looters were breaking windows, destroying plants, and ransacking the Mujal home. They were stealing anything and everything they could get their hands on.

"Oh my god!" yelled Roberto.

"Tico!" screamed Carmen.

Cesar floored it, and several people had to jump out of the way as he pulled the car into their driveway. The looters had spilled into the Machados' property, trampling all over it. Cesar pulled their car to a stop, and Carmen and Roberto rushed into their house. Cesar and Juana stayed outside, pleading with the wild crowd not to damage the Machados' home.

Ignacio stepped up and took charge. "Campañeros, compañeros, let's act civilized. Is anybody here from the SRD?" Several people responded. "Let's get some order around here. And don't anybody damage this house. This is the house of Captain Joaquin Quintana, one of the heroes of the revolution." Ignacio hugged Cesar and Juana. "Go on inside with your family. I'll watch the house." Ignacio and several others helped bring some order to the crowd that chanted, "Fidel! Fidel!"

"*Mami! Papi!*" squealed a very frightened Tico as he ran to them from his grandmother's arms.

"Tico, my darling!" said Carmen as she and Roberto both hugged their son.

"Thank God you're okay," said Roberto. He hugged Tico for a moment longer and went over to see after Rosa, who was sobbing and shaking.

Outside, the crowd still could be heard chanting, "Fidel! Fidel!"

Chapter 14

A WEEK LATER, on January 8, 1959, a huge victory motorcade made its way through Havana. Many of the comandantes, including Menoyo from the Second National Front of Escambray, who was much closer to Havana, had arrived in the capital soon after Batista fled in the early morning hours of January 1, 1959. It took Fidel a few days longer to arrive. He was coming from the Sierra Maestra mountains, which were all the way on the far eastern side of the island.

The celebrations were held up until the 8th, giving Fidel time to get to the capital. In the spirit of cooperation, it was understood by all the other groups that Fidel's forces were the main opposition. They gladly conceded power to Fidel with the understanding that there would be an all-inclusive government in which all groups would participate and that the constitution of 1940 would be reinstated as soon as possible. Fidel and the other comandantes, including Raul, Che, and Camilo, rode through the city on top of tanks and other military vehicles. Large crowds of people, excited to see their heroes, lined the streets to wave to them and cheer their victory. The rebels were smiling and filled with pride.

When the motorcade reached Havana's central plaza, there were hundreds of thousands of people waiting for them. Fidel made his way to the platform to give his first speech to the nation, and the crowd roared. Near the end of his speech, a flock of doves was released, and one of them perched on Fidel's shoulder.

"And now that this glorious revolution is victorious, Cuba can finally realize the dream of her apostle, Jose Marti." At the mention of Marti, the crowd erupted into cheers. Fidel continued, "And never again will we suffer through another dictatorship. To ensure this, I have appointed Justice Manuel Urrutia as interim president until elections can be held." Fidel turned to Camilo and, once again, as he had done several times during the speech, asked him, "How am I doing, Camilo?"

Camilo grinned leaned into the mike and said, "You are doing fine, Fidel."

Again, the crowd exploded into cheers.

Fidel finished up by telling the nation, "So go on and enjoy this day because this is your revolution. This is your victory."

Fidel walked down from the podium, and the crowd started to chant "Fidel! Fidel! Fidel!"

At the Machado home, the entire family had gathered to watch the celebration and speeches on television. Carmen was busy preparing an enormous amount of her famous chicken and rice.

On the TV, a reporter was giving a recap of the events. "You just heard Fidel Castro from Havana central plaza, where he and many key members of his Twenty-Sixth of July Movement addressed the crowd of more than half a million people who have gathered here today. Fidel was joined on the platform by his brother Raul, along with the charming Argentinean Che Guevara, and Camilo Cienfuegos, who had become a major symbol of the revolution. Also on the platform were other key members of his inner circle: Huber Matos, Juan Almeida, Ramiro Valdez, Joaquin Quintana, and others."

"That's Uncle Joaquin," said Tico.

"He looks so skinny," added Rosa. "And look at that beard."

The reporter continued, "And what has become another symbol of the revolution, Cuba's fighting women, notably Celia Sanchez and Vilma Espin."

"There's Elena!" shouted Diego.

"Look, look! She's wearing the rosary I gave her," said Cesar.

"They're all wearing rosaries or crucifixes." Rosa noticed. "That's nice."

"They're coming tomorrow," said Carmen. "Joaquin said he is bringing all his friends over. He sent us a bunch of chickens and kept telling me to make sure I make chicken and rice."

"My poor boy probably has not eaten since he left," said Rosa.

The television reporter finished with "Fidel ended his speech by mentioning Jose Marti like he did so many times and by once again asking his newly appointed army chief of staff Camilo Cienfuegos, 'How am I doing, Camilo?' People here today have picked up on that saying and are repeating it loudly and often. Reporting from the central plaza, Carlos Fuentes, CMQ News."

The next day, after all the parades and speeches, Fidel and most of his inner circle of comandantes started to arrive at the house of Joaquin's sister. The Machado backyard was full of family, friends, and soldiers of the revolution, including Camilo, Joaquin, Che, Elena, Menoyo, and Juan Almeida. A group of soldiers stood in front of the house, guarding it and the vehicles that had brought the guests.

It was the first time after their victory that almost all the principal leaders gathered to celebrate. All afternoon, people from the neighborhood came up to the soldiers outside with flowers, food, kisses, and hugs. It was a spontaneous display of thanks and appreciation for the heroes that had removed the dictator Batista from power.

Carmen came into the backyard from the kitchen with a big smile and sweat dripping down her face. Followed by Rosa, she walked up to Joaquin.

"Well, the food is done. Do you think your friends are ready to eat now?" she asked.

"Are they ready?" Joaquin laughed as he announced to everyone, "Compañeros! What we have all been waiting for, my sister Carmen's famous chicken and rice!"

The party burst into applause and cheers. Some whistled and jumped from their chairs.

"Finally," said Che, "after all these years of bragging. It better be good, Joaquin." He laughed.

"You have never tasted anything like this," answered Joaquin.

"It sure smells good," said Almeida, who was echoed by everyone else.

The soldiers rushed to form a line at the table, where three huge pots of the much anticipated meal awaited them.

"Camilo, you go first," said Joaquin.

"Don't let him go first," said Che. "There will be nothing left but bones."

All the soldiers laughed heartily.

Camilo moved toward the head of the line and scooped up Tico along the way. "Hey, little fellow, why don't you do the honors?"

Camilo lifted Tico up and carried him on one shoulder while Tico giggled and waved. As they approached the front of the line, Camilo saw that Carmen, Rosa, and Roberto were ready to dish out the portions.

"Please," he said, "you've gone through enough already. Allow us to do the serving. There are at least seventy-five people here. You folks won't have any time to spend with Elena and Joaquin. Besides, we are used to feeding this many people. Please, I insist."

"Thank you," said Roberto. "That is very nice of you."

They shook hands, and Camilo waved a couple of soldiers over to the serving line to dish out the food. Joaquin's soldier friends all agreed it was the best chicken and rice they had ever tasted. They kept coming to Joaquin to thank him and tell him that the chicken and rice was even better than he had predicted. He was happy to hear it but kept telling them to thank his sister Carmen instead. They all made their way to Carmen to tell her it was the best meal any of them had had in a very long time.

In Tico's bedroom, Diego and Elena were embracing, and Diego cried with joy and relief.

"I was so worried about you, Elena. Thank God you're okay. I missed you so much."

"I missed you too, Dad. I know you don't understand but…"

Diego cut her off. "I'm beginning to. For the first time, I see some hope for this country. You were right. I am so proud of you." He smiled a big smile and wiped his eyes. "I heard about your heroics. If you become half as good a physician as you were a soldier, you'll be one hell of a doctor." He gave her a big hug.

"I'm not sure I still want to be a doctor."

"Really? I'm surprised. What will you do instead?"

"There is still much work to be done for the revolution. I'm going to be part of that."

Diego, for the first time in his life, looked at her as an adult instead of a child. "Well, you've always been very smart. If that is what you want to do, I will respect your decision."

"Thank you, Dad. You don't know how happy it makes me to hear you say that."

She was sure that her father was proud of her, but she did not believe him when he said he understood her. He had no idea how much the revolution had to do to correct all the injustices that had been perpetuated for so long.

Again, they hugged, and each of them wiped away a tear. As Elena looked over Diego's shoulder, she saw the portrait Alejandra had painted of Tico. Alejandra still brought out angry feelings from her. She tried to push them aside but couldn't help feeling resentment toward her father's relationship with his new girlfriend.

He looked at her and asked, "Are you happy?"

"I am now. Are you happy?"

"You know I am," said Diego.

"Are you going to marry her?"

Diego was still apprehensive to talk to her about Alejandra, so he just said, "Maybe, but I need more time. How would you feel if I did?"

She forced a smile. "If it makes you happy." She could not help her distaste for such an idea, but she tried hard to hide it from Diego.

In the backyard, Camilo was in line for a second helping. Cesar was right behind him, followed by Bill Lima. Raul and Vilma entered the party. Fidel, Celia, and a few soldiers carrying bouquets of fresh tropical flowers were a few steps behind them.

Raul took one look at the gathering and became very agitated. "I can't believe you are all here at the same time. If somebody wanted to end this revolution, all they would have to do is bomb this house," said Raul.

Camilo whispered in Che's ear, "Hey, look. Little Fidel is here."

"Relax, Raul," said Che. "Have some chicken."

Joaquin sneaked up behind Raul, got close to his ear, and shouted, "Boom!"

Raul nearly jumped out of his skin. "That's not funny!"

"I think you are wrong," said Che. "It is funny."

"How would he know anyway?" Camilo laughed.

"Hey, hey, he laughed once. I was there," said Joaquin. "I saw it with my own eyes. It was in Mexico, 1956."

Almeida saw Fidel enter the backyard. "Attention!" he barked.

"Relax," said Fidel, "today is a day for celebration."

Joaquin approached them, and before he could say a word, Fidel asked him, "Joaquin, am I going to get to eat any of that chicken and rice or not?"

"Yes, we made sure Camilo didn't eat it all." The soldiers laughed again. "But first I have to introduce you to everyone. If I miss anybody, I'll never hear the end of it."

He started by introducing Fidel to his family. Fidel thanked them for their hospitality and told Carmen how famous her chicken and rice was in the mountains. Joaquin continued to take Fidel around the gathering to lots of smiles, handshakes, and congratulations. Vilma, Celia, Raul, and Gustavo were close behind. When they were introduced to Juana, Gustavo recognized her from the neighborhood where they had grown up and stopped to talk with her. After making the rounds throughout the party, Fidel, Celia, Raul, Vilma, Ramiro, Camilo, and Joaquin sat at one of the tables and began eating.

"Wow," said Fidel, "this really is delicious. I guess you were not exaggerating, Joaquin." The others agreed.

Tico came up to their table. "Uncle Joaquin, look what I got." In his hand, Tico held what looked to be baseball cards. But instead of baseball players, the pictures were of the members of Fidel's army. Tico pulled out Fidel's card from the stack.

"Look at this, Fidel," said Joaquin. "You never got your face on a baseball card, but now you have it on this." He handed the card to Fidel, and Tico put the rest of the cards on the table.

Camilo searched through the stack, found his card, and examined it. "Well, at least they used a better picture of me than the one on my wanted poster."

"Let me see those," barked Raul. He grabbed the cards from the table. "I cannot believe this. It has been less than two weeks, and the capitalists have already begun exploiting the revolution. They should not be allowed to do this." He turned to Tico. "Don't buy any more of these. It is wrong."

"What's the matter, Raul?" said Camilo. "Don't you like your picture?"

"It's offensive. I do not want to be a part of it. We fought to liberate this country, and they are making money from it. This is the worst form of capitalist exploitation."

"Relax, Raul," said Fidel, "this is neither the time nor the place."

"There is nothing wrong with these cards," said Camilo. "It's for the kids. Instead of looking at pictures of their baseball heroes, they will be looking at pictures of their revolution heroes. You should be happy and take it as a compliment."

"I think it's a great idea," said Joaquin.

"I just wanted to get all of you to sign them," said Tico, not knowing exactly how to react.

"I'll be glad to," said Camilo.

"I'll sign mine too," added Fidel.

"I will *not* be a part of this," growled Raul. He got up and stormed out of the party, followed by Vilma and Ramiro.

Fidel looked at Tico. "Don't worry about my brother. He's just a grouch."

"That's right," said Camilo. "Say, I'll trade you my jacket for Raul's card."

"Really?" exclaimed Tico, his eyes wide open with disbelief. Before Camilo could have a chance to take it back, Tico said, "Deal!"

Camilo took off his green army jacket and helped Tico put it on. The sleeves went past Tico's knees, and the bottom of the jacket almost reached the ground. They all chuckled, and Joaquin patted him on the back of the head.

"Now you look like a real soldier," said Camilo. Then he looked at Joaquin, winked, smiled, and held up Raul's card. "This is going on my wall."

PART TWO

Chapter 15

AFTER FIDEL AND his men had arrived in Havana and all the hoopla and celebrations of the rebels' victory died down, their new challenge was how to peacefully govern the country. During those first few days when they all celebrated in Havana, there seemed to be lots of harmony and common ground between all the other groups and Fidel's forces. But now, instead of a harmonious transfer of power from Batista to a new governing body, there were many disputes and disagreements.

Mostly this was due to the different philosophies among the rebels themselves and people like President Urrutia who had been appointed by Fidel to run the government. By February, Fidel himself had assumed the position of prime minister, taking over from Jose Miro Cardona.

The newly appointed president made it known from the beginning that he would not be a token figurehead. He emphasized that the reinstatement of the 1940 constitution and a free and open society was what everyone wanted and had fought for. He butted heads with Che and Raul and made it clear that he was not going to tolerate anyone interfering with the running of the country and the office of the president. Urrutia openly criticized the strong armed tactics by the newly formed militia and its increased meddling into people's lives. He said it was time to lift the state of emergency that had been instituted right after Batista's forces surrendered, restore the constitution, and allow the free market to take over.

In the open, Fidel was noncommittal about where his choices lay. He kept saying everything would work itself out and that the constitution would be reinstated soon. But behind the scenes, he was orchestrating a concentration of power that gave Raul and Che more and more responsibilities. Many socialistic ideas were being floated about, and word that the government was going to nationalize certain industries was buzzing around the country. Also, Fidel's handling of the trial of Batista's pilots gave an ominous glimpse of things to come.

A squadron of Batista's pilots was accused, by Fidel, of murder. They were brought up on charges for the intentional bombing of innocent people that were suspected by Batista's troops of working with the rebels. The pilots were arrested and tried for those offenses. At the trial, they were able to show evidence that they had not committed such an act. They were found innocent, but Fidel did not like the verdict. He said if the accused had the right to appeal a conviction, the state should have the right to appeal an acquittal. The pilots were retried in a televised kangaroo court that disallowed all of the pilots' evidence. The state made all kinds of unsubstantiated accusations against them that were accepted as fact. The pilots were found guilty and denied an appeal. They were all sentenced to death by firing squad. This did not sit well with many, including the newly appointed president.

The killing of the pilots was the beginning of thousands of firing squad executions to come. The executions came to be known as being sent to *"El Paredon"* which meant "against the wall." The *wall* was where those sentenced to death stood before the firing squad. In the eastern part of Cuba, where Comandante Huber Matos was put in charge of restoring order to the war-torn areas, the mood was completely different. An air of free enterprise and human ingenuity was openly practiced. Two different ideologies seemed to be taking root, the centralized socialistic model in Havana being pushed by Raul and Che and the more open free enterprise system in the interior of the country.

Camilo, now in charge of the armed forces, was trying to bring order to the transition from an army at war to one at peace and brought Joaquin along to help him. Camilo also had the delicate task of blending his army, the Escambray forces, and the underground rebels (like the SRD) into one cohesive unit. Because of this, Camilo and Joaquin found themselves left out of the loop and the dirty politics that were ensuing.

Also, due to the fact that all of Batista's armed forces personnel had disbanded, Camilo's regular units, along with Menoyo's Second National Front of Escambray, were replacing those positions. That left a vacuum of personnel, replaced by the new militia run separately from the regular armed forces though still, in theory, under army command.

That militia was mainly made up of new recruits late to the party but very eager to jump on the bandwagon of popularity with the revolutionary heroes. They couldn't wait to assert their new authority and question anyone's loyalty to their newly found "religion". The militia was run behind the scenes by Che, Raul, and men like Ramiro Valdez.

The militia was getting involved in anything and everything. Their convenient excuse was that they needed to look for and root out Counter-Revolutionaries. This had become their catch phrase, "The Excuse" to detain, question, and apprehend anyone deemed by them to be an enemy of the Revolution.

The mood of the country began to change; it could be felt in the air. Many people left Cuba shortly after Fidel took over but they were mostly people associated with Batista and his regime. Now the number of people leaving was not only increasing, but its make-up started to change from what had been referred to as Batistianos to regular people who did not want any part of what they had witnessed and what they believed was coming.

The tension between the president and others spilled over to include Fidel. Urrutia made public accusations about Fidel himself interfering in the affairs of the President, neglecting his duties as Prime Minister, failing to start the legislative process to institute the Constitution and lift all restrictions. Urrutia also openly disapproved of any industry or company being taken over by the government and the obvious mock trials that were being conducted. In response to this he withheld his signature from all bills in protest. It was only a matter of time before something would have to give. The balance of power and the direction of Cuba would have to choose a course. Eventually Fidel would have to tilt his hand and declare his true intentions.

Seven months later, Roberto sat at the desk in his office on a very hot July afternoon. He felt like his world was being turned upside down. He spoke on the phone with Carmen.

"You will not believe this. Two heavily armed militiamen just rushed in here and told me to clear out my office. They are nationalizing all foreign trade."

"What does that mean?" asked Carmen.

"It means I don't have a business anymore. They said the government will be handling all foreign trade from now on."

"They can't do that."

"Well, they just did. Thank God I'm still teaching."

"This is not right. You've worked very hard to make that business successful. We didn't steal anything from anyone."

"It's not only me," continued Roberto, "it's everyone. They told Marcelo next door the same thing. They're closing all the businesses at the airport, too."

"I can't believe this."

"Nothing can come in or go out of the country without the government handling it. I better call some movers. If I'm not out of here by six tonight they are going to confiscate everything."

Roberto said goodbye and hung up.

Carmen was stunned. She looked around her house, taking in all the pictures and mementos, a lifetime of memories. She had a terrible feeling that her whole life was about to make a dramatic change.

At that moment, Tico came running in and went over to her. He saw the sad look on her face and asked her, "Mommy, are you okay?" And he hugged her.

Carmen broke down and started to cry.

Havana was now in complete turmoil. Fidel had recently resigned as prime minister, saying he could no longer work with the president and making all kinds of accusations about Urrutia. He continued to meet with other ministers in open defiance of the president and was basically running the country from his hotel room.

Laws were being implemented without the approval of the president. Many in the government, like Menoyo, the Escambray rebels leader, who did not go along with Fidel, were being apprehended on all kinds of trumped-up charges, convicted, and sent to prison. Urrutia knew it would not be long before they would come after him. He signed his resignation letter on July 18 and quietly left the capitol building. He requested asylum at the Venezuelan embassy, where he released a statement to the press.

Roberto listened to the radio while packing up the materials in his office.

"President Manuel Urrutia has resigned," said the newscaster. "He has requested asylum at the Venezuelan embassy and, in a statement he read to the press, said he was no longer allowed to run the government, that it was obvious to him the constitution would never be reinstated, and that communists had taken over many positions of power without his approval. Fidel has denied these allegations from the president and is preparing to give a speech about the resignation."

In his speech, Fidel accused Urrutia of everything, including working for the CIA, conveniently forgetting to mention that Urrutia had been his own choice for president. Fidel still did not completely tip his hand and continued to refuse to give a clear answer about being a socialist, let alone a communist. But it was obvious, because of some of the ideas being implemented, like the nationalization of the port and other so-called vital industries, that Fidel wanted to move the country into a socialistic model.

Not long after President Urrutia resigned and sought asylum, Fidel rescinded his resignation as prime minister and went about remaking Cuba in his own vision. He appointed as president Osvaldo Dorticos, a doctor by trade and an old socialist political hack. The ultimate "yes man," Dorticos went along with everything Fidel wanted and signed any bill that was presented to him. The constitution was reinstated in name only. All its principles were completely ignored, and Fidel stopped any pretense about working with or listening to others. He next set his sights on the free press to muffle and control their reports and commentaries.

Fidel was now constantly giving speeches which contained more and more rants against the United States and imperialism. Many people that openly criticized Fidel and others in the new government, were automatically marginalized as Batistianos and, in many cases, taken to prison for what he referred to as "counter-revolutionary activities". Those were any "activities" of which the new revolutionary militia did not approve. A new intelligence unit, called the G2, was formed to combat the Counter-Revolutionaries. A pall descended over the people of Havana.

After the resignation by President Urrutia and his charges that Communists were taking over the government, the number of people wanting to leave the country increased dramatically. The US embassy was overwhelmed with applications for any kind of visa that would get people out of Cuba. The embassy, not wanting to turn anyone down, started to bypass the visa requirement. What one needed to leave Cuba for the United States became known as Visa Waivers. The majority of people in the country still had hope that things would calm down at some point and everything would work itself out. But more and more people now considered leaving. There was also a growing number of young men leaving Cuba with the intention to start an army that would come back and fight Fidel.

Meanwhile, Diego and Bill Lima were at the Telephone Company working on the computer system.

"So, when was the last time you heard from your daughter?"

"About three weeks ago," answered Diego, "right before she went to the Isle of Pine. She's so busy she doesn't have time for me anymore."

"What's she doing?"

"She is now part of the new militia. She just got promoted to lieutenant, but what she actually does, I really don't know. I can't get a straight answer from her. She keeps saying, 'The work of the revolution is not finished.'"

"So what are you going to do?"

Diego sighed. "What can I do? But I'm concerned about this new militia and all the secrecy." Diego sighed. "I don't know. I just don't know."

At that moment, several militiamen with large automatic weapons marched in. They were led by Captain Javier Lopez, an imposing and arrogant twenty-seven-year-old. He was followed by Lieutenant Ortiz, a much smaller man in his early twenties.

"Attention, everyone!" growled Captain Lopez. "As of now, the revolution, in the name of the Cuban people, is taking over all operations here."

"What?" protested Bill.

"The services of you and your employees are no longer needed," said Captain Lopez.

"By whose authority?" asked Bill.

Captain Lopez walked up to Bill until they were within an inch of being nose to nose and yelled at him, "By the authority of the people of Cuba, Yankee!"

"You can't do this," said Diego.

Captain Lopez turned to Diego, took some papers out of his pocket, and threw them at him. Diego made no attempt to catch them, and the papers flew all over.

"The orders have already been handed down. There they are." He pointed to the papers on the floor. "You can look at them yourselves." Neither Diego nor Bill made any attempt to pick them up. "From now on, this department will be run by someone deemed qualified by the revolution."

"Qualified?" said Bill with a chuckle. "I doubt there are fifty people in the whole world who know how to run this computer." He took a few steps toward the captain and told him with a smile, "In Cuba there are only two, me and him." He pointed to Diego.

Diego added, "They brought Bill from the United States specifically to run and maintain these computers. There is no one in this country who knows what these computers do, let alone knows how to run them. I have been training with him for over two years, and I barely know what I'm doing. And you just want to appoint anybody? Tomorrow you will be calling us to come back, but you won't be able to because nobody's phone will work."

The captain did not know what to say. Lieutenant Ortiz, although a younger man and of lower rank, seemed to be the most sensible of the two. He leaned over and said something to his superior.

Bill overheard Lieutenant Ortiz as he whispered to Captain Lopez, "Captain, maybe we should call headquarters and let them know what's going on. We should make sure that if we remove these two gentlemen from their post, we will be able to find someone who can run the capital's phone system."

"If you're going to call somebody, you had better do it quick," said Bill. "In less than two hours, the hard cycle goes down, and the mainframe memory has to be dumped into the secondary loop in order for the system to remain operational. If we don't start doing that real soon, there won't be a working phone in Havana, including Fidel's."

Bill turned away from the soldiers and winked at Diego.

Captain Lopez was now totally clueless as to what to do. He wanted to assert his authority, especially in front of this damn arrogant Yankee, but he could not run the risk of being blamed for the phone system shutting down. He walked around, mulling over his choices, and pretended not to be worried. Finally, he announced to everyone, as if it was his own idea, that he would go back to headquarters and personally make sure the right person would be sent to replace Diego and Bill. In the meantime, he would leave Lieutenant Ortiz in charge. Captain Lopez barked at the rest of his men to follow him and told Diego and Bill they had his permission to continue their work.

Early the next morning, Cesar was sorting mail with several of the other postal workers. Among them was Juan, a twenty-three-year-old with whom Cesar had been working for some time.

"Where is your brother?" asked Cesar. "I haven't seen him all week. Is he sick?"

"You don't know?" He leaned close to Cesar and said in a whisper, "The G2 went to Carlos's house in the middle of the night and took him away."

"The G2?" Juan motioned to Cesar to keep it down, and Cesar lowered his voice. "That's the intelligence agency. Why did they take Carlos? What did he do?"

Juan looked around and made sure no one was listening to them. "For no reason," Juan continued. "He was just complaining about the way President Urrutia was forced to resign. He was saying we should have free elections now. He was just talking, nothing radical, just expressing himself. Someone from the militia must have heard him because they accused him of being a Batistiano and a Counter-Revolutionary. Anytime someone thinks differently from the revolution and says anything these militia bullies don't like, they are automatically labeled a Batistiano and thrown in jail."

"They arrest people just for that?" Cesar was shocked.

"I'm telling you, Cesar, I am scared. Very scared."

Juan picked up his mailbag, and before he left, he leaned close to Cesar and told him, "During Batista, you could get incarcerated for doing things Batista didn't like. These people want to throw you in jail for just talking and thinking."

The look on Juan's face told Cesar just how scared he was. Juan left to make his deliveries.

Cesar continued to sort mail but couldn't help thinking about what Juan had said. Moments later, he heard a commotion coming from outside. He looked out the doorway and watched as several militiamen forcibly dragged Juan away. Cesar could not believe what he was seeing. Even during the worst days of Batista, he had never seen anyone dragged away at work.

He shook his head and said to himself, "What the hell is happening?"

Carmen was on the phone with Alejandra. The television was on, but she wasn't watching. "Are you kidding? The phone company too? Does Diego still have a job? Alejandra, what is going on in this country? I can't wait for Joaquin to get back from Camaguey so he can let us know why all this is happening. My god, what are they going to nationalize next, your studio?"

On the television, there was live coverage of Camilo trying to make his way to his headquarters. He had been away from Havana and all over the country, involved in the reorganization of the new armed forces. He was a breath of fresh air from all the politics and name calling that had been going on in the capital. A huge number of people were crowded around him, shouting things like "We love you" and "How am I doing, Camilo?"

The announcer described the scene. "It seems that, with every passing day, Camilo's popularity grows more and more with the people of Cuba. Some of them that you can see behind me have been waiting outside his headquarters for hours just to try to catch a glimpse of their hero, the chief of the army. Everywhere he goes, he draws big crowds, some even bigger than Fidel himself. The saying 'How am I doing, Camilo?' has become a national slogan."

Chapter 16

IT WAS SEPTEMBER, nine months after Castro and his forces had pushed Batista out of power. Joaquin had finally come back to Havana after being away with Camilo, helping him reorganize the new armed forces all over the island.

Joaquin sat with Diego in what had once been a bustling restaurant in Havana, but now it was half empty. Joaquin ordered pineapple juice, and Diego asked for a double whiskey.

"What's wrong, Diego?"

"You tell me what's wrong. Roberto's business has been nationalized, the militia storms into the telephone company and tries to fire everybody, and Cesar says they are dragging people out of the post office."

Joaquin shook his head and looked away. "I don't know what's happening either," he lamented. Joaquin turned and faced Diego with an exhausted and disappointed look on his face. "To tell you the truth, nobody seems to know where the hell Fidel is going with this revolution."

"What does Camilo have to say about all this? Isn't he still Fidel's right hand man?"

"Camilo has been swamped with the task of consolidating all the armed forces. We are so deep in bureaucratic bullshit we don't have time to sleep, let alone get involved in all this drama. Camilo and I are not much for the political games, but I can tell you, there's a big power struggle going on right now. Huber is pushing Camaguey toward democracy, Raul seems to be pushing Havana toward socialism, and Fidel is walking the fence. This whole mess started when President Urrutia resigned. I wish someone could have talked him out of it. We need a strong, independent president."

"Joaquin, I don't know exactly how communism works, but I can tell you that the government seems to be taking over everything. Do you think Urrutia is right? Is Fidel a communist?" asked Diego.

"In speech after speech, he keeps saying he is not. I was there in the mountains when he told that American reporter from the *New York Times* that he was not a socialist or a communist. He told him and always told all of us that his philosophy was representative democracy, social justice, and following the constitution. But he keeps giving Che and Raul more and more power. Those two have made it clear what their philosophies are."

"But why is he giving so much power to Raul? I thought he was a just a paranoid fool."

"He's Fidel's brother, that's why. He just made Raul the minster of defense. Camilo is beside himself over that and is having a meeting with Fidel about the new chain of command." The two men got quiet as the waiter returned with their drinks and put them on the table. After the waiter was out of earshot, Joaquin continued. "I just hope Camilo can talk some sense into Fidel."

Diego handed his whiskey to Joaquin. "I think you need this more than I do."

Fidel, Camilo, and Raul were meeting in Fidel's large but spartan office. The mood was tense. Camilo not only was upset about Raul now being his direct superior, but he could not believe what he was hearing from Raul and Fidel about Huber Matos. He had just left Camaguey and was with Huber the whole time. He knew Huber did not want to start any trouble; it was the other way around. He wanted to get out of the way. He was tired of dealing with Raul, and he did not want to do some of the things he had been asked to do by Raul and Che. So instead of continuing to constantly fight with those two, he just wanted to resign. Camilo was totally against accepting Huber's resignation and agreed with him about most of the things he was doing in the interior of the country.

"Listen, if Huber wants to resign, the revolution doesn't need him," said Fidel.

"We're losing a good man, Fidel," said Camilo.

"He's a traitor," said Raul. "This resignation is nothing but a trick. Just wait."

Fidel tried to calm his brother. "Raul, don't worry about him. If he wants to go, let him go."

"I don't trust him," answered Raul. "He is already running Camaguey and half of Oriente. He's in a perfect position to set himself up to lead a Counter-Revolution. I know it."

"You're crazy," countered Camilo. "He just wants to get out of the way and let you run things. You should be happy."

"Believe what you want," said Raul, "but this revolution has plenty to worry about without letting ex-comandantes do whatever they please. That's all we need, ex-Comandate Matos running around the country, telling everyone why he resigned and what he thinks is wrong with the revolution, fomenting trouble and dissent. We should have him arrested."

"First of all, Raul, he hasn't done or said anything. That is your imagination running wild," Camilo emphasized. "And what you call dissent others might call speaking their minds. I thought that's what we all fought for, being able to speak freely, to speak our minds."

Fidel took a big puff on his cigar and contemplated the situation. After a moment, he spoke. "Camilo, maybe it is nothing. Maybe he just wants to be free from the responsibility of following orders. But what if Raul is right? Let's play it safe. You should go to Camaguey tomorrow and arrest him."

Camilo was stunned. He could not believe Fidel wanted him to be the one to arrest Huber. It was obvious to Camilo that the decision had been made long before he came to this meeting, and he did not want any part of it.

"Let Raul go and arrest him," Camilo snapped. "It's his idea."

"But you are the chief of the army," said Fidel. "You should be the one to handle it."

"You made Raul minister of defense. He's above me. Let him do it."

Raul spoke up. He could not control his animosity for Camilo. "The minister of defense does not personally arrest people." He put his hand to his chin and thought for a moment. "But you are right. I am above you." He leaned closer to Camilo and told him with a sneer on his face and a dismissive wave of his hand, "So I'm ordering you. Go and arrest that traitor."

Camilo stood up. He was not about to be talked to that way by a man for whom he had no respect whatsoever. "I'm not taking orders from you!" he yelled at Raul.

"Calm down. Camilo, sit down, please," said Fidel. "Do it for me. I just want to make sure there is no treason here. If Huber is innocent like you say, he has nothing to worry about. Talk to him. You can make him understand my reasoning."

"That's right," said Raul. "You and that traitor speak the same language."

Camilo did not hesitate. All the animosity he had built up against Raul over the years bubbled to the surface. He lunged at Raul and punched him in the face. Raul went down but was able to grab Camilo's jacket and pull him to the floor with him. They wrestled, each trying to gain the advantage. Camilo put him in a half nelson hold around his neck and got in two good shots before some soldiers came in and broke it up. Fidel just sat there, witnessing it all and smoking his cigar.

The soldiers had restrained both men when Camilo said, "I don't care who or what you are. If you ever make an insinuation like that again, I'll kill you!"

The soldiers hustled Raul out of the room.

Fidel just sat there, shaking his head, puffing on his cigar. After a few moments, with a devilish smile, he said to Camilo, "You two don't like each other, do you?"

Camilo laughed. He straightened his jacket and ran his fingers through his long hair before he put his cowboy hat back on. He said to Fidel, "Your brother is an asshole, and you know it. He just doesn't like Huber for whatever reason, and he doesn't like me. That's what this is all about. Let's see what he says about me after this."

Fidel leaned over to the ashtray near Camilo, shook some ashes from his cigar, and looked at him. "You are right. My brother is an asshole. But he is my asshole, and I know he just wants to make sure he is covering my back." Fidel leaned on his chair and smiled at Camilo. "I know you have my back too, but it's never a bad idea to be careful. You know Huber. You are friends. That makes you the best man to do this. That way, you make sure he gets the respect he deserves. I don't really want you to arrest him. Just remove him from his command and have him come to Havana while you stay there and sort things out. We can have a chat with him and clear everything up."

Camilo sat down in silence, a grim look on his face.

With no response from Camilo, Fidel got very serious. "The revolution needs you to do this, Camilo. If Raul is right, our country is going to fall into a civil war, and that we cannot withstand. Cuba will fall into chaos. It's worth it to remove Huber now, just in case he has more ambitious ideas."

Camilo remained seated, saying nothing, looking at the floor and shaking his head.

Fidel finally said, "Are you going to do it or not?"

Camilo bit his lip and looked at Fidel. "I'll do it. But I'm telling you right now, I don't like it. Huber is not a traitor. He is doing exactly what we all fought for. The only person around here changing the rules is Raul." For the first time in all the years they had been together, he stared at Fidel with a look of defiance. "Maybe you should remove Raul from his command instead." He looked at Fidel, this time more with disappointment than anger, and said to him, "I'm telling you, Fidel. I don't like any of what's been going on around here lately."

With that, Camilo stood up and left. A few moments later, Raul returned, wiping some blood from his lip.

"See what I mean?" said Raul. He had been hiding in the office next door, listening in on Fidel and Camilo's conversation. He sat down and told Fidel, "I've been telling you for months he's a loose cannon. I don't trust him. If we think Huber is getting too ambitious, we should really be worrying more about Camilo." Raul sat there, looking out the window, nervously tapping his leg.

He turned and looked back at Fidel. "We must do something about Camilo, and we better do it quick before he gets any more popular. Don't believe for one minute he is not aware of it. Everywhere you go, it's Camilo this and Camilo that. People keep repeating that stupid saying, 'How'm I doing, Camilo?' He is getting caught up in his own popularity."

Raul shook his head in disgust. "People are actually going around saying he looks like Jesus Christ in a cowboy hat. In the streets, the word is he is even more popular than you. Some are openly saying he should be the leader. And the press is in love with him. He plays Mr. Humble like he's not into politics, but I'm telling you, he is a very big threat and a danger to you."

Again, Fidel puffed on his cigar. He thought for a long time. After all, he had created the monster himself. That funny line had come to bite him in the ass, and he knew

Raul was right. He was vulnerable to such a likeable guy as Camilo. But it was too risky to arrest him, especially at the same time he was arresting Huber. There could be a backlash that might build into something they would not be able to control. He knew Raul's dislike for Camilo would make it easier for his brother to do what had to be done. Huber could be put in prison, but Camilo had to be eliminated. He took one last puff of his cigar before he extinguished it in the ashtray.

He looked up at Raul and told him, "You're right. Take care of it."

The next day, Camilo made his way to Huber Matos's office inside a large military complex in Camaguey. He had just relieved Huber of his command and saw him off at the airfield. Huber was flown to Havana, not in handcuffs, but escorted by two soldiers. However, it was obvious he was being arrested, and Camilo was furious.

It had broken Camilo's heart to have to do this to his friend and such a brave man. Huber kept reassuring him that everything would be okay and told him not to worry. Huber was sure that once he talked to Fidel, he would be able to clear everything up.

He was so confident that he told Camilo, "I'm telling Fidel that if he can show me how I'm a traitor, I will willingly go to jail for twenty years."

He hugged his friend, got on the plane, and took off. A few minutes later, while still in the office, Camilo received a phone call from Joaquin. Camilo wanted to vent and started to tell his good friend about what he had just done. Joaquin kept trying to cut in, but Camilo went on.

"I told Fidel there is no treason here. I can see for myself. Huber just wants out. But it was like talking to a wall."

Joaquin finally jumped in and cut him off before he could say another word. "That's not the only thing that's wrong, Camilo. I called because Raul and Ramiro came in with a couple of soldiers and searched your office this morning."

Camilo's anger boiled. He knew that bastard would retaliate against him for what happened in Fidel's office, but he could not believe he was fucking with him so soon. He had to put a stop to whatever Raul was up to.

"That son of a bitch! I swear I'll kill him. Get me a plane. I'm going back to Havana today."

"I figured you would want to do that, so I started making some inquiries. But I can't get you a plane. Raul has ordered all pilots and planes on military maneuvers. I can't find a qualified pilot, let alone an aircraft."

Camilo knew that was not a coincidence. He was sure Raul was trying to keep him in Camaguey to cook up whatever he was planning against him. He had to get to Havana right away. "I'll find one somehow. Wait for me at the airport. I'll be there tonight." Camilo hung up and dialed another number. "Mirta, give me Fidel."

Mirta, Fidel's secretary, said, "Oh, hello, Camilo. He is not here right now. Let me see if I can find him for you." Before she could go and look for Fidel, Raul came and took the phone from her.

"Camilo, it's me, Raul. Fidel is not here."

"Are you searching Fidel's office too?"

Raul was not surprised that Camilo already knew what was going on. He had counted on Joaquin telling his good friend. "Camilo, I wasn't searching your office. There was a bomb threat, and we had to search everywhere."

Camilo knew Raul was full of shit, and he sarcastically asked him, "Since when does the minister of defense personally search for bombs?" Before Raul had a chance to respond to his question, Camilo yelled into the phone, "I need a plane, Raul! *NOW!*" He was determined to get back to Havana that day and put an end to all the bullshit once and for all.

"Sorry, all military planes are on maneuvers. But wait, let me see." Raul pretended to think. "Umm . . . there is a small plane, a Cessna, I think, coming from Oriente to Havana. I can have it stop in Camaguey and pick you up."

"I don't care what kind of a plane it is, just get me one." Camilo slammed down the phone.

Raul smiled and looked at the baseball type card of himself he had ripped from Camilo's office wall during the search. He held it in his hand, took one final look at it, then slowly crumpled the card, and tossed it into the trash can.

Camilo was never seen nor heard from again.

Chapter 17

THE DISAPPEARANCE OF Camilo's plane staggered the nation. Fidel made a big show of looking for him, but not a trace of the plane or Camilo was found. His disappearance was treated by everyone as a time for mourning, and a sense of tremendous sadness and loss was felt by all. After a few days, the search was called off, and everyone assumed Camilo had died in a plane crash.

A few days later, Fidel, Raul, Che, and Joaquin met in Fidel's office.

Fidel came from behind his desk and put his arm around Joaquin. "I know how upset you are. I know you two were the best of friends. Fuck, we are all brokenhearted about this," said Fidel as he slammed his fist against the wall.

"Camilo was my friend too. But damn it, the revolution must go on! Camilo would have been the first one to tell you so." He grabbed Joaquin by both shoulders, staring into his eyes. "That is why you have been promoted to comandante. Remember in the mountains when one of our brothers fell? The others took up the slack." He put his arm around Joaquin's shoulder, walked him to the sofa, and sat next to him. "We need you now more than ever, and we need you to take over naval operations. I need it run by someone I can trust."

Joaquin was still in shock. He didn't want to believe his friend was dead. He kept shaking his head, looking into his hat. "Camilo is the heart and soul of this revolution. We should keep looking for him. He might still be alive somewhere." He looked at Fidel and pleaded with him, "If he is alive, I know I can find him."

"No," said Raul, jumping out of his chair. "You are wrong. Fidel is the heart and soul of this revolution. You have been put in charge of naval operations. That is where the revolution needs you to be, and that is what you will do. You should stop questioning our judgment. You have your orders, Comandante Quintana. That will be all."

Fidel told Raul to stop and said to Joaquin, "You know my brother is not much for tact, but, Joaquin, we really need you to trust our judgment and follow your new orders."

Joaquin did not know what to say. He was still confused by Camilo's disappearance, and although he did not know what, he knew something was not right. But he had to tell them something, so for now, he figured he would go along with their plan. He stood up and told Fidel that he had always been a good and loyal soldier, that he appreciated his promotion, and that he would carry out his orders.

But the promotion felt like a bribe, like he was being bought off. Joaquin started to walk out but stopped short of the doorway. He turned and looked at Raul with an icy stare. "You know what, Raul? I was wrong. The men in the mountains have always known that you are the heart and soul of the revolution." He turned and stared at Che. Che had been there the whole time but had not uttered a single word. "Isn't that right, Che?"

Che remained silent, looking at the floor. Joaquin turned, saluted Fidel, and left.

"I'll talk to him," said Che, and he followed Joaquin out the door.

Raul looked at Fidel. "He's going to be a problem."

"Just watch him for now."

Later that day, a large crowd gathered in Havana's central plaza to hear Fidel speak about Camilo. The mood of the crowd was one of deep sadness. Some hugged and leaned on one another. Many were crying. Others stared sullenly at nothing in particular.

Fidel finished his speech by saying, "What is important to remember in this time of mourning for Camilo is that although some heroes will die, the revolution must live. We will all carry on, and we will all endure."

Joaquin assumed command of the small Cuban navy and went about his duties. But something had died inside him along with Camilo. He had a persistent feeling that things just did not add up. From then on, he questioned everything and dug for any information he could find.

Huber finally got his audience with Fidel. He told Fidel and Raul that he had no intention of interfering with the work of the revolution. He just wanted to go back to being a private citizen, write a few articles, maybe a book. The mention of writing articles was all Raul had to hear to be convinced Huber was going to foment trouble, and he said so. Huber assured them that was not the case and told Fidel what he had said to Camilo. If Fidel could show him how he was a traitor, he would willingly go to jail for twenty years. After a rigged trial in a kangaroo court, Huber was sentenced to just that, twenty years in prison for treason. He had dictated his own sentence.

It was now November 1959, almost a year since the revolution had taken over. Fidel decided it was time to control the comings and goings of the many foreigners that arrived in Cuba as tourists every year and ran around Havana at their leisure. In order to achieve that, he went after the very establishments that had traditionally catered to those people. Tourism had always been big business in Cuba, especially in Havana, which catered to a mostly

American clientele. Fidel saw tourism, particularly for American tourists, as a corruptive force against the ideals of what he wanted Cuba to be.

He first went after the tourist attractions he knew people would be in favor of closing. He began a public campaign to abolish all the sex shows and whorehouses that most people agreed were an eyesore to the country and a bad influence on the youth.

Not long after closing those illegitimate establishments, he proceeded to use the same excuse of bad influence on the youth of the country to close legitimate businesses that were tourist driven. The many casinos throughout the capital were shut down, and he went as far as expropriating famous nightclubs, like the San Souci and even the iconic Tropicana. Fidel saw allowing tourists to come into the country and freely roaming Havana as a roadblock to his plan to turn Cuba into his own personal vision. He said they would adversely influence the Cuban people, so he abolished all things that catered to that industry.

He did not stop with the tourist businesses. He went even further and announced the abolition of the upcoming carnival. All the colorful floats, beauty queens, and comparsas had been a Cuban tradition for many years and was another reason why so many tourists visited Havana.

As if that was not enough, even the winter baseball league was terminated. All professional baseball teams, like the Almendares Scorpions and the Havana Lions, the team Fidel himself had rooted for since he was a child, were disbanded. Fidel announced that because those teams played only in Havana, they were not a fair representation of the whole country. He declared that they were run not by Cubans but by foreigners. The association with American teams like the New York Yankees that had existed for almost thirty years was discontinued. Professional baseball players from foreign countries, mainly the United States, were barred from playing or conducting their spring training in Cuba, which was another popular tourist attraction. American tourists, who for many years had come to watch teams like the Yankees play exhibition games in Havana against the Cuban professional teams.

Fidel promised his baseball crazy countrymen that, in a year or two, a new national amateur league would be formed. He said teams from all over the island would compete for a national championship that would have a more fair and balanced competitive approach in the *beisbol* addicted country.

These actions erased any possible doubts anyone might have had. Cubans now knew for sure that nothing was untouchable. Things would never be the same in their country if even baseball became a target of the new regime. Their much adored professional baseball teams ceased to exist.

The following spring, Roberto was giving a lecture to one of his classes at the University of Havana. "Countries with a free market economy rely on a hard currency for its international trade value, either in gold or a secured currency, the US dollar being the one that is most commonly used."

Just then, several militiamen entered the classroom, led by two stern, unsympathetic lieutenants. "Roberto Machado?"

"Yes."

"I am Lieutenant Gallego, and this is Lieutenant Bosa. We are here to relieve you of your teaching post." Several students stood up and asked why. The lieutenant continued, looking only at Roberto, and told him with a sneer, "You are not a real professor. The revolution will no longer allow Batista's appointees to teach."

"I'm not a Batista appointee. I got this teaching job because of my work experience. I have run my own import/export business for years. Nobody did me any favors."

"And where is your business now?" asked Lieutenant Bosa.

"It was nationalized like everything else in this country, without compensation, I might add."

Lieutenant Gallego answered, "You don't have a business for the same reasons you don't have this position anymore. The revolution doesn't need antiquated bourgeois ideas. You have until Monday to clean out your office."

The students were astonished and visibly upset. Many of them voiced their opinions loudly and all at once.

Lieutenant Gallego addressed them, "Listen, everyone. I want you to listen to me. This class is no longer needed. It was based on the idea that the United States was the master of our economy. We are free from them now. You don't have to fill your heads with these exploitative principles anymore. You will never again be brainwashed by these outdated capitalist ideas. You are now free to think. So run along and forget about this class. Tomorrow, all of you go to the registration office and see what courses have been assigned to you. You are all dismissed."

The students began leaving, still grumbling and wondering about what was to become of their other courses and the university as a whole. Roberto could not let this goon have the last word, and he spoke up as his students walked out.

"Remember what Jose Marti said," he turned and looked at the militiamen, "whom Fidel loves to quote: 'Changing masters is not being free.'"

After his verbal act of bravado, Roberto was visibly shaken. He once again found himself being told to gather his belongings after losing his livelihood. He had no business and no teaching job. For the first time in a very long time, this man, who had always worked at several jobs, who had always made sure that his family had what he never had as a poor boy growing up, was out of work with no means to provide for his family. So many things seemed to be crashing down around him. He was afraid to think of what might happen next.

With tears rolling down his cheeks, he slowly walked across the university campus near the athletic field, carrying the books and papers that he knew he no longer had any use for.

That evening, Diego and Joaquin sat in the same restaurant where they had met before. This time they each ordered a double whiskey, straight up.

As soon as the waiter had gone, Diego spoke. "Roberto is taking his firing at the university very hard."

"I know. I heard from Carmen," said Joaquin.

Diego looked around and, in a quiet but tense tone, asked him, "Joaquin, what the hell is going on with this revolution? It looks like they are nationalizing everything. Has Fidel gone mad? He closes all the nightclubs, the casinos. He cancels the carnival and abolishes baseball. No baseball in Cuba? Is he for real? And now they are changing the currency on Monday?"

"That's Che's idea," said Joaquin, rolling his eyes. "Ever since Fidel appointed him as head of The National Bank, he has been looking for a way to make everybody financially equal. He came up with this harebrained idea, and Fidel has signed on to it. They are telling everyone the quickest way to accomplish equality is to give them each 200 pesos regardless of how much of the old money they turn in. That way, everyone will be financially equal and start out in a level playing field."

"So everyone will be equally poor."

"Exactly, except for the government, which will have and control everybody's money."

"Joaquin, this isn't what you fought for."

"You bet your ass it isn't," replied Joaquin, not able to hide his displeasure or his anger. He knew his brother never cared about politics, but he was happy to be able to tell someone. "Diego, after Camilo died, this revolution took a decisively hard turn to the left. I know that if Camilo were alive, none of this would be happening." He paused in silence for a moment. "Diego, that was no accident."

"What? What do you mean?"

"Listen." Joaquin leaned close and lowered his voice to a whisper. "I have found out, from good sources, that an aircraft followed the same flight path as Camilo's plane just a few minutes after Camilo's was supposed to have taken off. That pilot had to have seen what happened to Camilo's plane. Well now, the pilot of that plane has disappeared, and the traffic controller on duty that day was hit by a car and died the next day. The only witnesses to what might have happened to Camilo are either dead or have magically disappeared. And how could they not find any trace of Camilo's plane? Nothing, not a single piece of debris?"

He nervously looked around and moved closer to Diego. "I heard from good sources that the plane, after it landed from Oriente, never took off again. It was cut to pieces and buried near the Camaguey airport. Camilo and the pilot were shot and put in a metal drum filled with concrete and dumped in the ocean."

He tried to hold back his tears and quietly stared at nothing for a few moments. Finally, he said, "Diego, I did not want to believe it at first. But if they can do that to Camilo, to one of us who fought with them side by side, who gave everything to this revolution, you know what that means. It means they are willing to do this to anybody, and they are animals, worse than Batista."

He shook his head and sighed loudly. "They have deceived me, and they have deceived most of the men who fought with them in the mountains. They blatantly lied to us, Diego. They knew most of us would have never supported this revolution, let alone fought for it, if we knew what they were going to turn Cuba into." He got up disgusted, not knowing what to say or do.

He tightly held the back of his chair and leaned toward Diego. Rage poured from his eyes as he said, "They used us. They used our brain power, man power, and financial support. Then they turned around and coldheartedly got rid of the very people who helped put them in power. And they used any means to do it, including murder. Now they demand that we go along blindly with all their plans.

"Huber is not the only comandante that is in prison. They are jailing anyone in the army that hints at being a threat to them. Many within the armed forces who don't want to go along are accused of being traitors, given a one day trial and sent to prison for twenty years. Either that or they're dragged to *El Paredon* to be executed by the firing squads. First, these sons of bitches took over this country by lying and deceiving everyone. Now they are controlling the entire nation with fear."

"I can't believe this." said Diego.

"Well, believe it," Joaquin said to Diego as he sat back down. "Just look at what has happened so far. Huber Matos is in jail. Menoyo is in jail. Anyone that speaks up is being silenced, and now we are getting in bed with the Russians. You should see the weapons they are sending us. They've just announced the foreign minister of Russia, Mikoyan, is coming here. Why do you think that is? What happened to Camilo was way too convenient. By having him disappear in a plane accident, they got the most popular man and potential adversary out of the way without a fight." Joaquin again stared at nothing and shook his head in disbelief. He pounded on the table in total disgust, spitting out his words. "And then these bastards turn around and have the balls to use Camilo as a symbol of their own perversion, using Camilo's murder for their own benefit, parading his image and likeness as a symbol of their bastardized revolution, promoting the idea that Camilo was in total agreement with what they are turning Cuba into, which is disgusting and total bullshit. Camilo would have never gone along with any of this, it makes me sick."

"My god, Joaquin!" said Diego. "What about Elena? She doesn't answer my calls anymore. I can't even get past a secretary."

"Diego, I did not want to tell you this, but I think you should know. I have found out she is now in the G2. That's the intelligence agency that investigates Counter-Revolutionaries or potential Counter-Revolutionaries." He paused and shook his head. "It's sad to say it, but her job now is to arrest people who speak out for democracy."

Diego could not comprehend what he was hearing. What had happened to Elena and all her pure ideals? He told Joaquin, "I can't believe that Elena has been talked into this. She is so much smarter than that."

Joaquin felt horrible for Diego. He knew what Elena meant to him. He moved his chair close to Diego's, put a hand on his shoulder, and told him, "Castro's cronies prey on people like her, Diego. Remember I told you we were getting in bed with the Russians? Well, weapons are not the only things they are sending us. They are also supplying us with what they call political officers. They are here to teach how to brainwash people, especially the young and idealistic. Elena is both, which makes her the perfect candidate. She can easily be led. You will not be able to get through to her. Most of those who fought in the mountains are being replaced by wide-eyed, young, misguided idealists just like Elena. They are very easy to corrupt with the power of righteousness. They can easily be taught how to rationalize any behavior in the name of doing it for the greater good."

"I can't believe they have been able to get to her. She's way too smart for that."

"Diego, it doesn't have anything to do with how intelligent she is. Sure, she is smart, but intelligence is no substitute for experience. She doesn't know the ways of the world. She thinks she is saving it. She is so convinced she knows what's good for everyone that she is willing to enslave them all to save them from themselves."

They stopped talking for a moment when the waiter returned with their drinks. He set the glasses down on the table and left.

"How can you remain with this revolution, Joaquin?"

Joaquin downed his whiskey in one gulp and set his glass down. "Diego, the best thing I can do now is to stay in and play along with their bullshit. The minute I leave, I become a target, and I'm not going to run away and leave Cuba." He looked at his empty glass and sighed. "You won't believe this, but now we all have to go around calling each other *comrades*. It has gotten to the point that if you don't, they look at you with distrust." Joaquin reached over, took Diego's drink, and downed that one too.

"For now," he said to Diego, "I will go along with these son of bitches' program and try to get as much valuable information as possible. A lot of people are fed up. I might be able to help. Besides, what are my alternatives? End up in jail like Huber or dead like Camilo?"

Diego could not stop thinking about Elena and what these people were turning her into. Diego thought about it for a moment and said to Joaquin, "I want to help."

Joaquin was taken aback. He could tell by the look in his eyes that Diego meant it, but he was surprised. Diego had never had any interest in getting involved in anything to do with politics. Joaquin had only been talking to his brother about all this because he just wanted to vent.

He was getting a little drunk and could not help but laugh. "You? Since when do you want to help?"

Diego was annoyed that Joaquin seemed to find this funny. Angry and terrified, he said to him, "I want to help because I want to get my daughter away from those people. I never got involved or ever cared about politics like you and Dad, exactly because of things like this. This is the very reason I stayed away from all the bullshit. And now, surprise! Here we go again, trading dictators. But this time, you all really fucked up. Because if half of what you are telling me is true, this is beyond anything I ever thought could happen. It sounds like your ex-buddies, the Castros, not only want our possessions. They want our souls. I never cared about getting involved before. But not only can I not stand by and let them take my daughter's soul. This time, I cannot stand by and watch them do this to Cuba. These people have to be stopped."

Joaquin, under the effect of the whiskey, was at a loss for words. But he figured that, by tomorrow, Diego would go back to not giving a shit.

All he could manage to tell him was "Don't say a word to anyone in the family, Diego. I don't think they will be able to handle this. And the less they know, the safer it is for them."

On Monday afternoon, Carmen and Alejandra were watching TV as Fidel welcomed the Russian foreign minister, Mikoyan. Diego walked in from exchanging his old money for the new two hundred pesos, ranting about the injustice of it all, and Carmen just started to cry.

"Roberto was so distraught when he left this morning," she said. "He is taking the changing of the money very hard, harder than losing his business and his teaching job at the university. I'm telling you, Diego, I have a bad feeling about this."

"Where was he going after the bank?" asked Diego.

"He had to go to the university and finish cleaning out his office. I can't call him there. They have already taken out the phone. It's just been one thing after another. Why is this happening to us?"

Alejandra tried to console Carmen. "Don't worry. Everything will be okay. He'll be home soon."

Diego also had a bad feeling about Roberto's state of mind, so he decided to go and check on him. "Alejandra, you stay here with Carmen. I'm going to the university to look for him."

Cesar needed to talk to Roberto about something very important. He went straight from work to Roberto's office at the university and didn't even bother to go to the bank and make the money exchange. He was pretty upset about having to turn over all the cash he had saved for art school, but he needed to talk to Roberto about something more important. What was on his mind could not wait. Cesar's father had died when he was young, and he had always seen Roberto as his father figure. He loved his brothers and sister, but he had developed a special bond with Roberto.

When he got to the office, he looked around and did not see Roberto, but the window was open. He moved closer and realized Roberto was standing outside on the ledge. Cesar could not see it, but Roberto was clutching the two hundred pesos he had just been given in exchange for his life savings. Cesar did not know what Roberto was doing, but he knew instantly that something was very wrong with this scenario.

Very calmly, Cesar said, "Roberto, what the hell are you doing out there?"

There was no response from Roberto. He didn't even look at Cesar. He just stared off into space. Cesar climbed out on to the ledge and sat next to him. He made sure not to startle or spook Roberto. He reached in his mailbag and took out a sandwich. Cesar started to eat, treating the situation like nothing was wrong, and tried to engage Roberto in conversation.

"You want half my sandwich? It's a medianoche."

Roberto again did not respond, and Cesar kept trying his best to act like nothing unusual was going on. "Boy, this is really a great view. No wonder you like to come out here." He pointed to the athletic field that could be seen from Roberto's university office, to a man in track-and-field attire who was pole-vaulting all by himself. "Look at that guy, Roberto. How long do you think he has been jumping over that bar with that stick? He was there when I got here, and he just keeps going." He still got no response from Roberto. "Actually, he's pretty good. I wonder what competition he's practicing for." Roberto again said nothing, and Cesar kept talking. "Hey, are those big houses across the fields the embassies?"

Roberto finally spoke but continued staring at the money in his hands and looking at the ground several stories below.

"Two hundred pesos," he said between constant sobs that kept building. "My whole life savings are gone. I worked my ass off to save enough money so we could have something to fall back on. Now these people tell me all I deserve is two hundred pesos. Deserve?" he said, raising his voice. "My father was a *carbonero*. We delivered coal door to door. We had nothing. I could not have been any poorer growing up. I never took anything from anyone. Everything I got, I got through studying and busting my ass, but now everything I've worked so hard for is gone. I don't have a business, I don't have a job, and now these bastards have taken all my savings and tell me all I deserve is two hundred pesos." He looked up at the sky and cried out, "Why are they doing this to me?"

"I know. You got a raw deal, Roberto. But what can you do but regroup? You still have Carmen and Tico."

At that moment, Diego walked into the office. He heard voices coming from outside and walked to the window. "Oh my god!"

Cesar turned, looked back through the window, and put his finger up to his lips.

"I'm no good to anybody anymore," said Roberto.

"That's not true," said Cesar. "We all need you, especially me. You've been like a father to me. The reason I came over here today is that I need you now more than ever. I need your advice. I'm thinking about getting married, and frankly, I'm scared. I know the only way I'm going to make it happen is if you are there, next to me, as my best man."

"Cesar, I…"

"Get him in here!" said Diego.

Cesar quickly looked at Diego and told him, "Shut up." He looked back to Roberto. "Can we go inside and talk about it? I don't know about you, but I'm getting hungry. That sandwich sucked. I hardly had any of it, and I need to eat something. Come with me. We'll go downstairs, get a bite, and you can talk me out of getting married. Come on. Look, Roberto, even the guy with the long stick has gone."

Roberto stared at the ground below and was now loudly sobbing. "I don't know. I don't know anything anymore."

Cesar, still as calm as he could be, stood up. He was beginning to feel scared about what Roberto might do. With a little more of a sense of urgency, he told Roberto, "I want you to come inside with me, please."

Diego reached through the window and tugged at Cesar's pants. Cesar kicked him.

He paused for a moment, looked into Roberto's eyes, and told him, "I love you, Roberto. I need you. Carmen needs you. My asshole brother needs you. This whole family needs you, especially Tico. Roberto, forget about everything else, just think about how much your son needs you. Please come inside."

Cesar stepped back halfway into the room and held out his hand. He looked into his brother-in-law's eyes one more time and pleaded with him. "Roberto. *Please.*"

Roberto took one last look at the measly, freshly minted two hundred pesos. He slowly let go of the money and watched it gently swirl in the air as it floated away. He took Cesar's hand and stepped back inside his office.

Chapter 18

IN THE COMPUTER room at the phone company, Diego and Bill tried to teach the computer system to the official who had been assigned to them. The man was Antonio Diaz, a very paranoid and seemingly dimwitted young man whom the revolution had put in charge of Bill and Diego. Even though Antonio was in charge, he had no idea what he was doing. His purpose for being there was to learn the computer system from them.

The powers that be had reluctantly come to the conclusion that, for the time being, they had to continue to rely on the expertise of Diego and the Yankee Bill Lima if they wanted to have a working phone system. They hoped their man would learn fast and at least be able to keep the phone system running until they could get help from their new Russian friends.

Antonio was dressed in fatigues and was inspecting everything he could get his hands on. He did not really know what he was inspecting, but he threw his weight around to make sure Diego and Bill knew who was in charge.

Bill looked at Diego and quietly said, "Are you okay?"

"I don't know what I am anymore," answered Diego.

Antonio heard them whispering, and it made him nervous. He felt the need to know everything they had to say. He rapidly walked over and asked them, "What are you guys talking about? Is that something I am supposed to know?"

"It's nothing you are familiar with, Antonio," said Bill.

"What is it?" demanded Antonio.

"I was telling Diego to go pick up a box of the X24 reels. You don't know what those are."

"Yes, I do," answered Antonio, getting defensive.

"Boy, you sure learn fast," said Bill sarcastically. "They're in the annex building on the third-floor supply room."

Diego jumped in. "Bill, he really has no idea what they are. I'll get them. It's going to take him an hour and a half to find them, and he will still probably bring us the wrong ones."

Antonio was determined to assert his authority. He approached Diego and, in a quiet but angry voice, told him, "You are no longer in charge here. I am! I'll go get the reels myself." And he stormed out.

Diego sighed and said to Bill, "That guy is so arrogant and stupid it's frightening."

"Thank God he is an arrogant idiot. We don't need any smart ones around here." Bill put down the empty reel he held in his hand and stared at Diego. "Now, tell me, what's the matter? You seem upset and worried all the time. There's something bothering you."

Diego sat and put his head down. "It's this whole damned revolution, that's what's the matter! I'm one of the few people I know who still have a job. Roberto lost his business, his teaching job, and they took all his money that he's saved for years. He took it so hard. He had a nervous breakdown. That man has never been sick one day in his life, and now he's in a mental hospital. And he's not the only one. The hospital is full of people just like him. They're treating everyone like criminals. They have assumed that anybody who has anything at all got it by cheating someone else. There are a lot of honest, innocent, hard-working people getting hurt by all that's going on with these sons of bitches. Somebody needs to do something about these hoodlums in green fatigues."

"Are you really serious?" asked Bill. "You realize you're talking about your own daughter. Diego, her job is to track down people who think like you do."

Diego was puzzled and taken aback by what Bill had just said. "I never told you that, Bill."

"You don't know the half of it, Diego. You haven't seen her or talked to her in months. You have no idea how deeply she's gotten into this."

Diego got upset. Bill's tone made him worried and angry. He could not understand where Bill was coming from.

Diego looked at Bill with wild eyes and demanded, "How do you know so much? I think you'd better tell me how much you know about my daughter and how you know it."

"Diego, she is a member of the G2."

"What? How do you know that?" asked Diego. The anger built up inside him came out through his voice.

"Listen, Diego, if she knew we were having this conversation, she would throw us both in jail right now."

All the frustration and anger over his daughter's situation came pouring out of Diego. He grabbed Bill by the collar and slammed him against one of the computer tape drives. He made a fist and drew it back, ready to strike. Bill did not try to shield himself from Diego's blow.

Before he could hit him, Bill calmly looked straight at Diego and said, "You're fighting the wrong guy, Diego. I'm not the enemy. Right now, I'm the only friend you've got. You know you can trust me."

Diego continued to pin Bill against the computer drive but put his fist down. He was shaking. He felt like he was at the end of his rope with all that was happening with

Elena. And now this. How could Bill know all about Elena and what she did?

"Tell me where you are getting all this information about Elena! Right now, Bill! I trust no one."

Bill swallowed hard. "Diego, I work for the CIA."

Diego let go of Bill and stepped back. He was shocked. "You what?"

He could not believe what he was hearing. Diego had known Bill for over two years. How could this be? His head was spinning. He could not process all that was being revealed to him.

Bill straightened up and dusted himself off. "If anybody else finds out about me, I'm dead, Diego. That shows how much I trust you."

Diego did not know what to think. He just looked at Bill and mumbled, "You in the CIA? Why are you here at the phone company?"

"The CIA has always been very interested in what goes on in Cuba. I'm here because the phone company handles most of the communication in this city. The agency needs to know what is being communicated."

"But why are you checking on Elena so much?"

"Because I know what she means to you, and I want to make sure she is okay. And, Diego, she is not okay. She is in way over her head."

Diego knew Bill was right. He knew Elena was on a path of no return, and he was desperate. He looked at Bill with tears in his eyes and pleaded with him, "Please, Bill, I must save my daughter from these people. Just tell me what I need to do."

Bill knew Diego was at a point where he would do anything to help his daughter, and he wanted to warn him. "I don't want to mislead you, Diego. What we are talking about could be very dangerous."

"I don't care. I want to do something." He grabbed Bill again, this time not to hit him but to beg him. "I want to get my daughter back, Bill. Please help me." He paused for a second and let go of his friend. He stepped back and walked in a circle, debating whether to tell him about Joaquin. After a few moments of silence, he turned to Bill. "I think I know someone who might be able to help us."

Bill instantly knew whom Diego was referring to. His association with Diego had finally paid off. The agency was always looking for new assets, and Bill hoped to turn an insider like Joaquin into one.

"Well, my house phone is bugged," said Bill. "Yours probably is too."

"What about here at the office?" asked Diego.

"No bugs here yet. I just checked. But that won't last for long. We will need to meet somewhere else if we are going to talk about anything we don't want them to hear." He smiled. "I tell you what. I will meet you tomorrow night at Villalobos Park at ten o'clock."

Diego had a puzzled looked on his face. "But that's a homosexual hangout."

"I know. That is why it's a perfect place to meet."

Before Bill could say anything else, Antonio returned with the X24 reels in hand and gave them to Bill.

Bill shook his head at Antonio, turned to Diego, winked, and chuckled. "You were right, Diego, he brought us the wrong ones." Bill turned to Antonio, pointing to the reel. "We told you the X27."

Antonio stood in silence, not knowing what to say. He swore he had heard them say the X24.

Elena and Gustavo were having a meeting with Raul and Ramiro in Raul's office. They had originally met in the mountains when Gustavo trained her at the shooting range. There had been a mutual attraction between them from the beginning, and their romantic interest flourished when they were both assigned to the militia and later to the G2.

By this time, they had developed a relationship and were officially a couple. Both of them were young, eager, highly dedicated, and motivated, and they moved rapidly into a position of trust within the revolution. They had been summoned to what they were told was a very important meeting with Raul.

He welcomed them in and asked them to sit down. He thanked them for their loyalty and dedication and said he wanted to bring them up to date.

Raul stated, "Our worst fears have come true. Huber Matos was not the only one. We still have traitors among our people."

Ramiro spoke up, "Those bastards need to be weeded out if this revolution is going to survive."

Raul continued, "So what we have done is form a special group within the G2 to concentrate on them."

"These traitors are a very real threat to the revolution," interjected Ramiro again, "an even bigger threat than the Yankees. They are among us and in a position to destroy what we are working so hard to achieve."

Raul looked at Gustavo then at Elena. "We want you two to be part of that team. We have decided to promote both of you to captain. We want you to help us find out who these traitors are and who they are working with."

Elena looked at Gustavo, and he smiled at her. They were honored to be trusted with such an important task and proud to be promoted.

Gustavo sat up straight. "Thank you for your confidence in us, Comandate. When do we start to look for these traitors?"

"Right away," said Raul. "And no one is above suspicion except us and, of course, Fidel."

Ramiro folded his arms and looked right into Elena's eyes. "You two are going to be working together very closely. We know you are involved with each other. We don't think that is a problem." He looked at Raul, who nodded yes. "But if you do, we want to know now."

Elena returned Ramiro's gaze as she said, "Absolutely not."

Gustavo said, "No problem, Comandate. We make a great team."

Raul stood up from his desk and shook their hands. Ramiro did as well and told them they would report directly to him.

As they were walking out of the office, Ramiro reminded them again, "No one is above suspicion. Remember that."

It was ten o'clock the following evening. Bill, Diego, and Joaquin were in Villalobos Park, sitting together on a bench, talking about Bill and the CIA. The park was beautiful with greenery and wild flowers all around. It also had several great marble statues of past heroes and was at one time a park where parents would bring their kids to play during the day. But in the last few years of Batista's reign, it had become a place where homosexual men hung out and met at night. That evening, as usual, men could be seen approaching each other and talking.

Joaquin did not know Bill very well. He had only met him briefly at his sister Carmen's house during the big chicken-and-rice party. All Joaquin knew of Bill was that he was an American and he worked for IT&T with Diego. He was suspicious and skeptical about Bill being in the CIA.

"How long have you worked for the agency?" asked Joaquin.

"I was recruited right out of college. I have a degree in the new field of computer engineering, and the agency needed my expertise."

"I don't know." Joaquin scratched his head. "I just find it difficult to believe you are from the CIA. How do I know you are for real? The only reason I agreed to meet is because of Diego here. I've got a lot to lose. I need proof."

"That's fair. I would expect you to be skeptical." He looked at Joaquin and smiled. "But I don't have an ID or a badge with me. It would be suicidal for me to carry one." Bill stood up, looked around, and told Joaquin, "On October 28, Raul Castro ordered all military planes grounded while letting you and Camilo think they were busy on military maneuvers. Conveniently, this left Camilo with only a Cesna 310 coming from Orinte, piloted by a young officer that no one would miss."

"Hmm," said Joaquin as he listened, eyes wide.

"On January 2 and 3 of 1959, hundreds of Batista's men were forced to dig their own graves at San Juan Hill before they were shot to death. And here is a list of all the advanced weapons the Soviets have sent to Cuba in the last month, including dates and delivery locations. Do you need more proof?" Bill asked as he handed Joaquin the list.

Joaquin looked it over for a few moments and handed it back to Bill. He stood up from the bench and walked around in silence for a few seconds. Bill lit a match and burned the list.

With a look of sadness on his face, he said to Diego, "My god, I heard those rumors, but I never wanted to believe the mass killings were true."

"That's why we are here, Joaquin," Bill interjected, "to prevent it from happening again."

Joaquin paused for a moment, mulling over all that had been revealed to him and the documents Bill had shown him.

He sat back down on the bench and asked Bill, "Okay, what can I do?"

Bill handed him a small piece of paper. "For now, here is a number where you can pass information to us, especially anything to do with weapons delivery and Russian involvement with the Cuban military. But we need to find a way for you to get us documents like maps, blueprints, military papers, and so forth. And we can't continue to meet like this. It's too risky. I'm sure that because I'm an American working at one of their most vital enterprises, I'm being watched all the time. It took me a couple of hours running in circles around the city to make sure nobody followed me here. So we have to come up with another way to do this without arousing suspicion."

Diego finally spoke, "I want to know what you think about something, Joaquin. I don't even know if he'll do it, but Bill thinks Cesar, as a mailman, has the perfect cover to pass documents between us."

Joaquin could not help but laugh. "Are you serious? Cesar? You must be joking. Cesar has never been able to handle any kind of responsibility. Now you want to trust him with this? I don't like that idea at all. There has to be another way."

Bill jumped in and reassured Joaquin, "Cesar is our safest way to transfer documents. As a mailman, he will not attract attention. Plus no one will suspect Cesar."

"I think he is finally growing up. Joaquin," said Diego, "you know he is settling down and getting married. You should have seen the way he handled Roberto when he was out on that ledge. If it wasn't for Cesar, I swear Roberto would have jumped. How about if I just ask him? If he says no, that will be the end of it."

Joaquin kept shaking his head no, but knowing Cesar, he figured there was no chance he would agree to do it. He looked at Bill and Diego. "I just don't think it's a very good idea. But go ahead and ask him. He'll say no anyway."

"Good," said Bill. "Joaquin, you better leave now. You've been here too long already. As soon as you're out of the park, we'll go."

"All right we'll be in touch," said Joaquin as he got up from the bench and shook Bill's hand.

"Be careful," said Diego while he hugged his brother.

"You too". Joaquin turned around headed west and left the park.

Before Diego and Bill had a chance to leave, there was a commotion behind them. They both turned and saw a couple of policemen harassing some of the other men and making all of them leave the park.

Diego was very nervous as he saw the policemen coming their way. "Oh god, what are we going to do now?"

"Just act like we belong. Don't worry. All they'll do is chase us out of the park."

While the police yelled and blew their whistles, Bill grabbed Diego's hand and led him as they calmly walked east, hand in hand, out of the park.

The next day, Diego and Cesar sat together on the Malecon seawall along the edge of Havana Bay. Cesar was eating a sandwich and watching a group of kids who were fishing. They had been talking for a while, and Cesar felt like Diego was becoming more and more despondent.

"What's the matter?" Cesar finally asked.

"Everything, Cesar. Look around you. Look what they're turning Cuba into."

"I know. It's pretty bad. It seems like everybody is getting affected this time." He tried to lighten the mood a bit. In between bites, Cesar said, "Shit, I don't even have baseball to harass you with anymore. But at least we still have our family."

Diego was lost in thought. Quietly he said, "Not me. I don't have my daughter any longer."

"Oh, come on. You two might argue, but you know she loves you."

"Cesar, she doesn't visit me. She doesn't call. She doesn't even return my calls. I'm just as dead to her as Mercedes. She's has been brainwashed by these people."

Cesar put down his sandwich. He had not seen Diego this distraught since Mercedes died, and he did not know what to do. "Is there anything I can do to help?"

Diego paused and took a deep breath. "Actually, there is, but what I am about to tell you, you cannot repeat. Not to anyone."

Cesar, again trying to lighten the mood with his usual joking ways, put his hands up close to his face and waved his fingers in the air. "Oooh, what is it? The suspense is killing me." He smiled. "Oh, come on, relax! What can I do, really?"

"I'm very serious, Cesar. This could mean my life, and Joaquin's too."

Cesar's smile ran away from his face. He stared at his brother with a stone-dead serious look. "What the hell are you talking about, Diego?"

"Joaquin and I are working with the CIA."

"What?" Cesar could not believe what he just heard. For a moment, he thought Diego was trying to pull his leg. "Come on, you are not good at being funny. That's my department. So what are you talking about? Joaquin working for the CIA? Are you crazy?"

"He is, Cesar. We both are. Joaquin has come to the conclusion that the Castros murdered Camilo. He is convinced they killed him because they wanted him out of the way. Joaquin is on the inside, and he can see how they are handing Cuba over to the Russians. Soon our country will be turned into another communist state, and that is not what he fought for. We have been contacted by the CIA. The last thing the US wants is a communist state at their doorstep. We both have agreed to work with the Americans to get rid of these bastards, and we need your help."

Cesar looked at Diego and could see in his face that his brother was not joking. The conversation was now making Cesar very nervous. He wanted to forget what Diego just told him. He would much rather ignore it all and hope somehow things would work themselves out.

He nervously looked around and started to get angry. "I don't want to hear any more. I've got my own problems, Diego. Juana is pregnant."

Diego was a bit surprised. "So is that why you're marrying her?"

"No. No. That's not it, and don't give me that look like Mom does. I was going to marry her anyway. This is just a change in timing, that's all."

At any other time, Diego would have tried to talk his brother out of being railroaded into a marriage he thought was a big mistake, but there were more important things to deal with, so he just looked at Cesar and told him, "You can do what you want. Do what makes you happy. But we still need your help."

"I can't. Diego, I just can't."

"You mean you won't. I haven't even told you what I need."

"I don't care, Diego. I don't want to know what it is, and I don't want to get involved."

"Listen, Cesar, I'm not asking you to do anything dangerous. All we need is for you to pick up and deliver mail for us. Nothing more."

"Diego, please don't ask me to do this."

Diego knew that they needed Cesar's help, and all he could think about was getting rid of the people Elena had gotten involved with. He knew how much Cesar cared for Elena and how close they had always been, and he used that to pressure Cesar into helping them.

"If you don't want to do it for me or Joaquin, then do it for Elena. We have to get rid of these people before I lose my daughter forever. Please, Cesar. I have no one else to help me. Please."

Cesar stood up, furious at Diego for putting him in this position. He just wanted to run away and forget any of this had ever happened. But Elena meant too much to him, and he could not walk away. However, he knew in his gut that what he was about to agree to was a real bad idea. He wrapped up his sandwich and put it in his jacket pocket.

He said to himself, *This is a big mistake. I know it.*

He turned to Diego. "I'll deliver your damn mail. But don't ask me to do anything else." He turned back and angrily walked away without saying another word.

A few days later Diego, Alejandra, Cesar, Juana, Tico, and Rosa prepared to welcome Roberto home from the hospital. Roberto had been at the sanatorium for a month. He had fallen into a catatonic state of shock right after the incident on the ledge of his office. His depression was so deep they had to treat him with electroshock applications. It took twenty-two applications before he finally came out of it.

It had been touch and go for the first week, with nobody knowing if he would come out of the catatonic state or not. After two weeks, he finally responded to the treatments, and two weeks after that, he was released. Although still fragile, he was well enough to return to his family.

Carmen was nervous and excited to finally have her husband home again. She loved Roberto so much she could not imagine what she would do without him. That first week he was in the hospital had been horrible for her. She thought she might lose him forever and had to summon every bit of her strength not to have a nervous breakdown herself. Now she wanted everything to be perfect.

"Do you think we have enough picadillo?" Carmen asked. "It's Roberto's favorite." Her hand was shaking as she stirred the pot. "I want to make sure we have enough."

"You have made much more than we could possibly eat," said Juana.

"Does it taste all right? Do you think it needs anything?"

"Okay, okay, stop twisting my arm. I'll taste it." Cesar jokingly volunteered.

"Just taste it," said Rosa. "We want to make sure there is still some left for Roberto."

"Rosa, where did you get all this meat?" asked Alejandra. "They're rationing it now."

Cesar took a taste of the picadillo and said, "Joaquin got it. If you're in the military, you can get around the rations."

Tired of all the rationing, Juana spoke up, "That's what I've been telling you, Cesar. If you join the militia, we could be living like kings instead of standing in line for everything."

Diego leaned in close to Cesar and whispered, "Yeah, Cesar, why don't you sell your soul for a chicken?"

Cesar ignored him. He was still upset with Diego.

The doorbell rang, and Tico excitedly raced to answer it. "It's Daddy! I'll get it."

When he opened the door, there stood Elena in full military uniform, along with two other soldiers.

Tico looked back into the house. "Aunt Elena is here."

"Robertico, you've gotten so big," she said. "Soon you'll be old enough to join the young revolutionaries." She turned to the soldiers and said to the shorter one of the two, "You go back to the car and stay with the driver and guard the prisoners. And you," she pointed to the tall one, "wait out here. I won't be long."

Rosa came up to Elena and gave her a hug and a kiss. When Elena spoke, she was cold and distant. "It's nice to see you, too, Grandma."

Cesar was next to greet her. "I'm glad you could make it." He walked right up to her, grabbed her, and gave her a big hug. "Jesus, when was the last time I saw you? It's been months. What is keeping you so busy these days?"

Elena uncomfortably straightened herself up. "I'm rounding up counter-revolutionary scum. We had to make some arrests in the area, so I was able to spare some time."

Diego walked up slowly toward them and stared at Elena. "My daughter always made time for her family."

"I make time for my family. But now my family includes all the loyal brothers and sisters of the revolution."

"Who? All the hoodlums in green fatigues, bullying people for no reason, taking away everything decent people earned with hard work? Have you seen what your brothers and sisters of the revolution have done to your uncle Roberto? Tell me whom he took advantage of? Whom did he steal from?" Diego was so frustrated he could not hold back. "Thank God your mother is dead so she doesn't have to see you like this."

Rosa gave Diego a stern look. "Diego, please, stop it."

Elena ignored her father's comments and looked at Rosa. "I have more important matters to attend to. However," she looked at her father, "knowing Roberto's situation, I have gone out of my way to get him this." She handed an envelope to Rosa. "It's a government reeducation program. It's specially designed for people like Roberto whose capitalistic jobs are no longer needed by the revolution. At the end of the program, he will be placed in a job where the revolution will be able to utilize him."

"You mean brainwash him, don't you? Like they brainwashed you?" said Diego, raising his voice.

Cesar put his arm around his brother. "Calm down, Diego. It won't do any good to fight about this now."

Again, Elena ignored her father and looked only at Rosa. "Give my regards to Carmen and Roberto. I hope you all enjoy this day." She turned to Cesar and told him without a trace of sincerity, "Call my secretary and make an appointment. Maybe we can catch up. If you get tired of that postal job, the revolution can use you."

Cesar could not help himself. He did not mean to, but he let out a big laugh. "Oh, you know me. I'm not very good at following orders." He thanked her and told her he would think about it.

Elena turned and walked out of the house. She and the two soldiers got back in their car. In the backseat were two prisoners: Miriam Torres, Elena's roommate in the mountains, and Enrique from the hospital in New York. The weeding out of anyone suspected of having the slightest lack of loyalty was in full force.

After Elena left, Diego was mortified, his anger dissolving into a deep sadness. He was convinced he had lost his daughter forever. He went outside to the backyard of his sister's house, followed by Alejandra. She came over, put her arms around him, and tried to console him.

Diego rested his head on her shoulder and told her with tears in his eyes, "She hates me. I feel like I don't have a daughter anymore."

"She doesn't hate you. She's just young and confused and has too much power."

"Listen to how she talks, Alejandra. I've lost her. She's distant and cold like an iceberg. It's like talking to a stranger. You should have seen the way she looked at me. It was like I meant nothing to her."

Alejandra knew he was right, but she tried to lift his spirits and give him some hope. "When all these revolutionaries come crashing down to reality, she'll come back to you, Diego."

He knew she wanted to make him feel better but hoping and wishing would not bring Elena back, and Fidel and his goons were not going anywhere.

"This revolution will never come crashing down to reality. It's going to have to be brought down to reality." He knew he was not supposed to say anything to her, but it just came pouring out of him. He yelled, "And goddammit, I'm going to be one of the people to do it!"

Alejandra was confused and concerned by what Diego had just said. She had never heard him talk like that before. "What do you mean? What are you talking about?"

He was afraid he had already said too much, but he did not want to keep any secrets from her. He was torn as to what to say. Diego paused for a moment, trying to decide how much he should tell her. He paced the backyard in silence. He knew Alejandra meant too much to him to push her away, so he decided to go with his gut instinct.

"I've gotten involved with the CIA".

Alejandra's voice trembled slightly. She could not believe what he had just told her. All she could manage to say was, "What?"

"Bill Lima is my CIA contact. Joaquin is working on the inside, and even Cesar is helping out. Alejandra, this movement is growing every day. There are hundreds of us in Havana alone."

Alejandra's eyes began to tear up. She was overwhelmed with fear for his safety and felt like she had been hit across the face with a wet towel.

She hugged him and said, "Diego, I don't want to lose you."

"Don't worry. The CIA is behind us. The United States is going to make sure these sons of bitches don't turn Cuba into another Russia."

Alejandra was still holding on to him as tears trickled down her cheek. "I don't want you to do this, but I know what Elena means to you. I know I won't be able to change your mind." She looked right into his eyes. "I will never try to come between you and your daughter, but if you must do this . . ." She tried to compose herself. "Diego, it has taken me this long to find someone I love. Please don't shut me out."

"I won't. I promise. But I don't want you involved in any of this, and I beg you, not a word to anyone, including my family." They hugged and kissed. "I love you so much," he told her.

Alejandra hugged him as tightly as she could, repeatedly telling him to please be careful.

The car that brought Roberto home finally arrived. He was very fragile and somewhat disoriented. Joaquin had used his connections and had been the one to get Roberto admitted to the mental hospital. He had made all the arrangements, and now he was the one who had picked up Roberto from the hospital and brought him home. Carmen and Joaquin helped him out of the car and toward the house.

Tico, followed by the rest of the family, ran out to greet him.

"Papi, you're back," cried Tico. "I missed you!"

Roberto hugged his young son and began to cry.

Chapter 19

October 1960

THE SITUATION IN Cuba became more oppressive with each passing day. The government seemed to be confiscating everything from land to small businesses, and the free press had been totally silenced. All TV stations, radio stations, newspapers, and magazine were now run by the government. Their owners and management had been run out of the country under the threat of execution by firing squad. All of them were accused of being Batista apologists and charged with counter-revolutionary activities. Journalists who did not leave either became mouthpieces for the government or were sent to prison at the Isle of Pines just south of Cuba.

The Isle of Pines was Robert Louis Stevenson inspiration for the novel *Treasure Island*. The island had a maximum-security prison that was built back in the 1920s by another one of Cuba's dictators, Geraldo Machado. It was the largest prison in the whole country and was now filled beyond capacity.

Also, the firing squads had become more prevalent. They were held at La Cabana Prison, part of the historic Morro Castle in Havana. In charge of them was Che, who oversaw many of the executions himself. More than ever, people were desperate to leave the country.

Thousands of Cubans lined up for blocks outside the United States embassy to apply for visa waivers, which were being granted for the asking by the US embassy. The embassy was bending over backward to accommodate whole families that wanted to escape the situation in the country. Because it was so difficult for all family members to come to the embassy at the same time, they began to issue waivers for entire families and extended families without requiring that everyone show up. Plus the lines were so long already the last thing the US officials wanted was more people overrunning the embassy.

Every day a huge mob, organized by the government, lined up across the street from the embassy opposite those applying to leave the country.

All day long the mob would yell, "Worms, get out! Worms, get out!"

The expression *worm* was coined by Fidel, who had said, "It is good these people are leaving the country. They are nothing but worms that if they stay, will eat away at Cuba from the inside, the way a worm eats away at an apple."

From then on, anyone who wanted to leave the country was called a worm, and the word eventually became associated with anyone who was against the revolution. There was a tense and anxious feeling of panic spreading throughout country.

Bill Lima drove up through all the commotion to a Cuban military checkpoint. Soldiers guarded the entrance and checked everyone before allowing them to go inside.

"Are you an American citizen?" asked the guard.

"Yes, I am."

"Let me see your passport." After Bill handed it to him, the guard said with a sneer, "Are you leaving our beautiful country, Mr. Lima?"

"Oh, no, no. I just need to go inside so I can turn in my absentee ballot for the presidential election." Bill looked at the guard and smiled. "Of course, you wouldn't know anything about that sort of thing. By the way," he pointed to the mob chanting across from the embassy, "nice chorus. Do they know any other songs?"

The guard gave him a dirty look and motioned him through.

Bill made his way to the US Marines checkpoint. He flashed a US State Department ID that most CIA agents carried as a cover and was waved in. Once inside, Bill entered one of the offices and reported to his supervisor, who needed to be brought up to date.

"As you know, I have been cultivating my relationship with the Quintana family for over two years, and it's finally paying off. Joaquin is disillusioned with the revolution and is cooperating with us. He is a high-ranking member of Castro's inner circle, in charge of naval operations. He meets with Castro on a monthly basis and, as such, is in a perfect position to help us get to Fidel if we need to. Through Diego, I have set up a nucleus of Cuban nationals that can be utilized for whatever we require." Bill finished his report and was visibly upset. He had put a lot of time and effort into this operation but felt like he was being left out of the loop. He was determined to get some answers. "Now somebody needs to tell me what's going on. For months, the scuttlebutt has been that something big is being planned from the top, and it looks to me like the rumors are true. I've put a lot of hard work into this operation, and I deserve to know."

The person in charge of the operation and Bill's boss was none other than Beth Donahue, the jovial lady everyone knew as his girlfriend.

Beth looked at Bill from behind her desk. She knew he was right. She took off her glasses and slowly rubbed her eyes. She was hesitant to tell him the whole plan but felt he had earned the right to be brought up to speed and know the full extent of the operation.

She looked at him and said, "You are right. You should know." She took a deep breath and continued, "The Eisenhower administration has started training Cuban exiles in Central America in preparation for an invasion of Cuba. Both Kennedy and Nixon have agreed to continue the operation if they are elected. Right now, the invasion is tentatively set up to happen this spring." She leaned over her desk and emphatically said to Bill, "This information is to be divulged to no one. You have earned the right to know, but the plan for an invasion is for your knowledge only." She slowly leaned back in her chair. "Your new orders, when you get them, will be for some of your men to create diversions and small attacks in Havana. And some of your other men will concentrate on your new special orders." Beth paused for a moment. She knew that what she was about to tell him, Bill was not going to like. "They will take advantage of Joaquin's monthly State of the Navy Report to Fidel as the time for your men to eliminate him."

"What?" Bill thought he must be hearing things. He asked her, "I want to make sure I understand what you are saying. You want these guys, on their own, to assassinate Fidel Castro? Are you serious? These guys are not pros. They'll never be able to pull it off by themselves."

Beth countered, "It's your job to make sure they can pull it off. The invasion is the agency's number one priority, so the assassination plans might never be carried out. But we must proceed in case things change."

Bill wasn't happy. First they kept him in the dark for so long, then they sprung this on him?

Beth continued, "And remember, for now, you can't breathe a word about the invasion to any of your people. This is top secret."

Bill thought about telling her one more time how foolhardy it was having these amateurs try to assassinate Fidel. But he knew it would make no difference. The orders were coming from above, and Beth could not do anything to change them. He understood. These were his orders, and he must proceed accordingly. But he didn't have to like it. Instead he just sat there, looking at Beth and shaking his head.

After a couple of months of preparations, the big day for Cesar had arrived, the day of his wedding. He was getting himself ready with the help of Roberto, his best man. Roberto had come a long way since that horrible day at his office window ledge, and he had made a good recovery so far. Although the incident was a blur to him, he knew he owed Cesar his life.

The government had taken away Roberto's job, business, and life savings. He had to find some way to make a living. He did not want to go into the program Elena had arranged and endure all the propaganda and brainwashing that he was sure they would feed him. And he certainly did not want to go to work for the bastards that had ruined his life and were turning Cuba into another Soviet Gulag.

So, he started a small business making travel bags for the thousands of people who wanted to leave Cuba. The supply of suitcases had been exhausted, and people were desperate to find a way to carry their clothes and small possessions the government allowed them to take. When people left Cuba, they were forced to turn their house and everything they owned over to the government. It was the extortion price that had to be paid if they wanted to leave the island.

Since it was impossible to find materials anywhere to make the travel bag Roberto came up with a unique idea, he had the customers bring him their window curtains and shower curtains they would otherwise have to leave behind. People brought him the materials, and Roberto made the bags from the window curtains and lined them with the shower curtains. He had found an ingenious way to survive and feed his family. Now he was proudly helping Cesar on his wedding day.

People from both Cesar's and Juana's families were seated in the sanctuary. The middle class guests of Cesar's family and the lower-economic-class guests of Juana's made for a sharp contrast. But many on both sides of the aisle wore military uniforms. In the church rectory, Roberto tried to calm Cesar, who was battling the butterflies in his stomach.

"Stop being so nervous," said Roberto as he helped Cesar adjust his tie. "It'll be over before you know it."

"Stop telling me not to be nervous. Have you ever known anyone to stop being nervous because someone else tells him to? Every time you say that, it just makes me more nervous."

Alberto, Jose, and Armando, Cesar's friends, burst into the room. Jose was dressed in his militia uniform.

Armando said, "There he is, guys, just like I told you. He is really going through with it. He has the tux on and everything. That means I won the bet. Now, pay up."

"I think Cesar should be the one to pay," said Alberto as he and Jose put a few bills in Armando's hand. "He swore to us that he was never going to get married in a million years."

"This is all I need," mocked Cesar, "you guys coming here to make my life miserable. How the hell did you get in here anyway?"

Jose laughed. "It was easy. Now that I'm in the militia, I have friends in high places."

Alberto gave Jose a playful shove and said, "We came in when the priest wasn't looking. We just wanted to wish you good luck."

Cesar was happy to see them. They were always ribbing him, but he knew there was nothing they would not do for one another.

"Listen, the organist has started," said Armando. "You better hurry, or you will be late for your own wedding."

Cesar was always harassed for holding up everyone. But this time it was his wedding, and they had no choice but to wait until he was ready.

"You know what? Let them wait. This is my wedding, and they can't start without me."

In the church, Cesar's family was already seated in the first pew when Joaquin came in and joined them. A few moments later, Elena arrived with Gustavo. She half-heartedly waved to her family from across the chapel then sat with Juana's guests. Gustavo hugged Juana's mother, and the organist began playing the "Wedding March."

Diego was seated next to Alejandra and told her, "I can't believe she won't even sit with us." Then he turned to Joaquin. "Who is that guy she is with?"

"Gustavo Vela, one of Raul's snakes."

It was a typical Catholic wedding of its time. There was a full mass, the wedding couple took communion as well as some of the guests, and one of Juana's friends sang "Ave Maria." The wedding ceremony lasted over an hour, and when it was finished, the happy couple went outside, where they were showered with rice. They got into Cesar's convertible, said goodbye to all their friends and family, and left immediately for their honeymoon.

They had chosen Varadero Beach, the famous seaside resort, very popular with tourists as well as locals. It was considered one of the most beautiful beaches in the world. There was no reception because, even if one was in the militia, it was impossible to get supplies to feed that many people due to the fact that everything was rationed.

On January 1, Fidel gave a speech that was broadcast throughout the country to mark the anniversary of the revolution. Fidel, known for his long speeches, could rant about a topic for hours. He took this opportunity, on the anniversary of the revolution, to lambaste the decision of the United States to break formal ties with his government.

"I have been informed today that the United States plans to end formal relations with Cuba. Eisenhower has ordered all American citizens to leave the island within seventy-two hours. Well, the United States is going to have to learn that it is no longer our master. Cuba is a free and sovereign nation. We have the same rights as every other nation, and since the United States cannot accept that, let the Yankees go home."

The crowd immediately picked up on the saying and chanted, "Yankees, go home! Yankees, go home!"

After the decision to break off diplomatic relations with Cuba was made, the plan to assassinate Fidel was approved at the highest level of the CIA. At the same time, preparations for an invasion of the island were rapidly moving ahead with a group of Cuban nationals training in Central America. Bill had grown his assortment of anti-Castro men into a small but very efficient group. They had even carried out some minor sabotage missions just outside of Havana.

Bill sold the small group that now sat in before him on the idea that they should be proud to have been chosen to carry out the great task of eliminating Fidel. It was the best thing anyone could do to help bring down this deplorable revolution. The only promise Fidel had made good on was when he said everyone would be equal. Now everyone was equally poor.

It took very little arm-twisting on Bill's part to convince them to assassinate Castro. He found that all of them, especially Joaquin, who saw it as payback for the murder of Camilo, were more than happy to kill that son of a bitch Fidel. After all the misery he had brought to their island, what insulted them the most was Fidel's attitude. He expected them to appreciate it, to like what he had done to them under the perverted pretext that it was for their own good.

The only thing that worried Bill was Cesar because of his reputation as a slacker. But he only had to deliver the mail. And up to this point, Cesar had been nothing but reliable.

Bill knew that because his men were not pros, he had to hatch a plan that was uncomplicated, fast, and deadly if they were going to have any chance at pulling off the assassination. His plan was simple. Joaquin would leave a suitcase full of explosives near Fidel and set it off. He got the idea from the unsuccessful attempt on Hitler's life and he hoped that this time the plan would not fail. It was all going to depend on the logistics of his men getting and delivering the explosives and Joaquin having the balls to actually do it.

Some of the other anti-Castro men in Bill's group were training, unbeknownst to them, as a guerrilla support unit for the invasion. While the landing forces secured a beachhead, Bill's men would be part of the urban warfare that would create diversions in the capital to aid the invading forces.

The recall of all American personnel from Cuba, the fact that the Russians had taken over the phone company, and the termination of his job left Bill no choice but to leave the country. The powers of the revolution could not wait to get rid of Bill. They had only retained Diego at the phone company on a part-time basis, to run the American equipment until the Russians could convert it to their own system. By that time, Diego had become very much involved in all aspects of the rebel group and had been designated to lead it after Bill's departure.

Cesar still did not care anything about politics, but he was very worried about Elena. Remarkably, he not only delivered all the mail for them, but he was caught up, not in a sense of patriotism but in some sense of adventure. No one was more surprised about that than Cesar himself. As time went on, he got himself more and more involved in all operations. He still only delivered information that came to them through the mail. But he was the main go-between, passing documents that were crucial in planning the assassination. They received more information each day from the Americans, including orders to carry out small scale guerilla raids.

Bill's group had turned from an information gathering unit into an offensive force. Inside an abandoned warehouse near the seaport, the sound of fog horns could be heard in the distance. Diego, Bill, and Cesar were meeting with Cristobal and Hugo, the two other men who had been chosen for the agency's plan to terminate Fidel.

Bill addressed the group. "So the fact that I have to leave for the United States does not change anything. The plan to eliminate Fidel is still on."

"I heard from Joaquin," said Diego. "He is all set to give his naval report to Fidel so we know for sure that we are going in as planned. Are the rest of you all set?"

"Well, as you know, Felix left for Miami," said Cristobal. "We don't think he was compromised, but he felt he was being watched. We thought it would be better to play it safe and let him break away from the group. That means when the explosives and weapons are delivered, we'll be one man short." He looked at Cesar. "I was thinking maybe you could help us."

Even though Cesar's tone was that of the jokester, it was beginning to dawn on him how deeply he had involved himself in something that was so dangerous. "How did I go from just delivering mail to picking up explosives and plotting to assassinate Castro?"

Diego had been very surprised to see Cesar's transformation, and he wanted to encourage his brother, so he told him, "You should feel proud, Cesar. Do you know how many people want to kill that son of a bitch? When this is over, they're going to put your face on a stamp."

"More like a wanted poster," answered Cesar.

Diego ignored Cesar's comment. He walked over to Bill, and they engaged in their own conversation.

Cesar looked at Cristobal and half whispered, "I must be out of my mind. I've got enough problems already."

Juana had lost the baby, and Cesar did not find out until much later. To his surprise, the loss of the baby had hit him very hard. Juana had been bleeding when she made the trip to the hospital, all alone, and he felt guilty for not being around when it happened. People kept telling him the loss would bring Juana and him closer together. But the miscarriage had only pushed them apart.

Cristobal put his arm around Cesar's shoulder. "I heard, Cesar. I'm sorry Juana lost the baby."

"I wasn't even there when it happened. I'm just grateful Juana is all right. Thank you." He hugged Cristobal. Bill and Diego returned to the group.

"Okay, then we're all set," said Diego. "Let's wish Bill good luck, and starting next week, we will meet somewhere else."

The others left, but Bill and Diego stayed behind. These two men from such different backgrounds had created a bond between them with genuine respect and affection for each other. They hated to say goodbye and tried to make it short. They hugged, wished each other well, and each told the other to be careful. Bill dug through his pockets and found a small piece of paper. He looked at it and handed it to Diego.

"Here is a number you can call if the shit hits the fan."

A few weeks later, Fidel, Raul, Che, Ramiro, and Gustavo were in Fidel's office. The meeting was called to inform Fidel of a major development that had been uncovered by his intelligence people operating in the States.

Fidel puffed on a big cigar and said, "So, Ramiro, what is this good news you have for me?"

"Well, Comandante, as you know, we have spent a lot of time and resources on our intelligence apparatus in the United States, and it has paid off. We have discovered that the Americans are planning an invasion using Cuban exiles."

Fidel stopped smoking his cigar and put it out. He looked at all the men present and, with a slightly whimsical look, turned to Ramiro. "I thought you said it was good news."

Ramiro continued, "The good news is that we know where they will try to land, and we think we know when. Some of our men have infiltrated their ranks and are training in Central America right now. Their forces number about fifteen hundred."

Fidel said nothing, eyeing the men present.

Che wondered out loud to no one in particular, "What about US military involvement?"

"The word from our sources in Washington," Ramiro said, "is that, although Kennedy has been on board with the invasion since Eisenhower started planning it, he is afraid to risk American lives."

"I don't think he has the balls for it," snorted Raul.

Fidel looked back at Ramiro. "You said you know where."

"Our men in their camp are pretty sure that it's going to be on the southern coast. They are planning to land the worms on or near the Bay of Pigs."

"The Bay of Pigs. How poetic," said a smiling Fidel to the hearty laughter of the others.

Ramiro concluded, "Our men have told us they don't seem to have a definite date yet. But it looks like it will be sometime in April."

Fidel got quiet and thought for a moment, weighing his options. "All right," said Fidel, "let's keep a close eye on Guantanamo, but don't give the Yankees any reason to suspect we know what's going on. The outcome of this will depend on whether or not the Americans use their own troops. Fifteen hundred men are not enough to invade this island." He turned to Raul. "Step up the propaganda campaign in the United States against involvement in Cuba. I think you are right. This guy Kennedy looks a bit soft to me too. Any other good news?"

Gustavo hesitated, "I'm afraid so, Comandante."

"What is it? It can't be that bad," said Fidel.

Gustavo looked at Raul before he spoke. Raul nodded to him to keep going. "Well, Comandante, I'm afraid it gets worse. We have uncovered a counter-revolutionary ring that has members of our own."

Fidel stared at him.

Gustavo hesitated again before he told Fidel, "At this very moment, they are planning to assassinate you, Comandante."

Fidel's head snapped back with surprise at the news. "Who?"

Before Gustavo could answer, Raul spoke up, "Our old friend Joaquin Quintana."

Fidel was surprised but not stunned by this news. He knew Joaquin had not taken Camilo's death well. He thought Joaquin might suspect that he, and especially Raul, might have had something to do with Camilo's disappearance.

"How did you find out?"

Raul elaborated, "We had our man at the telephone company keep an eye on the Yankee Bill Lima. He was there under the pretext of being assigned to Lima to learn the computer system. Mr. Lima worked with Joaquin's brother Diego. They were very careful around our man at the beginning, but he did such a great job of playing stupid that the idiots eventually let down their guard. Our man, Antonio, is the best electronics bugger we have. He also had some help with a new device that our friends the Russians provided him. Lima turned out to be a CIA agent. He had been planted by the agency at the phone company even before we disposed of Batista and probably had been monitoring our phone communications from the beginning. Also, I'm sure the agency, knowing that Diego is Joaquin's brother, had cozied up to him so they could eventually get to Joaquin."

Raul gave them an "I told you so" look and said, "By the way, we all met Mr. Lima at the house of Joaquin's sister during that stupid chicken and rice dinner. Somehow, Mr. Lima got Diego involved, and in turn, Diego must have gotten to Joaquin."

When Raul finished, Gustavo added, "Also, Comandante, the militia was watching a suspect in a robbery at a food depot. He was trying to leave the country when they apprehended him. His name is Felix Solano. When they put the screws to him about the theft, he broke down and sang like a canary. He told them about some counter-revolutionary group he is involved with. The militia brought it to our attention as soon as they found out. I have interrogated him and he has been most cooperative. The dumb shits think Felix left for Miami, but he is in our custody. We know exactly what they plan to do."

Fidel thought for a moment. "Now that all the Americans are leaving, how will they communicate with them?"

Gustavo answered, "An old girlfriend of mine is married to their youngest brother, Cesar. She says he's been acting strangely. They are newlyweds, and they just lost a baby, but he is spending a lot of time out of the house. She thinks he might be cheating. I'm thinking since he works for the post office, he might be involved. I'm not sure if he is, but he is certainly in a perfect position to pass information without arousing suspicion."

"Check into it, Gustavo," said Raul. "And remember what I told you before. Not a word of this to Elena."

"Yes, sir."

Fidel sat back and lit another cigar. He told them what a great job they had done uncovering both plans. He knew that with the United States involved, it was crunch time, and the revolution itself lay in the balance. Either they repelled the invasion and foiled the attempt on his life, or everything would come crashing down. He dismissed them after making it clear they had to get to work on a way to stop both enemy plans, or the revolution would be doomed.

The Havana airport was exceedingly busy with all the Americans who had to leave the country. Cuban military trucks brought in hundreds of people to the airport whose sole purpose was to harass the departing Americans. The crowd brought in by the government stood behind barricades, constantly yelling, "Yankees, go home!"

Bill Lima and Beth Donahue, along with other US officials, sat in a Pan Am plane the state department had chartered to take United States employees back to America. Bill was not happy about leaving the unfinished plans he had put in motion. He was especially concerned about the safety and fate of the men he had recruited and gotten involved in such a dangerous operation.

Bill turned to Beth. "I still don't understand. Why are my people being kept in the dark about the invasion?"

Beth had heard Bill bring this up many times and had always been reluctant to give him any specific reasons while they were still in Cuba. Now that they were leaving the island, she felt she could come clean.

Beth answered, "It is to protect the secrecy of the operation that they are being denied information, Bill. If they are arrested, they won't be able to talk about the invasion because they won't know anything about it. No matter what the Castros do, your men won't have any information to provide the Cubans."

Bill was surprised to hear this and very concerned about what Beth was implying. He looked her in the eye and told her, "Beth, the way you're talking makes it sound like you already know they will be arrested."

Bill was not going to be happy with what she was about to tell him, but it was time he knew.

Beth sighed, "Bill, you were tagged. The Cubans have been on to you for over a month now. That supposed idiot, Antonio, they assigned to you and Diego turned out to be one of the best electronic spies they have. He has been working with the Russians, and they supplied him with new tools. It was through our spying on the Russians that we found out about Antonio and realized the Cubans were on to you. When we found out about it, the agency decided the best way to handle the situation was to continue the plan for assassination as if nothing had changed. You know as well as I do that the best way to salvage a blown operation is to use it as a form of misinformation. Now that they know, their focus is going to be in stopping the assassination attempt. That way we can keep Castro preoccupied with the threat to his life and draw their attention away from the invasion."

Now, more than ever, Bill was consumed with fear and concern for the lives of the men he had gotten involved in this mess.

"But my people don't know it is a blown operation," Bill stressed. "They will follow through. If we don't warn them, they are as good as dead."

Beth countered, "As far as we're concerned, nothing will change." She leaned in closer to Bill. "This is why we don't let ourselves become emotionally involved with foreign operatives. Face it, Bill. These people are expendable."

Bill could not believe what Beth had just said. He understood the nature and danger of the business he had chosen. But these were good decent men, with families being sent blindly to their deaths. He glared at her.

"As of today, Bill, you are no longer a part of this operation."

Bill looked at Beth with total disgust. He got up from his seat and moved away from her. He sat by himself, staring out the window as the plane took off, and he left Cuba for the last time.

Chapter 20

IT WAS FEBRUARY. By now all the news and information in the whole country was controlled by the government, but many rumors circulated around the island. In a society where there is no access to free information, rumors take on lives of their own and spread out of control. A rumor went around Havana that the government would soon require all children over the age of ten to attend boarding schools run by the state. The children would be removed from their homes and be taught at institutions outside their own provinces where they would live for the entire school year. The people felt it was an obvious attempt by the state to indoctrinate the kids and alienate them from their parents.

It was also rumored that the government might even cancel what was known as *patria potestas*. That was the legal term in Cuba for *parental rights*, the right that every parent had over their children. The rumor was that the government would transfer those rights to the state, make it a law, and give the state the rights over every child above that of their own mothers and fathers. Cuban parents were desperate to do anything to avoid having their children taken from them.

In response to this, the church started a program dubbed Operation Peter Pan. Parents could send their children to the United States, in many cases, to Catholic orphanages, to keep them from being brainwashed in the new state-run schools. Cuban parents tearfully sent thousands of their children on airplanes by themselves, supervised by priests and nuns. They didn't know when or if they would see their kids again. But to the parents, it was a preferable alternative to seeing their children turned into communist robots. The government had already started its brainwashing activities at all the schools, including private ones.

One day, to the horror of the nuns at Tico's Catholic school, the militiamen came storming in to one of Tico's classes and conducted a vile demonstration.

The captain of the militia looked out over all the young faces and asked, "Do you children believe in God?"

"Yes," the kids answered in unison.

He walked slowly between the rows of desks. The captain then asked, "Do any of you like ice cream?"

This time the kids all shouted in unison, "*YES!*"

He turned around and walked back through the rows of seated pupils and stood at the front of the classroom. "Close your eyes and ask God for ice cream."

The children did as they were told. After a few moments, the militiaman told them to open their eyes. Of course, the kids were disappointed that no ice cream had been delivered. The captain looked at all the children and smiled. He told them to close their eyes one more time.

When everyone's eyes were shut, he said, "Now, ask Fidel for ice cream."

The children again did so, and when they opened their eyes, the militiamen were passing out ice cream cones. The students cheered.

The captain got serious. "Boys," he said to all the smiling faces, "you cannot count on God, but you can always count on the revolution."

It was Tico's eleventh birthday, and the whole family gathered at the Machado home. The whole family that is, except for Elena. There were no other children at the party. It was a bittersweet celebration for Tico as none of his friends attended. He was not surprised, though. For weeks now, there had been no one in the neighborhood for him to play with. Many of Tico's friends had left for the United States or were being sequestered by their parents out of fear. Being a kid in today's Cuba wasn't as much fun as it used to be.

Everyone sang *Happy Birthday* to Tico, he blew out the candles, and they all cheered. After the candles were out, the ladies cut the cake and passed the pieces around.

Rosa asked Juana, "Where in heaven's name did you find a cake? We looked everywhere and could not find a thing. Not even Joaquin could get us one. They're even rationing sugar. Rationing sugar in Cuba. Can you believe it?"

Juana just smiled and told them she knew a baker and he did her a favor. Rosa and Alejandra went to the kitchen to make coffee. Juana stayed with the party.

While in the kitchen, out of Juana's range, Rosa said to Alejandra, "Cesar was out of his mind when it happened. No one was around, and he couldn't even find her for most of the day."

Alejandra said, "Poor Juana. It must be horrible to lose a baby."

"I can't believe how well she's taking it," said Rosa. "She must be in shock."

In the backyard, Joaquin, Diego, and Cesar were having a drink. Cesar was pacing and chain-smoking, lighting his next cigarette with the one he had just finished.

"Diego, have you communicated with Bill?" asked Joaquin.

"I don't have any way to get in touch with him. I have to wait for him to contact me. We are still getting information and orders through the mail, but it seems they want him to avoid any direct contact. They are playing it very carefully, and I can't say I blame them."

Cesar stopped pacing and faced his brothers. He was very nervous. The magnitude of the assassination plan weight heavily on him. He spoke up. "I don't like being the only carrier of information. Someone is bound to figure out what is going on."

"Cesar, you worry too much," said Diego. "Nobody is going to figure out anything. Relax and finish your drink."

Cesar ignored him, went back to his pacing, and lit another cigarette.

Joaquin asked, "And how about the plan? Has anything changed?"

"We haven't heard any different. Unless we hear otherwise, you leave the briefcase with the explosives in the bathroom behind Fidel's office just as planned. You know how to detonate the device. Just make sure you get out of there as fast as you can."

A few days later, Cesar was summoned to his supervisor's office. Before he arrived, Gustavo Vela walked out, just missing Cesar.

Cesar went up to the supervisor's desk, "Ernesto said you wanted to see me."

"Yes, Cesar. I wanted to tell you that you and Luis are switching routes."

Cesar froze. "Why? Is there something wrong?" stammered Cesar.

"No, nothing like that. We are just going to be switching routes from time to time."

Cesar did not know what, but he knew something was wrong. This was not good. He started to sweat.

"Well, does it have to be right now?" Cesar asked.

"Yes, starting today. It's not a big deal. You know each other's areas. You've covered for each other before."

He didn't know what to say. He did not want to arouse suspicion, but all he could think was *How the hell am I going to carry out the plans and continue to deliver the information? And what if they find out what I'm doing?*

He felt panic creeping up on him. All he could say was "Okay . . . okay."

When Cesar left the office, the supervisor dialed the phone. "Yes, I would like to leave a message for Captain Vela."

From then on, Cesar's old route and his new one were monitored by the G2. Every piece of mail was checked, all of Cesar's deliveries were watched, and his every move at the post office was noted.

March 10, 1961

Fidel met in his office with Raul, Ramiro, and Gustavo.

Raul said to Fidel, "We have some information we want to bring to your attention."

Gustavo spoke up. "Comandante, we have been intercepting letters from the CIA for the last three weeks.

They were being sent to a nonexistent address on Cesar Quintana's route. After reading the letters, we put them back in the undeliverable box, and Cesar has been observed taking them from the post office and delivering them to his accomplices."

Fidel nodded and said, "And what about my impending assassination?"

Ramiro answered, "The letters were written in code, but we were able to break it. We discovered the dynamite and weapons they intend to use will be picked up on April 10. Also, thanks to our friends the Russians and all the information they helped us get from our songbird, Felix, we know the time and place."

Raul interjected, "It looks like they have chosen your meeting with Joaquin on April 15 to carry out your assassination. That is about the same time our people are telling us the invasion is likely to take place. Although they appear to be two completely separate operations, the timetables are roughly the same. They figure if you are dead by the time of the invasion, our troops will be demoralized and will not fight back. I guess the CIA wants to make sure all their bases are covered. They want to get rid of you and stop this revolution one way or another."

Fidel sat there, digesting the information he had just heard. He thought for a few moments, tipped back his cap, and answered, "So it seems the invasion is to be a few days after the dynamite and weapons are delivered." They all nodded. He paused. "Okay, I don't want these worms arrested now. Let's wait until they pick up those weapons. That way the CIA will not have time to come up with another assassination plot." Fidel stood up. "Ramiro, I want you and Gustavo to handle these people. Make sure you stop them the minute they take possession of the explosives. Che and Raul, I want you two to concentrate on the invasion." He dismissed Ramiro and Gustavo and told them to get moving. He turned to Che and Raul. "Let's go over our plan to stop these traitors."

Later that day, Ramiro called Elena and Gustavo to his office. Ramiro was seated behind his desk. The situation before him was delicate due to the relationship of the would-be assassins to Elena, but he knew she was totally dedicated to their cause. He wanted to make sure she knew what was going on but did not want her involved.

Ramiro shook hands with both of them and said, "Elena, Gustavo, please sit down. Elena, I asked you to come here to fill you in on what is happening. What I am going to say will shock and even hurt you, but you need to know."

His comment made Elena feel unsettled. She could tell by Ramiro's tone this was very serious.

"What is it?"

"First, about the middle of April, the United States is planning an invasion of Cuba."

"Oh my god!" She could not believe what Ramiro was saying. An invasion was something she had not expected.

"Also," Ramiro paused for a second, "we have discovered a plot to assassinate Fidel at about the same time of the impending invasion."

Now she was really shocked. An invasion of the country plus an assassination of Fidel was beyond anything she could have imagined.

"By whom?" asked Elena.

There was a long, silent pause as Ramiro looked at Gustavo. Elena could tell there was more to this, and she was worried.

"What? Tell me."

Ramiro was about to tell her, but Gustavo jumped in before Ramiro had a chance to speak. He felt that, due to his relationship with Elena, he should be the one to tell her.

Gustavo looked at Elena and said, "Among others, your father, your uncle Joaquin, and your uncle Cesar."

Elena could not believe what Gustavo was saying. She was confused and could not digest this information. Joaquin, a traitor? Her father and Cesar involved? Was this a cruel joke? It had to be a mistake. Since when did her dad and Cesar care about getting involved in anything to do with politics? Gustavo had to be wrong.

"I can't believe that."

Ramiro interjected, "Elena, I did not want to believe it about Joaquin either, but we searched his quarters and found the phone number of a known CIA agent. I believe you know him."

"Who?"

"Bill Lima, your father's friend. He and your father got Joaquin involved."

Elena swallowed hard. "I still don't believe it."

"Elena," said Gustavo, "we have it on tape. You don't want to hear it."

Elena jumped up from her chair. "Yes, I do want to hear it." She had to hear it for herself, or she would never believe it, no matter what they might tell her. It was all too much for her to comprehend. "I have to hear it."

Reluctantly, Ramiro took the tape recorder from the bottom drawer, put it on top of his desk, and played the tape.

Diego's voice was heard. "Cesar, calm down."

Cesar answered, "I can't calm down. They are going to find me out. They just switched my route, and sooner or later, they will find the letters."

"No, they won't," said Diego. "All they will do is continue to put them in the nondeliverable basket like they do every other letter with a wrong address. Keep doing what you've being doing. Just be sure nobody is looking when you take them."

Cesar was in panic mode. "I don't like it. I don't like it at all. We better get this assassination over with soon, or we are all going to be dead."

At the time of the recording, Diego wanted to jump through the phone to shut Cesar up.

"Cesar, get a hold of yourself," said Diego. "And stop saying stupid things. I hope to God you are calling me from a pay phone. I can't secure every damn telephone in Havana. Now, hang up. We will get together with Joaquin and talk about this in person."

Ramiro shut off the tape recorder. Elena stood, speechless and stunned.

"Are you all right, Elena?" asked Gustavo.

Slowly she sat back down. She was crying.

"I can't believe this. I have no family left." She cried so hard she was shaking. She was estranged from her family, but this was the final blow. She would never again be able to have a relationship with any of them.

Gustavo walked behind her chair, put his arms around her, hugged her, and said into her ear, "I am your family, Elena. The revolution is your family."

She tried to compose herself and thought about what she was going to do now. Long ago, she had decided to dedicate her life to this revolution and had come to believe deeply in all the propaganda she had been fed. She decided she did not care that they were her father and uncles. They had to be stopped, and she was determined to be the one to stop them.

Elena wiped her tears and her nose with a handkerchief. Again, she stood up. "I want to be the one to arrest them."

Gustavo looked at Ramiro and back at her. "I don't think that is such a good idea."

She was furious. "The hell with what you think! I'm in the special unit of the G2 that was created to root out and stop this very thing. I've earned the right to stop these traitors no matter who they are." She turned to Ramiro. "Now when are we arresting them?"

Ramiro thought about it. He had always planned on Elena not being involved and still did not think it was a good idea. But she was determined. That was one of the things about her that made her such a good soldier. He looked at Gustavo, who just shrugged.

He turned back to Elena and told her, "I have to agree with Gustavo. I don't know about you getting involved in apprehending your father and uncles." He paused. "But you seem to have made up your mind." He sighed and shook his head. "If you think you can handle it, Gustavo is in charge of that. He will let you know when."

Chapter 21

THE SITUATION IN Cuba had reached a critical point. More and more people were fearful and desperate to leave the country. Cubans fleeing Cuba had begun with the Batista supporters followed by those affected by the confiscation of lands and businesses. Then it had escalated when parents sent thousands of their children to the US on the Peter Pan flights. Now, people from every social and economic level were willing to surrender all their possessions so they could leave Cuba and what it had turned into. The line at the American embassy seemed to have no end. Thousands of Cubans hopefully waited for their exit papers. In the early days of this exodus, the line had been a few blocks long. Now it had grown from those few blocks to over a mile.

And the harassment from the mobs, orchestrated by the government, continued to intensify.

Tico and Carmen were near the front. The entire scene was extremely overwhelming for Tico. He did not comprehend why all the people behind the barricades across the street kept yelling bad words and sometimes threw things at them. It was difficult for him to understand everything that was going on, but he knew his entire family was nervous and upset.

He was confused and scared. "How much longer, Mommy?"

Carmen did not know how to explain all this to Tico. She knew he was tired, and she could tell he was rattled by all the insults being hurled their way by those horrible people across the street from the embassy. She did her best to keep her composure for his sake.

"I don't know, Tico. We'll just have to wait as long as it takes." She gently put her hands on his shoulders and told him, "Don't pay any attention to that awful crowd across the street. They are just mean, stupid people who don't know any better."

Back at home, Roberto was talking to Rosa about leaving Cuba.

"Don't get me a waiver," she said. "I want to stay. I am too old to move to another country. I want to die and be buried next to my husband in Cuba."

Roberto sympathized with Rosa's apprehensions and could understand why she wanted to stay. But he also knew that Carmen would never leave Cuba without her. And they had to go as soon as they could. The new rumors were that Fidel would soon close the doors and no one would be allowed out.

Roberto tried his best to convince her. "Your husband would have been the first one to tell you to leave. Look around you, Rosa. This country is worse than ever. Look out the window. The line to leave this country is over twenty blocks long."

The Machados' home was a little over a mile from the embassy, and the line for the waiver papers had now almost reached their block.

"Everybody we know has either left or are planning to leave. Are you going to stay here all by yourself? Don't you want to see your grandson grow up?"

Rosa answered, "But what about Diego and Cesar? What about Joaquin and Elena? They need me too."

"Elena is a lost cause," said Roberto. "And it's only a matter of time before Joaquin will not want to be part of this shameful mess the revolution has turned into and your sons will want to leave too. We need you more than anyone. Carmen would never leave Cuba without you. And you know we can't stay. Look at what they are teaching Tico in school. Do you want him to grow up a brainwashed robot?"

"Of course not."

"Look at the animals who run this country, Rosa. You saw on TV what they did to the priests and nuns. They deported them then brought a mob to the airport to insult them on their way out. If that is how they treat priests and nuns, how do you think they are going to treat the rest of us?"

Shortly after the Catholic Church started the Peter Pan flights, which took thousands of unaccompanied children to the United States, all arranged and supervised by the church, Fidel started a campaign of retaliation. The Catholic Church was now an open target, and Fidel proceeded to expel as many clergymen and nuns as possible. On their way out, the priests and nuns were subjected to even worse treatment by the government mobs. Some nuns were even stripped and cavity-searched. They were accused of smuggling gold and jewelry out of Cuba.

Rosa wiped a tear from her eye. "I know, I know. You are right. I have to leave."

She knew what Roberto said was true. But at her age, it was so difficult to leave everything behind that she held so dear, especially her cherished memories of a lifetime in her beloved Cuba. Her tears gave way to sobs. Roberto came to her and put his arms around her in a tight hug.

"Don't worry," he said. "It's going to be all right."

April 10, 1961

At an ugly old house in a rundown section of Havana, Cesar, Cristobal, and Hugo finished unloading the explosives and other weapons. This was to be their safe house, the point from which they would carry out the assassination. The delivery of the explosives went without any problems, and the men felt confident.

"All right, that's the last of it," said Cesar. "Let's get out of here."

Hugo opened the front door and was stunned to see Gustavo Vela with several well armed soldiers behind him. None of the men planning the assassination had any idea they were being watched the whole time. Upon seeing Vela and the soldiers, Hugo took a couple of steps backward. Gustavo said nothing. With steely eyes, he drew his sidearm and calmly shot Hugo in the head. Hugo collapsed to the floor, while the other soldiers burst their way into the house.

Elena was the last to enter.

"Everyone is under arrest!" she shouted. Her eyes were fixed on Cesar. She walked right up to him and screamed, "I am Captain Elena Quintana of the Cuban Internal Security Forces. I am here to arrest you for treason!"

She reached into her pocket and took out the rosary Cesar had given her that Christmas Eve night that now seemed so long ago. She threw it at him, got closer to Cesar, and slapped him in the face.

She then turned her back and addressed the other soldiers. "Load these worms into the truck and take them to La Cabana for interrogation."

Cesar just stood there, stunned. He tried to say something to Elena, but the words wouldn't come out.

Cold and detached, Elena stepped over Hugo's dead body and walked out.

Diego had just been told that the phone company no longer needed his services because the Russians had finally brought their own equipment and phone experts and did not need his expertise. Although he no longer had a job, he was glad he did not have to deal with those people anymore. He called Alejandra from his office and told her the news. She asked him to come home so they could talk about it.

"I'm on way," he said, and Diego walked out of his office.

But by the time he got to the parking lot, he had changed his mind and decided to drop by the safe house to check on his men. He wanted to make sure everything had gone as planned. He drove up near the house and, from the corner, saw Elena and the soldiers loading the ammunition and weapons into their truck. Cesar and Cristobal, their hands cuffed in front of them, were carrying Hugo's dead body.

Diego was frozen in his car. As he watched the scene, he could not believe his eyes. His mind raced, and he tried to figure out what had gone wrong. Suddenly, he was overcome with fear, and his thoughts immediately turned to Alejandra.

"Oh my god! How did this happen?" He turned the car around and headed for his house.

On the car radio the announcer said, "A massive roundup of subversives has begun in Havana."

As Diego sped to reach Alejandra, the soldiers had already busted into his house, looking for him. When the soldiers arrived at the house, they saw Diego's car in the driveway and assumed he was there. But what they were not aware of was that Diego had taken Alejandra's car that morning because his needed to be repaired. They soon realized he was nowhere to be found. Only Alejandra was there when the soldiers, led by none other than Pablo, Juana's ex-boyfriend, came rushing in, guns drawn. Pablo was furious to find out Diego was not there.

The plan was to arrest Diego when he got home. Because Diego's office phone was bugged, Pablo himself had heard the conversation when Diego told Alejandra he was on his way home from the office. But Pablo was another example of someone being promoted because of his blind loyalty instead of experience or qualifications. Pablo, the newly appointed lieutenant, due to his arrogance and inexperience, had failed to assign anyone to follow Diego. He mistakenly thought he had everything under control. Pablo was sure Alejandra knew where Diego had gone instead of coming home and was determined to get it out of her. He had his men restrain Alejandra so he could interrogate her while several soldiers searched the place for evidence. Alejandra was handcuffed, sitting on a chair.

Pablo walked slowly around her and said, "We have no quarrel with you, so why don't you be a nice girl and cooperate? Now, I'm going to ask you just one more time. Where is he?" He pressed his face against hers and screamed, "Where is Diego Quintana!"

Alejandra looked at him with total disdain and screamed back at him, "Drop dead!"

Anger blazed in his eyes. He raised his hand and slapped her hard enough to draw blood from her lower lip. He grabbed her by the neck and again put his face close to hers.

This time, he leered at her, leaned in, and slowly licked her ear as he whispered, "I'm going to have some fun with you."

Alejandra was revolted by Pablo, and she spat in his face.

He slowly wiped off the saliva, grabbed her by her long hair, and slapped her again and again. "You are going to tell me where he is, one way or another!"

As the impending invasion approached, the arrest of the would-be assassins was only the beginning. Castro ordered a mass detention of anyone suspected of anti-government leanings. He left no stone unturned. Havana was in total lockdown. The arrests were so massive that the country literally ran out of jail spaces. People were detained in all sorts of places. They even had to use the famous

Blancita Amaro Theater, where they housed those suspects perceived to be the least dangerous.

One of the reasons the regime was so successful in apprehending so many suspects was due to a tactic Castro had used from the very beginning of his takeover of power. He had set up organizations that were anti-Castro and anti-revolution with the sole purpose of identifying those who were opposed to him. Because of this, Fidel had been able to keep tabs on the majority of people who wanted to bring him and the revolution down. He wisely did not act on those leads until it became obvious that the time had come to take advantage of such knowledge. He knew that as the news of the invasion became known to the people, many of those opposed to him would rise up to fight against him.

With this knowledge of his enemies, he made sure that very few spontaneous revolts would occur during the impending invasion. Fidel did not let it be known that the arrests were due to the invasion, making sure he would not tip off the Americans. Instead he used the excuse of the assassination as the reason for such actions. The massive arrests were conducted house to house in every neighborhood, especially in Havana, where almost every house in the capital was searched.

The doorbell rang at the Machados' home. Rosa answered it to find three militiamen standing on the front porch.

"Good afternoon, ma'am. I am Lieutenant Pino. We would like to come in and ask you a few questions."

Lieutenant Pino was a smarmy guy who tried to come across as friendly but was in fact a very suspicious and inept individual. He was typical of so many new militiamen who had jumped on the bandwagon of the revolution. Like Pablo, they were promoted to officer ranks not because of their abilities but because of their blind loyalty. Due to the state of emergency that the country was under, he had been given responsibilities that were above his level of competence. He was assigned to apprehend some of the suspects that were identified as potential threats. He was given a list of names and the Machado's neighborhood as the area to search for those individuals.

Rosa was not only surprised but apprehensive about these militiamen at her front door. The last thing she wanted was these men in her house. But what could she do? She was scared and nervous. She nodded hello and turned to call for Roberto.

"Roberto, there are some people here who want to talk to you." She looked back at Lieutenant Pino. "You better talk to my son-in-law."

Roberto came to the door. When he saw the militiamen, he immediately became concerned. Rosa excused herself and proceeded to go upstairs.

"Can I help you?" asked Roberto.

Lieutenant Pino said hello in his creepy-friendly sort of way and asked Roberto if he would be so kind as to help him. Even though Diego had never said anything to anyone in the family, Roberto had a feeling and suspected for some time that Diego might be involved with an anti-Castro group. He was afraid that Joaquin might be involved as well.

Pino handed Roberto a list of names. "We are looking for these people. We know for sure that two of them are students that live in this neighborhood. We need to ask you a few questions about them."

Roberto looked at the list. He thumbed through it, and on the second page near the bottom of the list, he saw Diego's name. His concern immediately turned to fear.

He did not want to appear scared, so he just said, "Come in."

Lieutenant Pino advised him that he was only looking for those names on the first page. The names on the other pages were the responsibility of a different group of militiamen. He was only interested in the students he had mentioned to Roberto. They had to search from house to house because they had not been able to find them in their own homes. He suspected the students might be hiding in someone else's house in the neighborhood.

At that moment, Carmen and Tico walked in the front door. They were back from the US embassy, where she had finally received the visa waivers for the family. Roberto immediately engaged them. He did not want the militiamen to know where she had just come from.

Before Carmen could say a word, he said, "Hi, honey. Did you guys have fun at the park today?" Tico almost corrected his father as to where they had been, but Carmen understood what Roberto was trying to do. She squeezed Tico's hand, and he said nothing. "This gentleman is Lieutenant Pino. He is looking for some student troublemakers in the neighborhood."

"Good afternoon, ma'am. I'm sorry to disturb you," said the lieutenant.

Carmen greeted him, and before she sat down, Roberto said to her, "Why don't you take Tico upstairs and get him ready for dinner?"

Carmen calmly walked Tico upstairs and found Rosa stuffing some papers into her bra.

Diego drove as fast as he could from the safe house to his home. He ran several red lights and almost ran over a couple of people that tried to cross the street in front of him. He got to his neighborhood, and by the time he was within a half block from the house, he saw soldiers and military vehicles all around. He was too late. His first instinct was to get out and run to Alejandra, but he knew it would be suicidal and futile to do so. He sat in his car and watched in total shock as two militiamen carried out the dead body of Alejandra.

He could not believe what was in front of him. How did this happen? How could this be? He felt like his entire world had collapsed.

He sat at the wheel, repeating to himself, "Oh my god! This is not happening! What have I done? What have I done?"

Diego burst into tears and pounded on the car's dashboard.

Roberto and Lieutenant Pino were talking. The lieutenant was apologetic.

"Roberto, I apologize but I have my orders," said the lieutenant. "I'm sorry to have to disturb you and your family. I'm just going to take a quick look around the house."

Roberto figured the best thing he could do was to cooperate so these men would conduct their search and leave the house as soon as possible.

"That's fine. Look anywhere you want." Roberto and the soldiers stood up.

Lieutenant Pino addressed his men. "Rogelio, you go look around upstairs, and don't make a mess. Ricardo, check around outside. I'm going to take a look down here."

He walked around the first floor of the house half-heartedly, searching for the students he had already figured out were not there. But he went about his search nonetheless.

Lieutenant Pino opened the door to Tico's playroom and saw Tico's huge arsenal of toy guns laid out neatly on the floor. He almost fell over when he saw all the rifles, pistols, and machine guns in Tico's playroom.

"What the hell is going on here?" he shouted.

He instantly dropped the nice guy act and drew his sidearm. He grabbed Roberto and pushed him up against the wall, pressing the gun to Roberto's head.

"What are you doing with all these guns?" demanded Pino.

At that moment, Tico came downstairs and saw the militiaman assaulting his father.

Tico ran to the two men and grabbed Lieutenant Pino by the leg. "Let my daddy go!"

The lieutenant grabbed Tico with his free hand and shoved him hard. Tico went sliding across the floor and hit the adjacent wall. Carmen, Rosa, and the other soldiers ran into the room to see what all the commotion was about. Carmen screamed at the sight of Roberto pinned against the wall with a gun to his head. Rosa went to hug Tico, who was shaken from hitting the wall. The soldiers did not know what to make of it all, so they pointed their guns at the entire family, including Tico, who was crying.

Through it all, Roberto remained calm. "They are toys. They are only toys. My son collects toy guns. Take a good look at them," he said to the lieutenant. The militiaman continued to press the revolver against Roberto's temple. Lieutenant Pino did not buy Roberto's explanation, and he decided to see for himself what kind of weapons they were.

Pino backed away slowly but kept his gun trained on Roberto. He inspected some of the toy guns and realized his mistake. He was at a loss for words and realized what a stupid blunder he had made. He did not know exactly what to do. He just shook his head and holstered his gun. He finally turned to Roberto.

"I'm very sorry," said an embarrassed Lieutenant Pino. "They looked so real."

Roberto tried to ease the situation and told the lieutenant it was a common mistake, that many people often took his son's toy guns for real ones.

Lieutenant Pino could not wait to leave the Machados' home. He was mortified at his stupid reaction to the toys. He again apologized to the Machados, especially Tico, who sniffed and rubbed his leg that had been smashed against the wall.

Pino leaned over to him, gave him one of his eerie smiles, and told him, "I'm sorry, little man. I was just doing my job."

He turned to his men, who were trying not to snicker, and barked at them, "Let's go!"

The guards were just about to leave when Diego showed up. He was stunned to see soldiers here, too. Diego had come back to retrieve the papers that he had given his mother to keep for him at the Machado home. He had not seen any military vehicles parked in front of his sister's house. The militiamen had left them parked by the suspected student's home while they walked the neighborhood, searching each house. He thought for sure that this was the end of the line for him. He was about to reach for his gun, but Rosa ran up to him the instant she saw him come through the door.

She grabbed him and hugged him while she whispered into his ear, "It's okay, it's okay." She kept her arm around him as she spoke loud enough for the whole group to hear. "Diego, these gentlemen are here looking for some students that live in the neighborhood. They're getting ready to leave now."

Diego had been put through hell, and it seemed like it would never end. Lieutenant Pino couldn't help but notice how nervous Diego was.

Lieutenant Pino introduced himself and said, "And who are you?"

Diego saw the list in the lieutenant's hand and said nothing. An awkward silence lasted for several seconds. The tension was thick in the air.

Lieutenant Pino was about to approach Diego and search him when he heard, "Lieutenant, arrest that man!"

It was Roberto shouting. Everyone was stunned for a second. Roberto continued, "He is the one who gave my son all those guns."

The tension was broken, and everybody laughed, especially the militiamen. The only ones not laughing were Diego and the lieutenant, who silently stared at each other. Pino was still embarrassed about the incident with the toy guns and did not want to press the issue with Diego and run the risk of looking like a fool in front of his men again. He gave his soldiers a dirty look, and they immediately stopped laughing.

"Let's go," ordered Lieutenant Pino.

He turned to the Machados and thanked them for their cooperation but still looked at Diego with suspicious eyes. He turned and left the house.

After they were gone, Rosa asked Diego, "What is it? What's wrong?"

Diego tried to steady himself. He did his best to hold it together and said to Rosa, "Alejandra is dead."

"What? What are you talking about?" asked Roberto.

"I can't go into details. But for some time now Joaquin, Cesar, and I have been involved in trying to throw these son of bitches out of Cuba. But something has gone terribly wrong. I have to find asylum in an embassy. I need the papers I left with you, Mom."

Rosa handed him the papers that she had hidden in her bra while the militiamen searched the house. She gave him a hug.

"What about Joaquin? Cesar?" she asked.

He couldn't think of what to say to his mother. He did not want to scare her and drive her into doing something that would get the others involved. He knew they were ready to leave the country, and he did not want to jeopardize that.

He just said, "I don't know. I'm sure they will be fine. I have to go now, Mom. I love you."

"I love you too." She wiped a tear from her eye. "Go, just go."

Diego turned to Carmen and Roberto. He told them he loved them, to be careful, and that he would soon see all of them again. He told Roberto to take care of his mother and sister. He went over to Tico and told him he too was in charge of taking care of the women.

He hugged Tico and said, "Next time I see you I will buy you the biggest ice cream you've ever seen." He turned for the door and was gone.

Chapter 22

THE COURTYARD OF La Cabana Prison, the old-style Spanish fort, was the scene of hundreds of executions by firing squad that were conducted daily. Many soldiers stood by with rifles over their shoulders. They watched as a newly killed corpse was untied and dragged away from the pole while they waited for the next set of convicted men and, in some cases, women who were to be executed. The arid dirt in front of *El Paredon*, the wall where so many had stood, had absorbed so much blood from the killings it was now a dark red mud.

Cesar was alone in his cell, semiconscious after having endured several beatings. The sounds of violence permeated the air. In the background, he could hear the cries and the horrible screams of men being beaten while interrogated. There was no furniture in Cesar's cell, and its walls and floor were stained with blood, both old and new. The distant echo of another firing squad execution could be heard cracking through the warm air.

Two soldiers entered his cell. They walked up to Cesar, who was lying on the stained floor, pulled him up by his arm, and dragged him down the hall. Cesar woke up from his stupor state, and fear took over his senses. He thought for sure they were taking him to the wall for execution. As the soldiers yanked him through the hall of cells, he could see the other prisoners packed like cows in a slaughter house, awaiting their fate in front of *El Paredon*. Inside the cells, he saw beaten and bloody faces. There was Francisco, the man Elena saved from the jabalina; Ramon, the student leader who got shot in the leg; Orlando, the big radio man from Che's columns; and Dr. Andujar, the elderly doctor from the mountains. They were all among those waiting to be executed.

Cesar cried out to the soldiers, "Where are you taking me?" There was no response. "Why won't you tell me? Answer me."

As they approached an office room, one of the soldiers finally spoke. "You have a visitor," grunted the soldier.

He opened the door, and they threw Cesar into the room where Juana was waiting.

Arms folded in front of her, tapping her foot, and nervously chewing gum, she looked at him without a trace of sympathy and demanded, "Cesar, what have you done?"

She looked him up and down with total disgust, seeing a beaten, defeated man lying on the floor in front of her. She yelled at him, "Oh my god, look at yourself!"

He was too weak to stand. He muttered, "I'm sorry."

"Who put you up to this? Who talked you into plotting against the revolution? And what is all this about you getting involved in a plan to kill Fidel? Are you crazy? Do you have any idea what you have gotten yourself into? And now, because I'm your wife, they want answers from me. I'm not going to pay the price for your stupidity. You better tell me what is going on, and you better tell me right now."

"I can't tell you."

"I'm your wife. Of course, you can tell me."

"I can't. Not here."

Juana was furious. She had not one ounce of concern or compassion for Cesar. All she could think of was how this whole mess would affect her.

"Yes, you can, Cesar. You better tell me, and you better tell them. Don't you see what you are doing? You are dragging me down with you. Tell them, Cesar. Tell them everything they want to know."

"No, please. I . . . I . . . can't."

Still tapping her foot, she stood over Cesar, anger pouring out of her. She leaned close to him and shouted, "Okay, you want to be a hero? Fine." She put her hands on her hips. "Be a hero. But you will be a hero all by yourself.

You are going to rot in this jail, and don't expect me to be waiting for you, if you ever get out."

Cesar was still too weak and groggy from all the beatings to muster any strength to argue with her. All he could manage to say as he tried to reach for her was, "Juana, please don't leave me now."

Juana quickly stepped back. She was disgusted and did not want to be touched by Cesar. She could hardly stand to look at him.

With total repulsion, she told him, "Look at you. Look at what you've become. Where is that strong, successful man I married? You're pathetic." She stopped for a moment, thinking as she moved further away. She got very serious and, with no remorse, spewed, "I wasn't going to tell you this, but I guess it doesn't matter anymore what you think. I didn't have a miscarriage."

"What?"

"I had an abortion."

Cesar was crushed. He could not believe the words coming out of Juana. All the while she only sneered at him.

"Boy was I wrong about you. I thought I married a man who was going to make my life better. Ha! What a joke. I started to have my doubts about you from the moment the revolution took over. I made the mistake of marrying you, but don't you believe for even one minute that I would have your baby! Do you think that I want my child to have such a weak, miserable nothing for a father? Think again. Look at you. Look what a loser you turned out to be."

Cesar was hurt and bewildered. He could not believe this woman he loved and married would do such a horrible thing and have so little concern for him.

He started to cry, and he pleaded with her, "I don't believe it. How could you do that to us, Juana? I thought you loved me."

She laughed. "No, you got it all wrong." She leaned closer to Cesar and screamed at him, "I thought you loved me!" She looked at him one last time and spat her gum on the floor. She walked to the doorway and yelled, "Guard, let me out of here!" Before the guard came over, she turned back to Cesar. "Go ahead and be a hero to your family, because to me you are nothing but a pitiful, pathetic loser."

The guard opened the door, and she left without looking back.

"Juuuaaannnaaa!"

She walked down the hallway and met up with Ramiro and Pablo.

"He wants to play hero. He won't tell me anything either."

"Just go home. We'll handle it," said Ramiro.

Pablo came over and put his arm around her shoulders; he looked at her and said, "I think you're going to need some company now."

She did not give it a second thought. Juana turned out to be nothing but a ruthless, heartless opportunist. She had come 360 degrees back to where she started. She dumped

Pablo when her fortunes seemed better with Cesar. And now that the poor man had been reduced to nothing, she went back to Pablo, who seemed to be going somewhere with the new regime.

Ramiro walked into Cesar's cell. Cesar was still on the floor, his face in his hands, crying like a little boy not able to deal with all that had happened to him. He felt like his life had turned to shit. He still could not believe Juana would just throw him away, like he had never meant anything to her.

"I want you to know," said Ramiro, "that you are not being brave. You are being stupid."

Cesar stopped crying. He did not want to give this bastard the satisfaction of seeing him this way. He wiped his nose with the sleeves of his prison garb and looked up at Ramiro.

"Leave me alone. I already told you I don't know anything," he rasped. "Ask Cristobal. Maybe he knows."

"Cristobal won't be telling anybody anything anymore."

Cesar's disposition immediately turned from sadness to anger. He yelled at Ramiro, "You killed him too? You son of a bitch!"

Ramiro just looked at Cesar and smiled. He walked up to him, grabbed him by his hair, and demanded, "Tell me who your contacts are on the inside and what their involvement is in this pathetic assassination attempt, and we will let you all live."

Cesar pushed Ramiro's hand off him and crawled away. He could not maintain his tough act any longer and broke down once again.

"I can't," Cesar sobbed. "I can't tell you."

Ramiro stood over Cesar for a few moments. He turned toward the door and called out, "Guards, take this piece of shit to the firing squad."

The guards dragged Cesar to the courtyard, and he kicked and screamed the entire way. Even in his weakened state, it took both guards to restrain him and tie him to the post.

Che could be seen nearby. He was leading the firing squad of another of the original comandantes accused of whatever charge they could pin on him, but basically for not toeing the line. There was a looming state of angst among the revolutionaries due to the impending invasion. People on the inside who were even slightly suspected of working with the Americans were disposed of daily. Their trials literally lasted minutes, and they were immediately sent to *El Paredon* to be put to death.

The sound of the firing squad discharging their rifles grabbed Cesar's attention, and he could see Che approach the slumping body. Che stood over it, raised his revolver, and put a final bullet through the head. Cesar was now hysterically pleading and begging. A soldier came over and put a blindfold on him. The firing squad loaded their rifles.

Cesar kept yelling, "Stop! Stop!"

Ramiro gave the order to the soldiers.

"Ready!"

"Don't kill me! Please don't kill me!" Cesar pleaded.

"Too late. You had your chance. Aim!"

"No, please don't. I beg you. Stop this!" cried Cesar.

Ramiro waited a beat and yelled, "Fire!"

The sound of gunshots cracked through the air. Cesar screamed and fell down into the dark red mud. For a moment, he did not know if he was dead or alive. He kept sobbing hysterically. Ramiro and the soldiers in the firing squad burst out laughing. Ramiro walked up to Cesar and again grabbed him by his hair.

"Next time there will be real bullets, you worm. Are you going to talk, or should we load the rifles?"

"No! No! I can't. I can't tell you anything. Please stop it. I don't know anything."

"Okay, you still want to play the hero, let's see how much of a hero you are going to be after you are dead. Load your weapons, men, with real bullets this time."

Cesar could not stand it any longer. He did not want to give up his brothers, but he had no will left in him. He dropped his head down and told them between his sobs, "It's my brother Joaquin. Joaquin and Diego."

Ramiro smiled a creepy smile. He slowly walked up to Cesar, got close to his face, and told him, "We knew that. I just wanted to hear you say it."

The firing squad put down their guns.

While Cesar was going through his mock execution at La Cabana, Joaquin, unaware of what was going on with Diego and Cesar, left his office and was about to get into his car. In the distance, he saw two military jeeps rapidly approaching. Before he could open his door, the military vehicles came screeching to a halt, blocking his path. Joaquin froze next to his car door when he saw Elena and Gustavo hastily exit their jeep while several soldiers, armed with automatic weapons, poured out of the other one.

Elena angrily walked up to Joaquin. She was practically shaking with fury as she got close to him and said, "Comandante Quintana."

Joaquin didn't move. He already knew in his guts what this was about.

With hate flowing from her eyes, she loudly told him, "You are under arrest for high treason." She threw the arrest papers at him and yelled, "You are a disgrace to the revolution!"

Joaquin grimly stared back at her. All kinds of feelings ran through him at the sight of his once beloved niece.

With sorrow and quiet resolve, he said, "No, you've got it wrong. All of you," he pointed to Gustavo and the soldiers that were now aiming their weapons at him, "and especially Fidel Castro, are a disgrace to Cuba." He paused for a second, still not believing the surreal scenario of his niece arresting him. Then he announced to the group, "This revolution was not fought for Fidelism or for Communism. It was fought for Cubanism. We fought so the people of Cuba could have a free choice, so they wouldn't have to, once again, live under an oppressive dictatorship. Don't kid yourselves for one minute as to what this revolution has become. This is a dictatorship. Fidel Castro is nothing more than a dictator with a manifesto. And you" he took his eyes away from Elena and pointed at Vela "you are nothing but a gangster. We used to import our gangsters from the United States. Now we home-grow them, give them military uniforms, and call them our comrades." Joaquin turned his attention back to Elena and, more with disillusionment than anger, told her, "And you, my little niece, Elena, you are an idiot."

Elena did not say a word to her uncle. She stood silently staring at him. Gustavo walked past Elena and grabbed Joaquin's arm. Joaquin forcibly took Vela's hand and pulled it away from him.

He looked at Gustavo and shouted, "Don't you touch me, you piece of shit!"

At this outburst by Joaquin, the soldiers, who had lowered their weapons, again pointed them at him and waited for the order to fire. Joaquin stood defiant, daring them to shoot him. When the order to shoot did not come, he straightened his uniform, ripped the comandante insignia from his epilates, and threw them at Gustavo.

"Here! Give this back to Fidel. Tell him I don't deserve to wear them. Only worthless scum like you deserve to wear these pieces of crap."

He did not wait for them to cuff him and hustle him into their vehicle. He calmly walked to their car as the soldiers lowered their guns. Before he got in, he turned and took a last look at Elena, remembering the times when she had been so warm and beautiful. Now she was nothing but a cold, heartless, unfeeling monster. He shook his head at her in total disgust and got in the car, and they took him away.

Chapter 23

DIEGO HAD LEFT his sister's house and was now on the run. If he didn't find a way out of Cuba, he was a dead man. In a phone booth on a busy Havana street, he continually looked around for fear of being apprehended. He dialed the number given to him by Bill Lima on the day they said their final goodbyes. It was the "when the shit hits the fan" number. The number he hoped he would never have to use.

A voice answered. "Hello."

Diego was relieved to hear someone on the other end of the line. "Can I speak to Lloyd?" he asked.

"This is Lloyd."

Diego relaxed as much as he could under the circumstances, hoping he now had a chance to escape.

"This is Diego. I need help."

"We know. We have been waiting for your call. Stay calm and try not to arouse any suspicion. We have everything covered. Be at Linea Avenue between A and B Streets today at 5:00 p.m. There is a sandwich shop on that corner. Don't look around and don't act nervous. Go inside, sit down, buy yourself something to drink, and wait. You will see a car with Honduran embassy license plates. When it stops in front of the shop, get in. And don't call this number again."

Diego began to ask if they knew anything about Joaquin and Cesar. "But what about…"

The line went dead. He stood there, receiver in hand, listening to the hum of the dial tone in is his ear. He hung up and walked out of the phone booth, looking in every direction. He did as he was told and hoped against hope that he could elude the militia until 5:00 p.m.

Diego walked down Linea, a busy avenue, not too far from Roberto and Carmen's house. He got to A Street, saw the sandwich shop, went in, and ordered a Coca-Cola, one of the few American products still available in Havana. He found a seat in front of the glass window that looked out onto the street, sat down, and waited. The official looking car approached the meeting place, and he saw the Honduran embassy tags. When the vehicle stopped in front of the shop, he walked out, moved cautiously toward the car, and opened the door.

There was a neatly dressed man in a suit in the back seat, looking out the other window. Diego got in. Once Diego had closed the door, the man in the suit turned to him and smiled. It was Gustavo Vela. Diego immediately recognized him as the man Elena was with at Cesar's wedding. Before he could react, Gustavo pulled out his pistol and pointed it at Diego.

"Hello, Mr. Quintana, remember me? May I have your gun, please?" Diego hesitated for a moment, and Gustavo, now looking at him very seriously, told him, "Please don't make me shoot you right here." Diego slowly reached into his waistband and handed him his gun. Gustavo took the pistol and tossed it onto the front seat. "We've been waiting for you." He chuckled and told Diego, "I want you to know that you didn't talk to Lloyd. You talked to one of our men. We have been onto you idiots from the very beginning." He pointed at the front seat of the car, sneered, and announced, "Oh, by the way, you remember your lovely daughter, Elena?"

The driver of the car slowly turned and stared at Diego sitting in the back seat. It was Elena, eyeing him with loathing and resentment. Gustavo watched this sorry scene between Elena and Diego and enjoyed a feeble laugh. Diego took his eyes off Elena while Gustavo took pleasure in his own pathetic giggles.

Without any hesitation, Diego pulled out a second gun he had hidden in his belt underneath his jacket and, mustering all the rage he had inside of him, fired it point blank into Gustavo's chest. Gustavo let out a muffled cry and slumped dead in his seat. Diego immediately opened the car door and got out.

Elena jumped at the sound of the gunshot. Shocked from witnessing her father gun down her lover, she was stunned for a few seconds. Quickly she snapped out of her stupor, jumped out of the driver's side door, pulled out her weapon, and pointed it at Diego as he walked away.

"Stop!" she yelled at him.

Diego kept walking.

She was watching her father get away.

Elena screamed, "Halt! Halt or I'll shoot!"

Hearing the threat of being shot coming from Elena, Diego stopped and turned around to face her. He did not want to believe the words coming out of his daughter. With his gun at his side, never pointing it at her, Diego stared back at Elena for a few seconds, which seemed like hours, millions of different feelings running through him. He looked into her eyes with sorrow on his face, but now empty of tears, he gazed at her one last time.

Diego looked at Elena with dejection and complete disappointment, not wanting to believe what she had turned into. The daughter he had always loved so much, the child he raised most of her life by himself. The daughter he had given his all for now stood pointing a gun at him, threatening to shoot him. He said nothing to her. There was nothing left to say. He just turned and walked away.

"Stop! Stop!" cried Elena.

She pointed her revolver at him. She took aim with the middle of his back square in her sights. She cocked her weapon and tried to muster the strength to shoot him, but she just could not bring herself to do it.

She collapsed to the ground, weeping uncontrollably. She dropped the gun and covered her face with her hands. But she continued to yell at Diego, "Stop! Stop!"

Diego was now running for his life. He turned the corner when a car with an Anglo-looking driver stopped right next to him.

"Get in."

Diego stopped and froze where he stood. He didn't know who this man was or what to do.

He yelled, "Who the fuck are you?" Diego lifted his gun and pointed it at the car.

The driver ignored the gun in Diego's hand and yelled back at him, "I'm David Jeffries. I'm with the Canadian Embassy. Get in. Now."

Diego stood frozen in silence. He did not know this man, and after all he had gone through and all the betrayals and fuckups, he was not about to trust some stranger.

Jeffries, seeing the look of distrust in Diego's eyes, pleaded with him and tried to reassure him.

"I'm a friend of Bill Lima. Now get in. Get in, or you're a dead man."

Diego hesitated for a moment. He turned back to look toward the car where he had just left Elena, where a herd of military vehicles now quickly approached. He looked back at

David, who now wildly waved at him to get in. He assessed the situation and realized he had no more time to waste and no other choice to make. He took a leap of faith and got in the car. Jeffries stepped on the gas, and they sped away.

A crowd of people gathered around Elena, who held Gustavo's body. She cradled his head and wept. When the military vehicles arrived, several soldiers jumped out and tried to take control of the situation.

While Diego made his daring escape, Ramiro and two soldiers entered Cesar's cell. Cesar was on the dirty floor curled in a fetal position, quietly sobbing.

"Come on, Cesar," he said. "We have a little surprise for you."

Cesar snapped his head and looked up at Ramiro, who had a diabolical smile on his face.

"You're letting me go?" he asked, hoping to God they might release him.

Ramiro let out a loud laugh. "Oh, no, no, Cesar. You're not going anywhere for a long, long time." He took a friendly tone. "But you helped us so much with the apprehension of Joaquin that we want to show you something that, thanks to you, we will be able to accomplish. We thought you might want to see the fruits of your cooperation."

"What?"

Cesar was confused. He did not know what the hell Ramiro was talking about. He sat on the floor with a baffled look on his face. He knew that, coming from these bastards, it could not be anything good.

Ramiro, seeing Cesar's expression, grinned and told him, "Just come with me, and I'll show you."

He motioned the soldiers to get him up. The two men grabbed Cesar by the arms and pulled him to his feet. They hustled him out of the cell and down the hall to the courtyard. He saw two other soldiers bring Joaquin to *El Paredon*.

Che supervised most of the executions, especially the ones that involved high-ranking ex-members of the revolutionary forces. And he had made it a point to be present for this one. Che met up with Ramiro and the soldiers that were dragging Cesar to the execution yard. Joaquin was there, being guarded by the soldiers of the firing squad. Joaquin was shackled but standing straight and appeared not to be scared. He looked at all of them with contempt, except for Cesar, for whom he felt sorry.

Ramiro and Che approached him.

Ramiro spoke, "Joaquin, you're looking good. We brought you a visitor. This is the man that fingered you. He has been most cooperative and helpful in your apprehension. I believe you know him."

Cesar could not believe this whole scenario. He was horrified to hear Ramiro tell Joaquin that he was the reason why his brother found himself in this situation.

"Joaquin!" yelled Cesar, now shaking and sobbing. "Don't believe them, please. They knew all along you were involved."

Joaquin felt terrible for his younger brother. He knew they should never have gotten Cesar involved in this mess. "Cesar, don't let these pieces of shit get to you. They are just fucking with your head. Don't give them the satisfaction of seeing you like this."

By now Cesar was crying uncontrollably. "I'm sorry, Joaquin. I'm so sorry."

Ramiro pulled him away. "Okay, Cesar, time for you to watch."

The soldiers dragged Cesar away from the area of *El Paredon* but held him nearby so he could witness the execution. Che moved close to Ramiro and stood next to him while Ramiro directed the firing squad. Che never said a word to Joaquin.

Cesar was inconsolable and kept pleading with them. "Oh god no!" he shouted to Ramiro. "Please tell me you're just messing with him the way you did with me. It's all fake, right? Isn't it?"

Che looked at Ramiro, and they both laughed.

Ramiro turned to Cesar. "Of course. We are just messing around."

A soldier went up to Joaquin with a blindfold.

Joaquin spat on him. "I don't want a fucking blindfold. I want to look all you cowards in the eye." He yelled at Che, "Especially you, you miserable, phony hypocrite! I always knew," he gestured toward Ramiro, "that he was a piece shit. But you, who pretended to be my friend and especially Camilo's, you are the biggest piece of shit of them all!"

Che ignored Joaquin's words but could not look him in the eye. Ramiro proceeded with the execution.

He shouted at his men, "Ready!"

Cesar did not want to believe this was really happening.

He kept imploring Ramiro, "It's all a joke, right? Oh god, please let it be just a sick joke. Please, God!"

Ramiro forged ahead with his instructions. "Aim!"

Cesar was trembling. He begged God to stop this. He looked at Joaquin and yelled, "I love you, Joaquin!"

At the exact moment, Ramiro yelled "Fire!" Joaquin shouted, *"VIVA CUBA LIBRE!"*

The guns went off in unison, and the bullets hit their target. Joaquin slumped dead on the post. Che calmly walked to where the dead body of Joaquin was tied, the body of a man he had called a friend, a man with whom he had gone through hell and shared so much in the mountains. This same man now meant nothing to him. He stepped up to the slumping body, took out his gun, and put a final bullet through Joaquin's head.

Cesar was horrified. He had prayed that they were going to do to Joaquin the same fake execution they had done to him. But the reality of what he had just witnessed completely overwhelmed him.

"No! No! You killed him. You sons of bitches killed him!"

Cesar went berserk. The soldiers that held him could not control him. He yelled, struggled, and fought with them. The soldiers finally were able to get a firm hold on Cesar and beat him with their truncheons until he lost consciousness. Limp and almost lifeless, they dragged him back to his cell.

Chapter 24

ROBERTO, CARMEN, ROSA, and Tico pulled up to the Havana airport in a gypsy cab, unaware of all that was going on with Cesar, Diego, and Joaquin. The scene at the airport was pandemonium. The area was extremely crowded with nervous, despondent people waiting to leave the country. As had become the norm, there was an even a larger number of people in the government organized mob, gathered nearby, demonstrating behind police barricades.

They shouted obscenities and chanted, "Leave, worms, leave!"

Rosa, already shaken by all that had gone on and unable to stop thinking about the fate of her sons, was startled to see the wild mob screaming such vile things and chanting that awful chant.

"Why are they screaming those things at us?" asked Rosa.

Roberto looked over at the mob across from them and back at Rosa, "The revolution promised everyone a job." He pointed to the wild crowd. "This is theirs."

The Machados and Rosa walked into the airport and got in line to be checked in. Inside the terminal, a long line of worn-out, weary people waited to be checked one final time before they could board the plane. The Machados waited for over two hours. Finally, they got to where they were second in line. A militia sergeant by the name of Garcia was in charge of the final check before they could board. He was one of the new converts to the revolutionary religion and spoke with harsh condescension to the woman in front of them.

By this time, he was more shouting than talking and told her, "This is the last time I'm going to say it! The new rules are that you are only allowed to take one change of clothes. That's it! Understand? If you want to get on the plane, put your suitcase on that pile." He pointed to one of the many stacks of suitcases that nearly reached the ceiling.

"But it's not even clothes. It's pictures and mementos of my family."

The sergeant, who had spent all day reciting the same thing to every person in line, snapped at her, "Old woman, you are just as stupid as the rest of the worms. What part of what I have told you so many times do you not understand?" He got in the face of the poor old lady and shouted at her, "You're allowed one change of clothes. That's it. Now move!"

The poor old woman shuffled along to where she was told to go, crying all the way. She took one final look at the pictures and her family relics, put the suitcase on one of the piles, and continued to sob all the way to the waiting room.

The soldier looked at the Machados and hollered, "Next!"

Roberto moved his family forward. Finally, after all the waiting, they were about to leave Cuba and the horrible place it had become.

"Your name?" said the soldier, not bothering to look at Roberto.

"We're all together," said Roberto, pointing to his family.

The sergeant looked up at Roberto and the rest of them. "Do all of you have the same last name?" asked Garcia.

"Yes, except for my mother," answered Carmen.

"I'll take her first," he said to Carmen and motioned for Rosa to come forward. With all the charm of a pit bull, he asked, "What is your name?"

"Rosa Quintana."

He looked her over, and with the same suspicious stare he gave all the other poor souls trying to leave, asked her, "Where are your release papers from the state?"

Carmen spoke up, "I have all of our papers."

"Just give me hers." He looked over the documents and said, "All right. Now, empty your purse and your pockets."

Rosa took everything out of her pockets and purse.

The soldier saw the few items that Rosa took out, leaned over to her, and with a mistrustful tone to his voice, asked her, "Are you sure that is all you have to declare?"

Rosa's voice cracked as she answered, "Yes."

He looked at her skeptically, got a little closer, and now with a threatening tone, asked her, "You're not trying to hide anything from us, are you?" He gave a cynical chuckle and continued to intimidate her. "Don't think we won't search you just because you're an old lady. We search anyone we think might try to smuggle things that don't belong to them anymore."

"No, I'm not hiding anything."

The sergeant rifled through her handbag. He took anything of value from her purse, including a brooch her late husband had given to her on their honeymoon. Then he handed the purse back to her.

Rosa pleaded with him. "Please don't take that. It is a present from my husband that I've had almost all my life."

Garcia laughed at her. "Well, guess what. You don't have it anymore. It now belongs to the people of Cuba." He dismissively waved his hand. "Okay, Grandma. Go ahead."

Rosa hesitated.

"What is it?" Garcia asked her. "I told you, you are not getting it back."

"Can I wait for them?" She pointed to her family.

"Yes, in the other room."

Rosa watched him put her precious brooch in his pocket. She trudged to the waiting area, turning several times to look at her family.

While Rosa walked away and the Machados waited to be processed, a lieutenant named Amaro marched up to the sergeant. He had some official-looking papers in his hand and whispered something in the sergeant's ear. The lieutenant looked at the papers, gave a weird look at Roberto, and walked away.

Sergeant Garcia gave Roberto a suspicious look. "Your name?"

"Roberto Machado and family."

Garcia continued to look at Roberto with the same mistrust and asked, "Papers?"

"Here they are," said Carmen.

The sergeant didn't bother to look or even glance at the papers.

Instead he demanded, "Empty your pockets, all of you."

They all took the contents from their pockets and laid them on the table. Again he checked the items, rifling through them, looking for anything he wanted to keep for himself. He took a few things from both Roberto and Carmen, including her earrings and Roberto's wallet. Even though the wallet was empty, it was a nice, expensive soft leather wallet, which Garcia obviously wanted for himself.

Carmen and Roberto did not bother to protest. They had lost everything they owned. They had turned it over to the state so they could be allowed to leave Cuba. They were resigned to that fact. What difference would it make to lose a few more items?

The soldier turned to Tico, who held the baseball type cards with the pictures of Camilo, Joaquin, and the other soldiers. He also wore a nice gold watch. Garcia saw the watch and immediately snatched it from Tico's wrist. He examined it and put it in his pocket.

"Hey, that's my watch," said Tico, demanding that the sergeant give it back to him.

Garcia leaned over to Tico and told him, "You can keep the cards but not the watch. Like I told your grandmother, these things now belong to the people of Cuba, not you. Not anymore, kid."

Tico defiantly told the sergeant, "Then why are you putting it in your pocket?"

The soldier ignored Tico's question and addressed Carmen. "You better tell your kid to shut up or none of you are going anywhere."

Carmen told Tico to please not say anything else, and the kid reluctantly got quiet. Garcia said to them, "You and the boy can go in, but, Mr. Machado, we have a problem. The State does not have any record that you turned in your car."

Roberto was astounded. He had never owned a car in his life. He never even bothered to learn how to drive. He had no use for a car. Just like in New York City, there were plenty of cabs in Havana, and that was what he had always used to get around.

He asked the sergeant, "What car? I've never owned a car."

The soldier ignored Roberto's comment and looked back at Carmen. "I said you and the kid can go in."

"Not without my husband, I'm not."

Carmen was not about to leave Roberto alone with this jackass bent on making their lives miserable up through the very last minute they were in Cuba.

"Then nobody leaves."

Roberto did not want to separate from them either. He also did not want to run the risk of the whole family not being allowed to leave.

Quietly he spoke to his wife. "Carmen, please just go on in. I will handle it. No matter what happens, I beg you, get on that plane."

Carmen would not hear of it. She was determined to stay with Roberto no matter what might happen. "I'm not leaving without you."

Garcia impatiently watched the exchange between them. He was not about to waste one more minute. He shouted at them, "Make up your minds or get out of the line!"

Roberto saw the look in the sergeant's face and knew he had to talk Carmen into going ahead or they would all be thrown out of the airport.

Roberto grabbed Carmen by her shoulders and looked into her eyes and pleaded with her, "Carmen, for Tico's sake, please go. They are not going to let any of us leave if you don't do what he says, and you know that we cannot let Tico grow up in this country. I promise you I will get to Miami somehow. Now go."

Carmen hesitated for a moment, but she knew Roberto was right. If there was any hope of them leaving, she had to do what this monster in fatigues was telling them to do. She did not want to leave without Roberto but could not run the risk. The last thing she wanted was to see Tico raised in the hellhole Cuba had turned into. Carmen started to cry and fell into Roberto's arms. The family all hugged each other and they all began to cry. Tears streamed down Tico's face.

"Please, come with us, Papi."

Roberto held Tico in his arms and told him, "You are the man of the house now. Go with your mother. She needs you to protect her. I promise I will be with you as soon as I can."

The sergeant looked at all of them with total disdain and said, "Okay, okay. Enough of the crying and the hysterics. Go in or get the hell out of here."

Carmen and Tico made their way to the room where Rosa waited for them.

Roberto turned back to the soldier. "What do you want from me?"

"Your car."

"I told you I don't own a car."

"Then bring me the paper that proves it." He shoved Roberto out the way and yelled, Next!"

Chapter 25

OUTSIDE OF LA Cabana prison, many inmates, including Cesar, were loaded into a closed, windowless truck. They stood jammed together like sardines in their tin can. Cesar was one of the first to enter the truck. The captain of the watch handed the prisoners' transfer papers to the driver while two soldiers taunted and struck the prisoners as they got in the truck. This same scenario was repeated many times daily as the number of prisoners kept increasing in this oppressive nightmare Cuba had become.

The number of those killed in front of *El Paredon* had now surpassed a thousand souls in Havana alone. A very large number of militia personnel was needed just to keep up with the arrest and execution of so many Cubans. The soldiers that herded them into the truck were relentless in their abusive taunting.

"I hope you all enjoyed your stay at La Cabana," the soldiers mocked. "If you thought you got good service here, just wait until you see your splendid accommodations at the Isle of Pines, you worms."

The captain of the watch at La Cabana went over the transfer papers one more time with the driver while the two guards continued to load and taunt the prisoners.

He told the driver, out of earshot of the guards, "Take these men to pier 12 and make sure they are all loaded onto the *Esperanza*. The count is seventy-two."

The driver nodded and wrote down the number.

When the truck arrived at the docks, the many beaten and sore prisoners waited to get out. Most of them were sick and could hardly breathe after being squeezed into the truck that was made to hold no more than fifty men. Because Cesar was one of the first to get in, he was at the back of the truck.

While the enclosed truck sat in the hot sun, the prisoners felt even sicker, waiting for the ferry captain to arrive at the pier. He was taking his sweet time. He couldn't have cared less about the men in the truck or how miserable they might be.

The truck driver finally went to look for him and found him leisurely having his morning coffee. The driver walked into the captain's office, saluted him, and told him the men were ready to be loaded onto the boat. The captain told him to sit down, have a cup, and relax.

"There's no rush," he said.

But the driver insisted the men be let out before they suffocated.

"Okay, okay. What's the big deal anyways? You think they are going to be any better off in their lovely prison cell in the Isle of Pines?" The ferry captain reluctantly got up from his chair and asked the driver, "How many did you bring me this time?"

The driver handed him the transfer papers and told him, "Seventy-one."

The captain barely glanced at the papers and told the driver, "You count them going out, and I'll count them going in."

The driver, followed by the ferry boat captain, approached the men who guarded the truck. He walked up to the two guards, while the captain went over to his boat, the *Esperanza*, and prepared to receive the prisoners.

The driver told the guards, "The captain wants both of you by the gangway, loading the prisoners and counting them as they go in. I'll count the prisoners as they get off."

When the driver opened the door of the truck, the smell of vomit filled the air. One by one, the prisoners got down from inside the truck and, like zombies, walked to the gangway. Cesar was the last one in the truck, and when it was his turn to get off, the driver stopped him.

"You wait right here."

That was when Cesar, to his amazement and surprise, realized the driver was his good friend Jose. He could not believe his luck and tried to say something, but Jose told him to be quiet and stay in the truck. Jose walked over to the *Esperanza* and told the captain all the men had been let out and that he could leave now. The two guards stayed on the boat so they could watch and help unload the prisoners when they arrived at the Isle of Pines prison. The truck, now empty except for Cesar, took off.

Jose drove to a desolate beach house on the outskirts of Havana and got out. He looked around to make sure no one was watching. Then he cautiously opened the back of the truck and helped Cesar out.

"Get in the house quick, Cesar. If they spot us we're dead."

Cesar got out, grabbed his good friend, and hugged him. He kept thanking Jose for getting him out and saving him from the hell at the Isle of Pines.

Cesar asked him, "Why don't you come with me, Jose? You're a good man. You don't belong here."

Jose was tempted by Cesar's offer, but he told him, "I can't, Cesar. This country is all I know. I'm not going to go to the United States and be an immigrant. That just won't work for me." He looked at his old dear friend and told him, "You go ahead and go. You have no choice. If you stay in Cuba, you will spend the rest of your life in jail, or they will kill you in front of *El Paredon*. Me, I need to stay in Cuba. Someone has to stay to keep things in check. Maybe when all this madness settles down, Cuba can become what the revolution originally meant it to be." He hugged Cesar for the last time and handed him a bottle of rum, just like the bottles he used to sneak and share in the nightclubs with his buddies.

Jose smiled and said, "Just remember the good times."

Cesar watched his friend get back in the truck and drive off. He entered the beach house through the back door. At first he did not see anyone but soon, out of the shadows, he saw to his astonishment his two friends, Armando and Alberto waiting for him.

"Jesus," smiled Armando, "do you always have to be late?"

Cesar started to laugh and cry at the same time.

He ran up to them, grabbed them, and said, "I can't believe you fucking guys."

The three of them hugged one another in a tight embrace. Now all three laughed and cried together.

Across the athletic fields of the University of Havana sat Embassy Row, where a lot of countries had built their embassy compounds. One of the few that did not was the United States, who had built theirs by the Malecon sea wall not far from the Machados' home.

The track-and-field grounds of the university were directly across from the Canadian embassy. Today, like every other day, right outside their embassy, the pole vault jumper Cesar and Roberto had seen from Roberto's office ledge joked around with the Cuban guards. It had become a daily routine for him to stop and chat with them before and after he practiced his pole vaulting. The guards were there to prevent people from sneaking in and asking for asylum.

Every embassy now had their own detail of Cuban guards assigned to do the same. There were a great many people that were sought out for arrest who wanted to request asylum. That made it impossible for them to openly apply for the visa waiver that the United States was issuing to all that requested it. To do that at this point would be especially dangerous because so many were being hunted by the Cuban militia due to the impending invasion.

The athlete let the guards hold the pole and play with it, and he talked about how he needed to practice every day because his goal was to go to the Olympics and represent Cuba. He told them how he wanted to win the gold medal and make Fidel proud. The guards laughed and joked around with him. They did not take him seriously since he was not an official member of the Cuban Olympic team. They all thought if this guy wasn't crazy, he was definitely eccentric. When the jumper wasn't looking, they made fun of him and made crazy signs behind his back.

Inside, the Canadian ambassador had gathered a small group of asylum seekers, including Diego. The ambassador was a career diplomat, an older no-nonsense type of guy. He had been the Canadian ambassador in Cuba for some time now and was not a fan of the Castro regime. He was a fair-minded man who said what he meant and meant what he said. He was known to not pull any punches. He had gathered the group of asylum seekers to tell them of some news he had just gotten from his country's prime minister.

"I have good news for you," he began, "the Cuban government has agreed to let you all leave the country." There was a murmur of excitement by those assembled in front of him.

A woman in the group who could not believe the government would be so accommodating piped up, sarcasm in her voice, "To what do we owe this wonderful display of generosity?"

The ambassador dismissed her sarcasm. He understood what these men and women had been through and why they would be skeptical.

He patiently told her, "Canada has decided not to follow the United States' lead in breaking ties with Cuba, and the Cuban government is very grateful."

This seemed to appease the woman, and she gladly accepted the ambassador's explanation. They were all very pleased to hear the good news. Most of them were strangers thrown together into something over which they had no control. Relieved and thankful, many of them shook hands and patted one another on the back, knowing they had been blessed after their terrible ordeal. Diego was happy to hear this too, but he wanted to know why those in the room had been chosen.

Diego asked, "Why us in particular?"

The ambassador turned to Diego and explained. "The government of Canada has requested you because you have all been sentenced to death. Believe me, the Cuban government was not too happy to oblige our prime minister's request, especially for your release, Mr. Quintana. The Cuban government seems to have a special interest in your arrest. But Cuba cannot afford, at this time, to deny any of my country's requests. After a few hours of negotiation, they finally agreed, and now that Cuba has given you your release, we can have you in Ottawa very soon."

The ambassador dismissed the group and went back to his office, happy that his country was able to at least spare these poor souls' lives. Many of those saved looked for an available phone to tell the good news to their families.

Diego had no one to call. He prayed that his mother, sister, Tico, and Roberto had been able to get on their flight and make it out of Cuba. He went back into the yard while he waited. He thought about Cesar and Joaquin and wondered what had become of them. He had seen Cesar apprehended with his own eyes, and he knew that Joaquin could not have possibly avoided detention. He prayed to God that both would make it out alive.

He also thought over and over as to what could have gone wrong with the operation. *What the hell happened?*

When he thought of Alejandra, he began to cry. He was inconsolable and completely blamed himself for her death. How cruel life had been to him. After all those years of being alone and loveless, he had finally found the new love of his life, only to have her violently snatched away.

And Elena. *Oh my god, Elena*, he thought. What could he have done differently to save her from those animals? How could she have become such a brainwashed robot? His beautiful, intelligent daughter had been turned into a monster he no longer recognized, pointing a gun at him, threatening to shoot him dead. He would never be able to get that image out of his mind.

He tried not to think about it. He walked over to the fence and looked out into the streets of Havana and tried to take in as much as possible. He would soon leave Cuba, the only home he had ever known, and he realized he would not be able to come back ever again. He gazed out at his homeland for one long last look.

Roberto had left the terminal. He had put up a brave front with Carmen and Tico, but now he was nearly in a state of panic.

Those militia sons of bitches would not let up. It wasn't enough that they had confiscated his business, fired him from his university post, and taken all his savings. Now they demanded that he turn in a car he never even had. That asshole sergeant told him to bring papers that proved he did not own a car. What papers? They didn't issues papers for cars that didn't exist. How could he prove he had never owned a car? He didn't even know where to start.

There was an office of transportation a couple of blocks from the airport. But they only dealt with air transport, not ground vehicles. However, the Department of Transportation was located in the center of Havana. Roberto did not have enough time to go back to the city. The airport was too far away. There was no chance he could get there and be back in time. And that didn't take into account the time it would take to sort out this mess. Before he got a chance to get back, the plane with his family would be gone.

His mind raced at a million miles a minute. He was even more afraid that if he wasn't back in time, Carmen would not get on the plane, and they would all be stuck forever in this hellhole, leaving Tico to be raised under this horrible system.

He began to run. In the distance, he could still hear the government mob chanting, "Leave, worms, leave!" He ran the couple of blocks to the Department of Air Transportation and stumbled into the building. He burst through the door and rushed to the desk, startling the secretary, who was taken aback by his appearance and crazy demeanor. Out of breath and in a frenzy, he told her his name and tried to explain the situation he found himself in. But she couldn't make any sense of what he was saying.

He kept repeating, "I need some document that proves I don't own a car."

The secretary at the front desk tried to calm him down.

"Mr. Machado, I understand that you are very upset. But we don't deal with car registrations in this office. Not only that, but we are swamped with all the planes that are trying to take off and land. I don't think Mr. Godina will be able to help you, but if you want to see him, you still need to make an appointment. Mr. Godina is very busy. The soonest he will be able to see you," she rifled through the appointment book and looked back at Roberto, "is a week from Monday."

Now Roberto was hysterical. The man had been through hell and back and had practically lost his mind in the process. He was close to losing it again.

"A week from Monday? I don't even have an hour. My family is waiting for me at the airport right now. If I don't get back very soon, I may never see them again."

At that moment, Mr. Godina's office door opened. He had heard all the commotion at the front desk and had to see for himself what all the racket was about. When he stepped out of his office, he was surprised to see a man screaming and crying in the lobby.

He walked up to Roberto. "Professor Machado?"

Roberto saw that Mr. Godina was none other than Ignacio, his former student. Roberto was even more surprised than Ignacio. He had lost contact with his students and had no idea Ignacio was in charge of this department. After getting over the initial shock of seeing his former pupil, he grabbed Ignacio and pleaded with him.

Roberto explained the absurd circumstances he found himself in and the ridiculous demand to turn in papers about a car he had never owned. Ignacio did not quite understand all that Roberto was talking about, but he knew his mentor was in a terrible situation and was about to have a nervous breakdown right there in his office.

He told the secretary to call two of his soldiers and get him a car. Roberto, Ignacio, and the two soldiers got in the official government car and zipped back the short distance to the airport. Ignacio, Roberto, and the two soldiers marched through the crowded terminal, and when they got to the gate, they could see the Machados' plane was still on the tarmac. But the steps were being taken away, and the door had begun to close. Roberto was at least relieved to see that Carmen had listened to him and had not made the mistake of getting off.

The same soldier who had checked in the Machados was still at the desk. He saw Ignacio's rank of captain, stood at attention, and saluted. He saw Roberto next to him and was confused as to what this was all about.

"Who is in charge here?" demanded Ignacio.

Now the weasel Garcia started to worry. This was not looking good for him. He answered, "Lieutenant Amaro. But he is not here now, sir."

"Are you the soldier who gave Mr. Machado a hard time?"

Now Sergeant Garcia was really worried. He had a man standing in front of him with the rank of captain, demanding answers he either did not have or was afraid to give. He started to shake.

The soldier stammered his answer. "Captain, it was Lieutenant Amaro who told me to make sure he turned in his car."

Ignacio was furious. He was not about to allow this idiot to give him the run around. He got in his face and told him, "I don't care who told whom what. I've known this man almost all my life, and I can personally vouch that he has never owned a car. If you know what is good for you, you'll make sure he gets on that plane."

The sergeant was at a loss for words and didn't know what to do. "I can't, sir." He pointed to the tarmac where the plane was starting to taxi off. "The plane is already leaving."

Ignacio got even closer to Garcia and, in a loud and threatening tone, ordered him, "Then I guess you better call the tower and stop it." He looked into the sergeant's eyes and screamed, "I couldn't care less who started this mess! I am ordering you to fix it. Call the tower right now and stop that plane, or I swear," he pointed at the two soldiers that had come along with him, "I'll have my men throw your ass in jail for insubordination. I'm ordering you to stop that fucking plane *NOW!*"

He grabbed Garcia by the collar and, in a more quiet voice, told him, "And you better return his son's watch and everything else you took from him and his family."

"Yes, sir."

The sergeant was now literally shaking in his boots. He got on the phone and desperately tried to get a hold of someone in the tower. While he was on the phone, the little weasel started to go through his pockets to find the items he had taken from Rosa and the Machados. He found everything and gave it all back to Roberto.

Tears trickled down Roberto's cheeks, and he hugged Ignacio.

"Thank you, Ignacio. Thank you so much. How can I ever repay you for this?"

Ignacio put his arms around Roberto. "This doesn't even begin to repay you for everything you have done for me, Professor. I'm the one who will never be able to repay you for all your help and generosity. Not only do I owe you for my education, but I owe you my life. I'm sure those Batista goons would have put a bullet in my head the day the revolution took over. If it wasn't for you, I would not be standing here. Now go and join your family."

In the distance, one could see the plane turn around and come back toward the gate. Roberto hugged Ignacio one last time and ran to the tarmac. Ignacio turned his attention back to Garcia and, once again, chewed him up one side and down the other. Lieutenant Amaro returned, and Ignacio tore into him as well.

Chapter 26

DIEGO SAT ON the grass at the Canadian embassy grounds. He and the other asylum seekers, along with the Cuban guards on the other side of the fence, were watching as the pole vaulter practiced. The man took several jumps until he seemed exhausted. When he finished his workout, he picked up the pole, put it on his shoulder, and trotted toward the guards.

Many times, the guards had watched him do this. After his workout, he would run toward them until he got close. Then he would stop, put down his pole and chat with them. As usual, they looked at one another as he approached, laughed, and made the usual jokes and comments about the crazy guy.

This time, he seemed to run faster than usual. They wondered if this nutcase was going to barrel right into them before he had a chance to stop. But instead of slowing down, he picked up speed, his knees high and face set with determination. The guards nervously looked at one another and began to move out of the way of the long pole that was coming right at them. The pole vaulter did not slow down at all. Instead, he took off right past the startled guards and, in a lightning move, pole-vaulted himself over the fence, right into the embassy yard. He turned around, looked at the dumbstruck guards and, with both hands, gave them the finger.

All the equally startled people on the embassy grounds stood and cheered. They ran up and surrounded him with hugs and handshakes. Then, almost in unison, many of the asylum seekers turned toward the guards and gave them the finger just like their new hero had done. They hoisted the pole vaulter onto their shoulders and paraded him around the yard and in front of the guards. Many of them ran to the fence that separated them from the soldiers to laugh, point their fingers at the Cuban guards, and mock the totally confused and pissed-off soldiers.

Diego stood up and watched this spontaneous celebration from the asylum seekers, these desperate people with so little to celebrate for such a very long while. For the first time in what seemed like forever, he started to laugh and clap his hands. He remained there and kept on clapping along with the others until it turned into a huge ovation.

The guards were flabbergasted, and a loud argument ensued amongst them, each trying to blame the others. They also felt disgraced, watching the people inside the embassy grounds mocking and ridiculing them. Some of the guards took out their weapons and pointed them through the fence at several of the more vociferous offenders, threatening to shoot if they did not stop. This only made the asylum seekers laugh and mock them even louder.

Some of them might have been shot if the captain of the watch hadn't arrived after hearing all the commotion. He yanked the guns away from the guards who were pointing them at the people inside the embassy. Then he cursed at his soldiers and ordered them to stand down before they created an international incident.

The celebration seemed to go on forever. Someone brought out a small portable radio, and many started to dance by the fence, right in front of the guards. They enjoyed the fact that the guards couldn't do anything but stand there and bite their tongues. For many, if not all, it was their first opportunity to openly defy Fidel's goons, and they loved it.

This went on until the ambassador, who had gotten a call from someone in the Cuban government, came out in the yard and implored them to please stop. He tried to remain serious, but even he could not help but smile. He invited the pole vaulter into his office, and the celebration slowly died down and came to an end.

Diego remained outside even after most of the others had gone back into the embassy building. He looked out once again, trying to take in as much as he could before he had to leave Cuba forever.

The next morning, the ambassador gathered those he had met with before, the ones sentenced to death by the Cuban government. He asked that they follow him, then walked them toward a Canadian embassy van and handed each of them their papers.

He personally shook everyone's hands and said, "Goodbye and good luck. You will all be in Ottawa by late this afternoon. Congratulations, you are all free men and women again."

The van drove to a private landing strip, and they all boarded a Canadian diplomatic plane. Diego walked up the steps, and before he went in, he turned around and took one last look at Cuba. Then he boarded the plane for Ottawa. He sat in his seat, sadly looking out the window as the plane taxied and took off. He silently said goodbye to his island home, never to return. Elena came to his mind, and he couldn't help it; he broke down and started to cry.

When Diego's plane arrived in Canada, it was sunset on the outskirts of Havana. Cesar, Alberto, and Armando prepared to board a small boat that was barely seaworthy.

They were concerned the damn thing might not hold them, let alone be able to make the ninety-mile journey that they were about to embark upon. With trepidation, they carefully got into the boat and said a prayer. They looked around to make sure no one was watching as they silently rowed out to sea.

They tentatively paddled out into the calm waters and waited until the Cuban coast was beyond the horizon before they hoisted their makeshift sail. Alberto was the only one among them who had ever sailed a boat, and Armando and Cesar kept asking if he was sure he knew what the hell he was doing. Alberto reassured them that he had everything under control.

"Will you both stop bothering me? Please, just sit down and shut up."

Cesar held on to the mast and kept repeating to no one in particular, "I hope to God this boat makes it."

After a day at sea, which seemed like months, a boat approached them. They were exhausted and their makeshift sail had cracked and broken. Cesar had found some paint in the beach house, and even in this state of mind, his sense of humor could not be denied. On the back of their small sailboat, he had beautifully painted *Granma II*. As the boat got closer, they realized it was a US Coast Guard cutter. They jumped up and down to make sure they got the coast guard's attention. With all their exuberant jumping and waving, they almost capsized their little boat. The US ship caught sight of them and eased right up alongside. The sailors helped them onto the coast guard cutter, where they were given dry clothing, water, and something to eat.

They were at last safe at sea and on their way to freedom. It was a bittersweet triumph for Cesar. After all the beatings he had endured, the betrayal by his wife, witnessing the assassination of his brother Joaquin, and not knowing the fate of Diego, he was at last on his way to the United States to start a whole new life. He had no idea where it would take him, but he was thankful that he had made it alive. He prayed that Diego and the rest of his family had been as fortunate.

Roberto had made it to the plane, practically jumping from the tarmac into the cabin, hardly waiting for the steps to be set. When he got inside, the other passengers that had witnessed his ordeal stood up and cheered. They patted him on the back as he ran down the aisle to his wife and son, and they all embraced and cried out of relief and joy. Rosa was crying too, and Roberto was happy and proud to hand her the precious brooch the little weasel Garcia had taken from her. She immediately stopped crying, hugged him, and planted a big kiss on his forehead. He turned to his son and gave him back his watch. Tico gave out a small cheer. The plane finally took off, and they were on their way out of Cuba and on to the United States.

Their plane landed in Miami late in the afternoon, and Rosa and the Machados were met by US Immigration and taken to a waiting area to be processed. They were now newly arrived refugees. They had to fill out lots of paperwork, and they had to be questioned one by one before the immigration officials could release them from the airport and into the city of Miami, which would become their new home. They waited in the holding area of the Miami airport long into the night with many other families.

An immigration officer came up to the group that had now been given their release papers and were almost ready to be let out.

"Welcome to the United States," he said. "Thank you all for your patience. Please follow me. There are still a few more details we need to take care of, but it won't be much longer before all of you can leave."

They followed the officer, and Roberto picked up the sleeping Tico. When he did, Tico dropped his cards with the pictures of the heroes of the revolution. The faces of the early leaders like Joaquin and Huber could be seen among the cards on the floor. As the new refugees exited the holding area, a janitor came by to clean up. When he got to where the Machados had been, one could see, among the other pictures on the floor, the photograph of Camilo with his wide smile and distinctive cowboy hat. The janitor's broom swept them away.

Epilogue

IT WAS SEPTEMBER 15, 1980, one of those rare but not unheard of rainy days in Miami when the sun shined brightly in the sky. A hearse followed by several cars drove up to a cemetery, and a large group of people exited their cars. They gathered in front of a canopy where several chairs had been arranged in front of the burial site. As soon as they all arrived, as if on cue, the rain stopped, and the sun began to shine even brighter.

Six men, among them Tico and Cesar, pulled the coffin out of the hearse and walked it over to the platform that had been built to lower Diego's remains. Next to the burial site, there was a grave with the name Rosa Quintana etched on a marble headstone. Rosa had died not long after arriving in the United States, officially of a heart attack but, in reality, from a broken heart. She never got over the death of her son Joaquin in front of that firing squad at the hands of those miserable bastards that had taken over Cuba.

Among those in attendance was Carmen. She had aged prematurely from all the misery she had endured and the loss of her beloved mother and brother, but still she remained a beautiful woman. Roberto sat next to her, holding a cane, looking old and frail. Although he had recovered from his breakdown, all those electroshock applications had finally taken a toll on his health. Tico came over and sat on the other side of Carmen. He now went by his adult name of Roberto. He was a successful businessman who had studied and worked hard to make something of his life.

Like so many of the children of those first Cuban refugees to arrive on the US shore, Roberto (Tico) felt a sense of debt and gratitude to his parents for taking him out of Cuba. They had saved him from a life of misery in that communist wasteland. He had succeeded and had made them proud. Not only had he become a successful businessman but also a community leader, having been recently elected as councilman to the city of Miami. Politics still ran deep in the veins of this family. So many children of those refugees, including the fourteen thousand kids from the Peter Pan flights, most of whom were able to reunite with their parents in the States, were determined to succeed and make sure their parents' effort and sacrifice did not go to waste.

Behind them sat Cesar. He looked older but still retained much of his youthful appearance, although by this time he was almost three hundred pounds. It seemed all his gluttony had caught up with him. He sat next to a beautiful young woman, his new bride. She was his third. Some things would never change. He was now the owner of one of the biggest and most sought-after commercial art firms in all of South Florida. Cesar had achieved his goal of becoming a commercial artist. And he never forgot his buddies Armando and Alberto. He not only employed them but gave them a big piece of his business, making them rich. They now stood next to him.

Standing beside them was Bill Lima. He was still somewhat heavy but not fat. He had finally learned to control his eating. He also had been one of the pall bearers who carried Diego's coffin. Shortly after leaving Cuba and arriving in the US, Bill had quit the CIA over their betrayal of the Quintana brothers. He was disgusted and ashamed and could not spend one extra minute working for the agency. He tried his best to make up for it.

He had saved Diego's life by having his Canadian friend David rescue him from the grasp of the militia. And when Diego touched the soil of the US, Bill was there to greet him. Bill and Diego resumed their friendship. Bill opened his own security firm specializing in computer surveillance and brought Diego along to work with him and eventually made him his partner. They had made a fortune setting up security for many large corporations and had become like brothers. He now stood there brokenhearted over the death of his good friend.

Elena, as promised, never came or even bothered to acknowledge the death of her father. She remained a steadfast communist, moving up the ranks of the revolution to become one of its leaders.

A priest walked to the front of the burial site and spoke to all who had gathered; some were sitting, some standing. He invoked a prayer and told the crowd of Diego's heroics and the sacrifices he and the Quintana brothers had to endure. He brought up Joaquin's name and spoke about what a hero he had been and reminded them that if not for some bad luck, all of them might still be in a free Cuba.

The cemetery workers waited until the sermon was finished then proceeded to lower the coffin into its burial spot. The sound of soft weeping filled the air, and when the coffin reached the bottom, people stood and walked over to say their final goodbyes. Many held flowers and threw them into the grave.

The Machados and Quintanas along with Bill, Cesar, and his two friends, stayed after the others had left and held hands for one final prayer.

Cuba officially became a communist country when Fidel finally announced it to the world after the failed invasion. The invasion of the Bay of Pig was a total disaster. President Kennedy refused to commit American troops or even provide air cover for the poor souls that were left behind to die on the beach of Playa Giron or be captured by Fidel's forces. The failure of that invasion solidified forever Fidel's hold of power.

The exodus of Cubans by now had reached over a million people, 10 percent of its population, the equivalent of thirty million Americans leaving the United States. Although plagued by many dictatorships, the beautiful island of Cuba had been a prosperous country. It was among the best in all categories in all of Latin America. But now, thanks to Fidel's cronies and his communist policies, it had been reduced to the status of Haiti.

Fidel still ruled with an iron hand, and continued to shamelessly use the image of Camilo Cienfugos as a symbol of the Revolution, as if Camilo would have gone along with the perverted way the revolution he and so many fought for had turned into. And although some things had been achieved by the revolution, like educating most of the people, nothing had been accomplished for the good of those people. Everything that was achieved was done for only one reason, to be able to better utilize them for the good of the regime.

In the late twentieth century, no one needed slaves to pick their cotton. They needed people educated enough to efficiently run the machinery and fill an army that would keep the regime in power. On the other hand, those Cubans that left for America as refugees, the very same people that were harassed and called useless worms, became some of the most successful immigrants in the history of the United States.

About the Author

AL ROMERO IS a graduate of Florida State University and resides in South Florida with his wife Marie and their dog Bailey, they also have a daughter, Alexandra.

Mr. Romero is an Actor, Comedian and Writer who performs regularly on Cruise

ships, in Las Vegas and Atlantic City casinos and has written several screenplays.

Mr. Romero was born in Cuba and experienced first-hand Fidel's revolution.

Some members of his family, who were with Castro from the beginning eventually turned against him.

One of Mr. Romero's uncles while a member of Castro's Army, became disillusioned with how Fidel betrayed the very ideals that they all fought for and started to work with the CIA to over throw him and was killed in a firing squad.

Mr. Romero's two other uncles also got involved with the CIA. One was apprehended and sentenced to thirty years of hard labor, while the other one barely escaped the grasp of Fidel and his henchmen.

Mr. Romero wrote *Revolution* by incorporating his family experiences with the plight of other Cubans as well as historical facts, to tell this compelling story. It illustrates how Fidel lied, cheated, and murdered his way into power, making Cuba into a Soviet puppet.

It is the hope of Mr. Romero that this novel will finally bring to light what really happened in Cuba and how Castro enslaved that beautiful island.

About the Contributing Author

The contributing author Dave Kelley, is a graduate of the University of Missouri School of Journalism. Mr. Kelley worked as an educator for many years and is the author of the children's book *Cuckoo Elementary,* and the humor book, *Trump to English Dictionary.* A close friend of Mr. Romero for many years, Mr. Kelley helped the author with research for the book and traveled to Cuba, where he visited the childhood home of Mr. Romero as well as other locations that are mentioned in the book. While doing research in Havana, Mr. Kelley was detained for several hours by the Cuban authorities for taking pictures on the streets of the neighborhood where Mr. Romero lived as a child.

CPSIA information can be obtained
at www.ICGtesting.com
Printed in the USA
JSHW021137060722
27621JS00003B/6